Baker + Taylor   4/5/19   $17.99   Lincoln Nmn 2020

# sadie

# also by courtney summers

Cracked Up to Be

Some Girls Are

Fall for Anything

This Is Not a Test

What Goes Around

Please Remain Calm

All the Rage

# sadie

## courtney summers

WEDNESDAY BOOKS
NEW YORK

SADIE. Copyright © 2018 by Courtney Summers. All rights reserved. Printed in the United States of America. For information, address St. Martin's Press, 175 Fifth Avenue, New York, N.Y. 10010.

www.wednesdaybooks.com
www.stmartins.com

Designed by Anna Gorovoy

The Library of Congress Cataloging-in-Publication Data is available upon request.

ISBN 978-1-250-10571-4 (hardcover)
ISBN 978-1-250-10572-1 (ebook)

Our books may be purchased in bulk for promotional, educational, or business use. Please contact your local bookseller or the Macmillan Corporate and Premium Sales Department at 1-800-221-7945, extension 5442, or by email at MacmillanSpecialMarkets@macmillan.com.

First Edition: September 2018

10  9  8  7  6  5  4  3

*To my grandmothers, Marion LaVallee and Lucy Summers,*
*for their unwavering love and support*

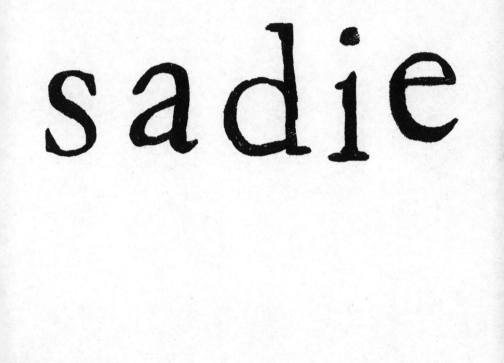

**DANNY GILCHRIST:**

It's a beautiful day in the city. The sun is shining, not a cloud in the sky. I had a great lunch in Central Park, a chicken shawarma from the Shawarma Stop, which was overwhelmingly recommended to us by our listeners after last week's episode on NYC's best kept secrets. Thanks for that, you guys. It was so good, it just might be my dinner too. From WNRK New York, I'm Danny Gilchrist and you are listening to *Always Out There*.

Today, we're doing something new—something big. Today, we're pre-empting your regularly scheduled episode of *Always Out There* to launch the first episode of our new serialized podcast, *The Girls*. If you want to hear more, you can download all eight episodes—that's right; the entire season—on our website. We're pretty sure you'll want to hear more.

Created and hosted by one of our longtime producers, West McCray, *The Girls* explores what happens when a devastating crime reveals a deeply unsettling mystery. It's a story about family, about sisters, and the untold lives lived in small-town America. It's about the lengths we go to protect the ones we love . . . and the high price we pay when we can't.

And it begins, as so many stories do, with a dead girl.

# THE GIRLS

## EPISODE 1

*[THE GIRLS THEME]*

**WEST McCRAY:**
Welcome to Cold Creek, Colorado. Population: eight hundred.

Do a Google Image search and you'll see its main street, the barely beating heart of that tiny world, and find every other building vacant or boarded up. Cold Creek's luckiest—the gainfully employed—work at the local grocery store, the gas station and a few other staple businesses along the strip. The rest have to look a town or two over for opportunity for themselves and for their children; the closest schools are in Parkdale, forty minutes away. They take in students from three other towns.

Beyond its main street, Cold Creek arteries out into worn and chipped Monopoly houses that no longer have a place upon the board. From there lies a rural sort of wilderness. The highway out is interrupted by veins of dirt roads leading to nowhere as often as they lead to pockets of dilapidated houses or trailer parks in even worse shape. In the summertime, a food bus comes with free lunches for the kids until school resumes, where they are guaranteed at least two subsidized meals a day.

There's a quiet to it that's startling if you've lived your whole life in the city, like I have. Cold Creek is surrounded by a beautiful, uninterrupted expanse of land and sky that seem to go on forever. Its sunsets are spectacular: electric golds and oranges, pinks and purples, natural beauty unspoiled by the insult of skyscrapers. The sheer amount of space is humbling, almost divine. It's hard to imagine feeling *trapped* here.

But most people here do.

**COLD CREEK RESIDENT *[FEMALE]*:**
You live in Cold Creek because you were born here, and if you're born here, you're probably never getting out.

**WEST McCRAY:**
That's not entirely true. There have been some success stories, college graduates who moved on and found well-paying jobs in distant cities, but they tend to be the exception and not the rule. Cold Creek is home to a quality of life we're raised to aspire beyond, if we're born privileged enough to have the choice.

Here, everyone's working so hard to care for their families and keep their heads above water that, if they wasted time on the petty dramas, scandals and personal grudges that seem to define small towns in our nation's imagination, they would not survive. That's not to say there's no drama, scandal or grudge—just that those things are usually more than residents of Cold Creek can afford to care about.

Until *it* happened.

The husk of an abandoned, turn-of-the-century one-room schoolhouse sits three miles outside of town, taken by fire. The roof is caved in and what's left of the walls are charred. It sits next to an apple orchard that's slowly being reclaimed by the nature that surrounds it: young overgrowth, new trees, wild-flowers.

There's almost something romantic about it, something that feels like respite from the rest of the world. It's the perfect place to be alone with your thoughts. At least it was, before.

May Beth Foster—who you'll come to know as this series goes on—took me there herself. I asked to see it. She's a plump, white, sixty-eight-year-old woman with salt-and-pepper hair. She has a grandmotherly way about her, right down to a voice that's so invitingly familiar it warms you from the inside out. May Beth is manager of Sparkling River Estates trailer park, a lifelong resident of Cold Creek, and when she talks, people listen. More often than not, they accept whatever she says as the truth.

**MAY BETH FOSTER:**
Just about . . . here.

This is where they found the body.

**911 DISPATCHER *[PHONE]*:**
911 dispatch. What's your emergency?

**WEST McCRAY:**
On October third, forty-seven-year-old Carl Earl was on his way to work, a factory in Cofield. It's an hour's drive from Cold Creek. He'd barely begun his commute when he noticed black smoke marring the early morning horizon.

**CARL EARL:**
Started out like any other day. Least, I think it did. I imagine I got up, had breakfast and kissed my wife on my way out the door because that's what I do every morning. But I honestly can't remember a thing before I saw the smoke and everything that happened after that . . . well.

I wish I could forget it.

**CARL EARL** *[PHONE]:*
Yeah, my name's Carl Earl and I just want to report a fire. There's an abandoned schoolhouse off Milner's Road and it's all lit up. It's about three miles east of Cold Creek. I was just driving by and I noticed it. I pulled over to call. It's lookin' pretty bad.

**911 DISPATCHER** *[PHONE]:*
Okay, Carl, we're going to send someone out.

Are there any other people around? Anyone in need of assistance you can see?

**CARL EARL** *[PHONE]:*
Just me out here, far as I can tell, but I might not be close enough . . . I could maybe get a little closer and see—

**911 DISPATCHER** *[PHONE]:*
Sir—Carl—please stay clear of the fire. I need you to do that for me, all right?

**CARL EARL** *[PHONE]*:
Oh, yeah, no—I wasn't going to—

**CARL EARL:**
So I did as I was told, even though a part of me wanted to play hero. I'm still not sure what compelled me to stick around because I couldn't afford to miss the work, but I stayed 'til the cops and the firemen came. I watched 'em go at it until the flames were under control and that's when I noticed . . . just beyond the schoolhouse there, I saw—I was the, uh—I was the one that saw her first.

**WEST McCRAY:**
The body of Mattie Southern was discovered between the burning schoolhouse and the apple orchard, just out of sight. She'd been reported missing three days earlier and here she was, found.

Dead.

I've decided the gruesome details of what was uncovered in that orchard will not be a part of this show. While the murder, the crime, might have captured your initial interest, its violence and brutality do not exist for your entertainment—so please don't ask us. The details of this case are easy enough to find online. In my opinion, you only really need to know two things.

The first is the cause of her death was blunt force trauma to the head.

The second is this:

**MAY BETH FOSTER:**
She was only thirteen years old.

**CARL EARL:**
I don't sleep great anymore, since it happened.

**WEST McCRAY:**
Mattie left behind a nineteen-year-old sister, Sadie; a surrogate grandmother, May Beth; and her mother, Claire; but Claire's been out of the picture for a while.

I first heard about the Southern murder at a gas station outside Abernathy, about thirty minutes from Cold Creek. I was with my crew in the eastern plains and we'd just wrapped interviews for a segment of an episode of *Always Out There* dedicated to profiling small towns in America. You know, the kind on a rambling decline. We wanted their residents to tell us what those places lost, not because we thought we could restore them to their former glory but simply so you knew they existed. We wanted to give them a voice before they disappeared.

**JOE HALLORAN:**
It's a nice thought, anyway. That somebody gives a damn.

**WEST McCRAY:**
That was Joe Halloran, one of the Abernathy residents we interviewed. I wasn't thinking about his words when I was standing behind the guy ahead of me at the gas station, listening as he told the clerk *exactly* what happened to the Southern kid. The grisly facts didn't inspire me to stick around. My crew and I had gotten what we came for and we were ready to go back home. It was a terrible thing, sure, but we live in a world that has no shortage of terrible things. You can't stop for all of them.

A year later, I was sitting in my office in New York. It was October, a year to the day Mattie died, actually, the third—and my attention kept wandering from my computer screen to the window, where I could see the Empire State Building. I liked my job at WNRK, and I liked my life in the city, but maybe some part of me—the same part that let me walk away from Mattie's story the first time without a second thought—was overdue for a shake-up.

It arrived in the form of a phone call.

**MAY BETH FOSTER** *[PHONE]*:
Is this West McCray?

**WEST McCRAY** *[PHONE]*:
It is. How can I help you?

**MAY BETH FOSTER** *[PHONE]*:
This is May Beth Foster. Joe Halloran told me you give a damn.

**WEST McCRAY:**
There'd been no new developments in the Mattie Southern case, no suspects named to the crime. The investigation seemed to have ground to a halt. But that wasn't the reason May Beth contacted me.

**MAY BETH FOSTER** *[PHONE]*:
I need your help.

**WEST McCRAY:**
Three months ago, in mid-July, she'd gotten a call from a police station in Farfield, Colorado, a town many, many miles from Cold Creek. They'd found a 2007 black Chevy parked on the side of the road and inside of it, a green bag full of personal effects belonging to Mattie's older sister, Sadie

Hunter, who had disappeared that June. Sadie herself was nowhere to be found. She still hasn't been found. After a cursory investigation, Sadie was declared a runaway by local law enforcement, and, having exhausted all possible avenues available to her, May Beth Foster reached out to me. I was her last hope. She thought maybe I could bring Sadie back home to her alive. Because Sadie *had* to be alive, because—

**MAY BETH FOSTER** *[PHONE]*:
I can't take another dead girl.

# sadie

I find the car on craigslist.

It doesn't matter what kind, I don't think, but if you need more than that to work with, it's boxy, midnight black. The kind of color that disappears when it's next to any other. Backseat big enough to sleep in. It was offered up in a hastily written ad in a sea of hastily written ads, but this one riddled with spelling errors that suggested a special kind of desperation. *Make an offer, pleas* settled it for me. It means *I need money now* which means someone's in trouble or they're hungry or they've got a chemical kind of itch. It means I've got the advantage, so what else can I do but take it?

It doesn't occur to me that meeting someone on a road outside of town to buy a car for any amount of money I'm willing to pay might not be the safest thing in the world but that's only because what I'm going to do once I have the car is even more dangerous than that.

"You could die," I say, just to see if the clean weight of those words off my tongue will somehow shock their reality into me.

It doesn't.

I could die.

I grab my green canvas backpack off the floor, shrug it over my shoulders and run my thumb over my bottom lip. May Beth gave me blueberries last night and I ate them for breakfast when I woke up today. I'm not sure if they've stained my mouth and I have a hard enough time with good first impressions as it is.

The screen door on the trailer is rusted out, sparks a whine into all our surrounding Nowhere That Matters, but if you need a visual, picture a place far, far less than suburbia and then imagine me, a few more rungs down that ladder living in a trailer rented from Fed-Me-Blueberries May Beth for as long as I've been alive. I live in a place that's only good for leaving, is all that needs to be said about it, and I don't let myself look back. Doesn't matter if I want to, it's just better if I don't.

I grab my bike and ride my way out of town, briefly stopping on the green bridge over Wicker's River where I stare down at the water and feel the dizzying pull of its raging current in my gut. I dig through my bag, pushing aside clothes, bottles of water, some potato chips and my wallet until I find my cell phone tangled up in a ball of underwear. Cheap piece of plastic; doesn't even have a touchscreen. I throw it in the water and then I get back on my bike and ride out to Meddler's Road, off the highway, to meet the woman who wrote the craigslist ad. Her name is Becki *with an i*. She'd write that, *with an i*, like I couldn't see it for myself in every email she sent. She's standing next to the boxy, midnight-black car, one hand rested on its hood and the other on her pregnant belly. Behind her, another car is parked, a little newer. A man sits at the wheel with his arm hanging out the open window and he's tense until he sees me and then all his tension seems to melt away. It's offensive. I'm dangerous.

*You shouldn't underestimate people,* I want to call out. *I have a knife.*

It's true. There's a switchblade in my back pocket, a left-over from one of my mother's boyfriends, Keith. Long time ago. He had the nicest voice of all of them—so soft it was almost fuzzy—but he was not a nice man.

"Lera?" Becki asks, because that's the name I gave her. It's my middle name. It's easier to say than my own. Becki surprises me, the way she sounds. Like a scraped knee. Long-time smoker, I'd bet. I nod and take the cash-fatted envelope from my pocket and hold it out. Eight hundred in all. Okay, so she countered my initial offer of five but I know it's a good deal. I'm more or less paying for the repairs they made on the body. Becki says I should get a good year out of it at least.

"You sounded a lot older in your email."

I shrug and extend my arm a little farther. *Take the money, Becki,* I want to say, *before I ask you what you need it for.* Because the man in the car does look pretty itchy; unfixed. I know that look. I'd know it anywhere, on anyone. I could see it in the dark.

Becki rubs her swollen belly and moves a little closer.

"Your mama know you're out here?" she asks and I settle on a shrug, which seems to satisfy her until suddenly it doesn't anymore. She frowns, looking me up and down. "No, she don't. Why'd she let you come out here all alone to buy a car?"

It's not a question I can shake, nod, or shrug to. I lick my lips and steel myself for the fight. *I have a knife,* I want to tell the thing that likes to wrap its hands around my voice.

"My m-mom's d-d-d—"

The more I *d-d-d* the redder her face gets, the less she knows where to look. Not at me, not directly in my eyes. My throat feels tight, too tight, choked, and the only way I can free myself is if I stop attempting to connect the letters altogether. No matter how hard I try in front of Becki, they'll never connect. I'm only fluent when I'm alone.

"—ead."

The stutter's hold loosens.

I breathe.

"Jesus," Becki says and I know it's not because of the inherent sadness of what I've just told her, it's because of the broken way it came out of my mouth. She steps back a little because that shit is catching, you know, and if she gets it, there's a 100 percent chance she'll pass it on to her fetus. "Should you—I mean, can you drive?"

It's one of the more subtle ways someone has asked me if I'm stupid, but that doesn't make it any less maddening coming from a woman who can't even spell the word *please*. I tuck the envelope back in my pocket, let that speak for me. Mattie used to say it was my stubbornness, not my stutter, that was my worst quality, but one wouldn't exist without the other. Still. I can afford the risk of pretending Becki's ignorance is more than I'm willing to fork over for her used-up car. She laughs a little, embarrassed. Says, "What am I talking about? Of course you can . . ." And again, less convincingly: "Of course you can."

"Yeah," I say, because not every word I speak turns itself into pieces. The vocal normalcy relaxes Becki and she quits wasting my time, shows me the car still works by bringing the engine alive. She tells me the spring on the trunk is busted and jokes she'll let me keep the stick they use to prop it open at no extra charge.

I *hmm* and *uh-huh* my way through the transaction until it's official and then I sit on the hood of my new car and watch them reverse out, turning left onto the highway. I twirl the car key around my finger while the early morning heat slowly envelops me. The bugs find me an affront to their territory and make a feast of my pale white, freckled skin. The dry, dusty smell of road tickles my nostrils, speaking to the part of me that's ready to go, so I slide off the car and roll my bike into the brush, watching it fall unspectacularly on its side.

May Beth gives me blueberries sometimes, but she also collects expired license plates, displaying them proudly inside the shed behind her double-wide. All different colors and states, sometimes countries. May Beth has so many license plates, I don't think she'll miss two. The registration stickers are courtesy of old Mrs. Warner, three trailers down from mine. She's too frail to drive and doesn't need them anymore.

I muddy the plates up and wipe my dirty palms on my shorts as I round the car and get in the driver's side. The seats are soft and low and a cigarette burn marks the space between my legs. I slip the key into the ignition and the motor growls. I push my foot against the gas and the car rolls over the uneven terrain, following the same path out Becki took, until I reach the highway and then I go in the opposite direction.

I lick my lips; the taste of blueberries long since left them but not so long I can't still imagine their puckered sweetness enough to miss it. May Beth will be so disappointed when she knocks on my door and finds me gone, but I don't think she'll be surprised. Last thing she said to me, my face cupped firmly in her hands, was, *Whatever you're thinking, you get it out of that damned foolish head of yours right now.* Except it's not in my head, it's in my heart, and she's the same woman who told me if you're going to follow anything, it might as well be that.

Even if it is a mess.

# THE GIRLS

## S1E1

**WEST McCRAY:**
Girls go missing all the time.

My boss, Danny Gilchrist, had been talking for a while about me hosting my own podcast, and when I told him about May Beth's call, and about Mattie and Sadie, he urged me to look into it. It seemed a little kismet, he thought, that I was in the area when Mattie died. Still, those were the first words out of my mouth:

*Girls go missing all the time.*

Restless teenage girls, reckless teenage girls. Teenage girls and their inevitable drama. Sadie had survived a terrible loss, and with very little effort on my part, I dismissed it. Her. I wanted a story that felt fresh, new and exciting and what about a missing teenage girl was that?

We've heard this story before.

Danny immediately reminded me of why I was working for him, and not the other way around.

**DANNY GILCHRIST** *[PHONE]*:
You owe it to yourself to dig a little deeper. Don't decide what you *don't* have before you know what you do. You're better than that. Get down there, see what you find.

**WEST McCRAY:**
I left for Cold Creek the same week.

**MAY BETH FOSTER:**
It broke Sadie, Mattie's murder. She was never the same after, and rightfully so, but that the police never found the monster who did it, well. That had to have been the final straw.

**WEST McCRAY:**
Is that what Sadie said?

**MAY BETH FOSTER:**
No, but she didn't have to. You could tell just by lookin' at her.

**WEST McCRAY** *[STUDIO]*:
There's been no justice for Mattie Southern.

It's impossible for residents of Cold Creek to accept that a crime so heinously and chaotically executed would go unsolved. Television has provided their point of reference; after all, on shows like *CSI*, they'd catch the murderer within the hour, often working with less than what was discovered in that apple orchard.

Detective George Alfonso of the Abernathy Police Department, who headed the investigation, looks like a movie star past his prime. He's a six-foot-tall black man in his early sixties with short, graying hair. He expresses dismay over the lack of leads, but given the circumstances, he's not necessarily surprised there are so few.

**DETECTIVE ALFONSO:**
We didn't realize we were dealing with a murder, initially. We got a call about a fire and unfortunately, much of the crime scene was compromised by the fire department's efforts to put it out.

**WEST McCRAY:**
The DNA evidence they've recovered has been inconclusive and in need of a match. So far, there's no real suspect pool to pull from.

**DETECTIVE ALFONSO:**
We've filled in the gap between Mattie's disappearance and death as best we can. As soon as we got the call she was missing, we put out an AMBER Alert. We searched the local area and looked into several POIs—people Mattie had been in contact with in the hours before she vanished. They were cleared. We have a single witness who says they saw Mattie get into a pickup truck the night she went missing. It was the last time anyone ever saw her alive.

**WEST McCRAY:**
That witness was Norah Stackett, who owns Stackett Groceries, the only grocery store in Cold Creek. Norah is fifty-eight, a white, redheaded mother of three grown children, all of whom she's employed at her store.

**NORAH STACKETT:**
I was closing for the night when I saw her. I'd just turned the lights off and there was Mattie Southern at the corner, getting into some pickup. It was dark enough I couldn't tell if it

were blue or black, but I think black. I didn't get a look at the plate or driver either, but I've never seen that truck before and I haven't seen it since. Bet I'd know it if I saw it again, though. Next day, I hear there's cops all over Sparkling River and I'll just say I figured she was dead. I just knew. That's weird, isn't it—that I just knew? *[LAUGHS]* Givin' myself the creeps.

**WEST McCRAY:**
The girls lived in Sparkling River Estates. It's a small park, no more than ten trailers to it, some better kept than others. Cute little lawn ornaments and flower beds adorn one, while a rotting couch surrounded by garbage accents another. There's no sparkling river nearby, but if you follow the highway out of town, you might come across one.

As I mentioned earlier, it's managed by May Beth Foster, the girls' surrogate grandmother. She shows me the girls' trailer, a double-wide, exactly as Sadie left it. May Beth has found herself in a suspended state of grief where she can't bring herself to clean it out, even though she also can't afford not to rent it.

I don't know what I'm expecting when I step inside, but the place is spare and clean. For the last four years of their lives, Sadie raised Mattie here on her own, but still—she was a teenager and when I think of teenagers, I think of some sort of natural disaster; a tornado moving from room to room, leaving carnage in its wake.

It was nothing like that in the place they called home. There are still cups in the kitchen sink and on the coffee table in front of the old television in the living room. A calendar on the fridge that hasn't been flipped since June, when Sadie disappeared.

Things get downright eerie in their bedrooms. Mattie's room looks like it's waiting for her to come back. There are clothes on the floor, the bed is unmade. There's an empty glass with water stains coating its inside on the nightstand.

**MAY BETH FOSTER:**
Sadie wouldn't let anyone touch it.

**WEST McCRAY:**
It's a direct contrast to Sadie's room, which looks like it knows she's never coming back. In her room, the bed has been neatly made, but aside from that, every available surface is bare. It appears to have been stripped clean.

**WEST McCRAY** *[TO MAY BETH]:*
There's nothing here.

**MAY BETH FOSTER:**
I found all her things in the dumpster back of the lot, the day I realized she was gone.

**WEST McCRAY:**
What kinds of things?

**MAY BETH FOSTER:**
She got rid of her books, movies, clothes . . . just everything.

It makes me sick to think about her throwing her life in the garbage like that because that's what it amounts to. Every little bit that made her, everything, was all in the trash and when I found it, I just started to cry because she'd . . . it wasn't worth anything to her anymore.

**WEST McCRAY:**
Did you see this coming at all? Did she give you any kind of indication she was planning on leaving?

**MAY BETH FOSTER:**
That week before she left, Sadie got really quiet, like she was thinking about doing something stupid, and I told her whatever she was thinking . . . don't. I said to her, "Don't you do it." But by that point, I couldn't reach her about much of anything.

Still, I never imagined *this* . . .

I have to tell you, it's killing me to be in here. I just, I'd really like not to be.

**WEST McCRAY:**
We continue talking in her trailer, a cozy double-wide at the front of the lot. She has me sit on her plastic-covered couch, which squeaks very loudly every time I move. When I tell her that's not so great for an interview, we end up in her small kitchen, at the kitchen table, where she serves me a glass of iced tea and shows me the photo album she's kept of the girls over the years.

**WEST McCRAY:**
You did this?

**MAY BETH FOSTER:**
I did.

**WEST McCRAY:**
Seems like something a mother would do.

**MAY BETH FOSTER:**
Yeah, well. A mother should.

**WEST McCRAY:**
Claire Southern, Mattie and Sadie's mother, is not a welcome topic of conversation, but she's an unavoidable one because without Claire, there would be no girls.

**MAY BETH FOSTER:**
Less said about her, the better.

**WEST McCRAY:**
I'd still really like to hear it, May Beth. It could help. At the very least, it'll give me a better understanding of Sadie and Mattie.

**MAY BETH FOSTER:**
Well, Claire was trouble and there was no reason for it. Some kids are just born . . . bad. She started drinking when she was twelve. At fifteen, she was into pot, cocaine. By eighteen, heroin. She'd been arrested for petty theft a few times, misdemeanors. Just a mess. I was best friends with her mama, Irene, since Irene started renting from me. That's how I come into their lives. You never knew a soul as gentle as Irene. She could've had a firmer hand with Claire, but there's no use in dwelling on that now.

**WEST McCRAY:**
Irene died of breast cancer when Claire was nineteen.

**MAY BETH FOSTER:**
Before Irene died, Claire got pregnant. Irene was trying so hard to hold on for her grandchild but it wasn't . . . it wasn't meant to be. Three months after we put Irene in the ground, Sadie was born. I'd promised Irene on her deathbed I'd look

out for that little girl, and that's what I did. That's what I've always done because, well—you have any kids of your own?

**WEST McCRAY:**
Yeah, I do. A daughter.

**MAY BETH FOSTER:**
Then you know.

# sadie

Three days later, I dye my hair.

I do it in some public bathroom along the way. The ammonia mingles with the stench inside the dirty stalls and makes me gag. I've never colored my hair before and the end result is a muddy blond. On the girl on the box, it was golden, but that doesn't matter because all it's meant to look is different.

Mattie would've hated it. She would've told me so. *You never let me dye my hair,* she'd whine in her thin voice and by thin, I don't mean papery or weak. It just never came completely into itself. When she laughed, it would go so shrill and hurt my ears but I'm not complaining because when Mattie laughed, it was like being on a plane at night, looking down on some city you've never been to and it's all lit up. Or at least how I imagine that would be. I've never been on a plane before.

And it's true too. I never let her dye her hair. When she was burning through every rule in my book (*call if you go to a friend's house, don't text boys without telling me, put your phone away and do your goddamn homework already)* that was the only one she chose to honor: *no dyeing your hair until you're fourteen.* Just missed it.

I think the real reason Mattie never touched her hair was because she got the blond from Mom and couldn't stand the thought of losing what little pieces of her she had left. It always made me crazy how much the two of them looked alike, with their matching hair, blue eyes and heart-shaped faces. Mattie and I didn't share a father and we didn't look like we were sisters, not unless you caught us mirroring each other's expressions in those rare instances we felt the exact same way about something. Between her and Mom, I was the odd one out, my unruly brown curls and murky gray eyes set upon what May Beth always called *a sparrow's face.* Mattie was scrawny in a way that was underdeveloped and awkward, but there's a special kind of softness that goes along with that, something less visually cynical compared to my makings. I'm the result of baby bottles filled with Mountain Dew. I have a system that doesn't quite know how to process the finer things in life. My body is sharp enough to cut glass and in desperate need of rounding out, but sometimes I don't mind. A body might not always be beautiful, but a body can be a beautiful deception. I'm stronger than I look.

It's dark when the sign comes up for Whittler's Truck Stop.

A truck stop. Closest thing to a pause button for people living on fast-forward, only they don't pause so much as dial themselves down to twice the speed the rest of us operate on. I used to work at a gas station just outside of Cold Creek and my boss, Marty, never let me work nights alone was how little he trusted truckers passing through. I don't know if that was entirely fair of him, but it's how he felt. Whittler's is bigger than what I come from, but doesn't seem as clean.

Or maybe you get so used to the mess of home you convince yourself over time everything's exactly where it belongs. Nothing here is really trying for its best. The neon lights of the gas station sign seem duller than they should be, like they're choosing to slowly go out rather than ending themselves with that sudden *pop* into darkness.

I head for the diner, *Ray's* written in cursive paint on a sign that's too small for the building it rests atop, making everything appear dizzyingly askew. BEST APPLE PIE IN GARNET COUNTY! a sloppy cardboard sign boasts from the window. TRY A SLICE!

I push through the heavy glass door and fall into the fifties. Ray's looks just how it was described to me, red vinyl and turquoise, the waitresses in dresses and aprons styled to match. Bobby Vinton plays on an honest-to-God jukebox in the corner and I stand there, absorbing the nostalgia, the gravy-and-potatoes smell of it all, before I make my way to the counter at the back. The serving station and the kitchen is just beyond it.

I perch on one of the stools and rest my hands on the cool Formica countertop. To my right, a girl. Girl. Woman. She's hunched over a plate of half-eaten food, thumbs moving fast across her phone's screen. She has frizzy brown hair and she's got so much exposed pale skin, it makes me shiver to look at her. She's wearing black pumps, short-shorts and a thin, tight tank top. I think she works the parking lot. *Lot lizards.* That's what they call girls like her. My eyes travel up for a better look at her face and it's the kind of face that's younger than it looks, skin ravaged by circumstance, not passage of time. The lines at the corners of her eyes and the edges of her mouth remind me of cracks in armor.

I rest my elbows against the counter and bow my head. Now that I've stopped, the drive is catching up with me. I'm not used to that kind of push behind a wheel and I'm fucking tired. The muscles in my back have tied themselves into tight little knots. I focus on tunneling each individual ache into a single pain I can ignore.

After a minute, a man comes out of the kitchen. He has olive skin, a shaved head and beautiful, full-color tattoo sleeves on both arms. Skulls and flowers. His black *Ray's* T-shirt strains across the front of him, tight enough to show off the parts of his body he must've worked hard for. He wipes his hands on the greasy towel hooked in his belt and gives me a once-over.

"What'll it be?"

His voice sounds like a knife that sharpens itself on other people, intimidating enough that I can't even imagine what it would sound like if he yelled. Before I can ask if he's Ray, I notice the name tag on his shirt says SAUL. He turns his ear toward me and asks me to repeat myself, like there were words here and he only just missed them.

Mostly, my stutter is a constant. I know it better than any other part of myself, but when I'm tired, it can be as impossibly unpredictable as Mattie was when she was four and started playing hide-and-seek all over the neighborhood without ever telling anyone she'd begun the game. I have talking to do here but I don't want to waste a possible spectacle on someone I'm not sure will give me what I need, so I clear my throat and grab the small, laminated menu next to a basket of napkins and skim it for something cheap. I give Saul a pointed look, gesture to my throat and mouth *sorry* like I'm fucking laryngitic. I tap the menu so he realizes this is me, communicating. His eyes follow my finger and its *tap-tap-tap* to COFFEE . . . $2.00.

A minute later, he's sliding a mug under my nose, saying, "Just so we're clear, you can't be nursing that all night. Drink it while it's hot or add a meal to it."

I let the steam curl around my face before I take that first sip. The coffee scalds my tongue and my throat, waking me up faster than the caffeine ever would, but it tastes strong enough for me to be able to count on that too. I set the mug down and notice a woman at the service window. She's wearing a black *Ray's* shirt, like Saul, and she reminds me of a slightly younger May Beth, except this woman's hair is dyed black. May Beth's is all salt with a little pepper. They both have similarly peachy faces and pointed features, though, and everything after their necks is rounder and much less defined. Soft. May Beth used to wrap me in her arms and hold me close when there was no one else to do it—until I got too old for that sort of thing—and I loved that softness. I let the memory inspire a careful smile to play across my mouth. I give it to the woman. She gifts me with one of her own.

"You're looking at me like you know me," she says.

That's something else that separates her from May Beth, besides the hair—her voice. May Beth's voice is crumbling sugar cubes. This woman's is tart apple pie. Or maybe it's not that she sounds like that, it's what I'm smelling. There's a pie rack a few feet down the counter, the diner's famous apple sitting on top with its soft, syrupy pieces of fruit tucked into a beautifully flaky crust. My mouth waters and I know I've been hungrier than this in my life, but that caramel-cinnamon-sugar kiss is making it hard for me to remember when. My stomach growls. The woman arches her eyebrow and it's then I notice the name tag pinned over her right breast says RUBY. It'll be a bitch pushing that one past my lips.

"Forget it, Roo," Saul says from behind the service station. "She can't talk."

Ruby turns to me. "That true?"

"——"

I close my eyes. A block: a feels-like-forever moment

where my mouth is open and nothing happens—at least, not on the outside. Inside, the word is there and the struggle to give it shape makes me freeze, makes me feel like I've been disconnected.

"Y-you l—" I fight for the *L*, fight my way back to myself. I open my eyes. I feel the woman beside me staring. Ruby, she doesn't even blink and it makes me grateful but I fucking hate that too, because the kind of decency everybody ought to live by isn't something that deserves my gratitude. "You l-look like s-someone I know."

"That a good thing?"

"Yeah." I nod, faintly pleased with its successful landing. *Yeah.*

"Thought you didn't talk," Saul says, unimpressed.

"You want something with that coffee?" Ruby asks.

"I'm g-good."

She purses her lips. "You know you can't be nursing that all night."

Jesus. I clear my throat.

"I w-was wondering if I c-could ask y-you s—" *Something.* "A question."

That's a thing I can do sometimes: fake out my stutter. I psych it up to ruin one word and switch it out with another at the last minute and it somehow never manages to catch up to me. The first time I discovered this, I thought I was finally free, but no; I was being held hostage in a different way. It's exhausting, doing all that thinking for the kind of talking no one else has to think twice about. And it's not fair but there's not much in life that is.

"Sure," she says.

"Is R—" I close my eyes briefly. "Ray around?"

She winces. "Died a few years back."

"S-sorry." Shit.

"What do you need Ray for?"

"Have *you* w-worked here l-long?"

"Going on thirty years." She peers at me. "What's this about?"

"T-trying to f-find someone."

There's a faster way to do this. Before she can respond, I press my lips together and hold up my finger. She waits the minute I'm silently asking for while I open my backpack and take out a photograph. It's eight years old, but it's the only picture I have that holds the face of the particular person I'm looking for. It's a summer scene, all of us posed outside May Beth's trailer. I know it's summer because her flower beds are in full bloom. She's the one who took the photo and I took it from her, where it was nestled in the album she keeps of me and Mattie. This is the only picture of us that includes Mom—and Keith.

He has a hard face, a week's worth of beard and deep crow's feet I can't believe he ever got from smiling too much. He looks like he would step out of the photograph just to hate you up close. He has a child on his hip and that child, with the messy blond hair, is Mattie. She was five. The eleven-year-old girl in pigtails out of focus in the far corner of the shot is me. I remember that day, how hot and uncomfortable it was, and how I could not be coaxed to pose alongside them until my mom finally said, *Fine, we'll do it without you,* and that didn't feel right to me either so I crept into the frame and became the moment's blurry edges. I stare at it too long, like I always do, and then I point to the pen in Ruby's apron pocket. She hands it over. I flip the photo and scribble quickly across its back:

*HAVE YOU SEEN THIS MAN?*

But I already know the answer because I heard about Ray's from Keith. He used to talk about this place, said he was a regular, used to cradle Mattie in his arms and run his hand through her hair and say *one day, maybe,* he'd take her to Ray's for a slice of apple pie because *baby, you never tasted anything so good* . . . if Ruby's been here as long as she says she has, I know she's seen him. I pass the photo to her. She holds it careful as anything while I lean forward, watching her closely for some flash of recognition. Her face gives nothing away.

"Who wants to know?" she finally asks.

My heart hopes as little as I'll let it. "H-his d—his daughter."

She licks her lips and I notice her lipstick has faded and all that's really left is the harsh red of her liner. Then she locks eyes with me and sighs in such a way I wonder how often this happens, girls asking after men who have nothing in them to give.

"We get a lot of men in here and they don't really stand out unless there's something wrong with 'em. I mean— more than what's usually wrong with 'em." She half-shrugs. "He might've come through, but I don't remember him if he did."

I can hear a lie a mile away. It's not some superhero perk from stuttering, being in tune with other people's emotional bullshit. It's just what happens after a lifetime of listening to liars.

Ruby is lying.

"He s-said he w-was a r—a regular. Knew R-Ray."

"Well, I'm not Ray and I don't know him." She slides the photo back to me, the tone of her voice taking a saccharine turn. "You know, my daddy left me when I was younger than you. Trust me when I tell you sometimes it's just better that way."

I bite my tongue because if I don't, I'll say something ugly. I make myself stare at the counter instead, at a dried coffee splotch that hasn't been wiped up. I put my hands in my lap so she can't see them curl into fists.

"You said he's a regular?" Ruby asks. I nod. "What's your phone number?"

"D-d-don't have a f-phone."

She sighs, thinks on it a second, and then reaches for a take-out menu from the neat stack next to the napkins. She points to the number on it.

"Look, I'll keep my eye out. You call, ask for me, I'll tell you if I've seen him. I can't make any promises." She frowns. "You really don't have a phone?"

I shake my head and she crosses her arms, the look on her face wanting a *thank you,* I think, and it just makes me madder. I fold the menu and shove it and the photograph in my bag, trying to ignore the hot flush working its way across my body, the awful shame of not getting what I want. Bad enough it happens in the first place, worse to be forced to wear it.

"Y-you're lying," I say because I won't let her make me wear it.

She stares at me a long moment. "You know what, kid? Don't bother calling. And you're done with your coffee."

She heads back into the kitchen and I stare after her. *Good job, Sadie. You fucking idiot, now what?*

Now what.

I exhale slowly.

"Hey." The voice sounds featherlight, uncertain. I turn my head and the woman is staring at me. "Never seen anybody call Ruby on her bullshit before."

"—" I push past the block, letting out a small gasp. "You n-know w-why's she's b-bullshitting me?"

"Haven't been around that long. Just long enough to know she can be a real bitch when she wants to be." She looks at her hands. Her nails are pink and long and pointy, and I imagine the feel of them clawing across skin. Every little thing about you can be a weapon, if you're clever enough. "Look, there's a guy . . . sometimes he's hanging around behind the diner, sometimes, it's the gas station . . . if he hasn't been chased away from them, that is. If he has, you can usually find him by the dumpsters at the back of the parking lot. Name's Caddy Sinclair. He's tall, skinny. He might be able to tell you something."

"He a d-dealer?" I ask, but it's a question that answers itself, so she doesn't bother. I slide off the stool, tossing a five on the counter, because I know where I have to go now. "Thanks. A-appreciate it."

"Don't thank me yet," she says. "He doesn't do anything for free and no one talks to him unless they have to so you might want to think long and hard on whether or not you really do."

"Th-thanks," I say again.

She reaches over for my half-drunk coffee, wraps her hands around it and says, bitterly, "I know a thing or two about missing dads."


"You here for the Ruby Special?"

The voice is like phlegm, thick and unappealing. I cross from the light into the long, outstretched shadows of the truck stop until I'm in front of Caddy and Caddy is in front of me. I circled the diner and the gas station, and he wasn't there. He's in the last place I was told to look—the back of the parking lot next to the dumpsters. He's leaned against one of them, contoured by darkness that, for one moment, almost gives him extra dimension until my eyes adjust and I see how pathetically built he really is. He's thin, his eyes cloudy and lifeless. Stubble shades his jawline and pointed chin.

"N-no."

He's smoking, takes a deep drag off the cigarette nestled between his long fingers. I watch the cherry flare and fade and my neck prickles uncomfortably at a memory of Keith. I don't want to get into it, but I still have the scar on the back of my neck and I was afraid of fire for a long time after I got it. When I was fourteen, I forced myself to spend a night with a pack of matches and I made them burn bright, held them for as long as I could stand it. My hands would tremble, but I did it. I always forget fear is a conquerable thing but I learn it over and over again and that, I guess, is better than never learning it.

Caddy tosses the cigarette on the pavement and grinds it out. "Didn't your mama tell you about approaching dangerous men in the dark?"

"W-when I see a d-dangerous man, I'll k-keep that in m-mind."

I've got no sense of self-preservation. That's what May Beth used to tell me. *You wouldn't care if you died for it, so long as you were gettin' the last word.* It was hard enough having the stutter, let alone being a smart-ass on top of that.

Caddy slowly pushes himself from the dumpster and sets his murky gaze on me.

"Wuh-wuh-wuh-wuh *will* yuh-yuh-yuh *you*?"

It's not the first sorry imitation of myself I've ever heard, but I still want to pull his tongue out of his mouth and strangle him with it.

"I n-n-n—" *Calm down,* I think and then I want to slap myself for it. *Calm down* doesn't do anything. *Calm down* is what people who don't know any better tell me to do, like the difference between having a stutter and not having one is a certain level of inner fucking peace. Even Mattie knew better than to tell me to *calm down.* "I n-need to talk t-to you."

He coughs, spitting something resembling drying Elmer's Glue onto the ground. My stomach turns at the sight. "That right?"

"I w-w-want—"

"Didn't ask you what you want."

I take the picture out and hold it right in front of his fucking face because it's already pretty clear that I have to do this differently than I did it with Ruby. What's that saying: *better to ask forgiveness than permission?*

But I've never been good at saying *sorry* either.

"D-do you know this m-man? I n-need to know where t-to f-find him."

Caddy laughs and shoves past me, his bony shoulder slamming into mine, forcing me into a graceless backward shuffle. There's something confident about the way he moves his body for a guy who can't be a buck twenty soaking wet. I try to memorize it, the way his shoulders lead.

"I'm not goddamned Missed Connections."

"I can p—I can pay."

He stops and turns to me, running his tongue over his teeth as he contemplates it. In one quick clean stride, he closes the space between us and rips the photo from my hands. If I'd clutched it any tighter, I'd still be holding half of it. My first instinct is to make a grab back, but I catch myself in time. Sudden movements don't seem like they'd work in my favor.

"What do you want with Darren Marshall?"

I try not to wear the shock of this name on my face. Darren Marshall. So that's what Keith's calling himself now. Or maybe Keith was the name he gave himself when he lived with us and Darren is his real name—part of me wants that to be true. There's something about peeling back a layer this fast that feels good. I haven't felt good in a long time.

Darren Marshall.

"I'm his d-daughter."

"He never mentioned no daughter."

"W-why w-would he?"

He squints and holds the picture up in what little light

there is and the long, loose sleeves of his shirt creep down enough for me to see a constellation of track marks on his left arm. May Beth used to tell me it's a sickness and made me tell Mattie the same thing, but I don't believe it because people don't choose to be sick, do they? *Show a little compassion for your sister's sake. Hate the sin, love the sinner.* Like my junkie mother's addiction was my personal failing because I couldn't put my *compassion* ahead of all the ways she made me starve.

"Got somethin' to say?"

He knows exactly where I'm looking.

"No."

"Well, I'll be damned." He smiles faintly and gets close to me again. "Is it a money thing? You didn't give a fuck after he left but now you're hungry, that it? Why you think a man owes you more'n the life he gave you, huh?" He quiets for a moment, studying me. "Gotta say, kid, I don't see much of a resemblance." I raise my chin and he chuffs softly, slightly incredulous as his gaze returns to the photo. "You ever heard of a fool's errand?"

*Fool's errand.* Noun. I think. Like chasing after nothing, but sometimes nothing is all you have and sometimes *nothing* can turn into *something.* And I've got more than nothing. I know the guy in the picture is alive. If he's alive, he can be found.

I grab the picture from Caddy. "Then I'm a f-fool."

"I knew Darren but he hasn't been around in a long damn time. Might know something about that too," he says, and my throat gets tight because like I said, I can hear a lie a mile away.

Caddy isn't lying.

"It'll cost you," he adds.

"Already s-said I'd p-pay. How m-much?"

"Who said anything about money?"

I grab the picture back and he grabs me by the arm and the surprising grip of his spider-leg fingers makes me want to separate from my skin just so I don't have to feel it. The heat of him. A door slams somewhere beyond us. I turn my head to it.

There's a truck, a big black dog of a thing idling in the dark. A girl runs toward it. She's small in a way that reminds me of Mattie, and I stare at her tiny body, made of tiny bones, watching as she comes to a halt at the passenger's side. She stares at it for a long, painful moment and there's nothing I can do to stop what happens next. I watch as this girl, who isn't Mattie, pulls the door open. The cab of the truck lights up briefly as she climbs inside. She closes the door. The truck's interior lights dim, swallowing her whole.

Caddy digs his fingers into me, his nails sharp.

"L-let m-me go."

He lets me go, coughing into his elbow.

"It'll cost you," he says again.

He tilts his head to the side, his eyes drifting over me and then—a little more tentatively than he did the last time—he puts his hand on my arm and walks me farther into the darkness. He brings himself closer to me, fumbling for his belt buckle, whispering the kind of nothings in my ear that can't even pretend to be sweet. His breath is sour. I look into his eyes and his eyes are red.

# THE GIRLS

## S1E1

**WEST McCRAY:**
The first half of the photos in May Beth's album are only of Sadie. She was a small, happy baby, with brown hair, gray eyes and healthy pink skin. She didn't look anything like her mother.

**MAY BETH FOSTER:**
Sadie was the spitting image of Irene and Claire couldn't stand it, and if you saw Claire with Sadie, you'd wonder why she'd even have a baby in the first place. She hated holding her, nursing her, soothing her. I'm not being dramatic. She. *Hated.* It. I loved on Sadie best I could, but it was never enough to make up for what she wasn't getting from her mother.

**WEST McCRAY:**
Who was Sadie's father?

**MAY BETH FOSTER:**
I don't know. I don't think even Claire knew. She said his last name was Hunter so that's what she put on the birth certificate.

**WEST McCRAY:**
According to May Beth, Sadie had a lonely childhood those first six years without Mattie. Claire's addiction superseded all affection, and left her daughter attention-starved.

Sadie was also painfully shy, due to the stutter she developed when she was two. There was no clear cause. It might have been genetics. Hereditary. No other members in Sadie's known family stuttered but her paternal side is unaccounted for. May Beth unearthed a recording she made when Sadie was three; we had to hunt down a cassette player to listen to it.

**MAY BETH FOSTER [RECORDING]:**
You wanna talk into the recorder, honey? [PAUSE] No? I can play it back for you and you can hear what you sound like.

**SADIE HUNTER [AGE 3] [RECORDING]:**
Th-th-that's m-magic!

**MAY BETH FOSTER [RECORDING]:**
Yeah, baby, it's magic. Okay, talk into right here, just say hi!

**SADIE HUNTER [RECORDING]:**
B-but I w—I want t-to, I w—I—

**MAY BETH FOSTER [RECORDING]:**
We just have to record it first.

**SADIE HUNTER [RECORDING]:**
B-but I w-w-want t-to *hear*!

**WEST McCRAY:**
Sadie never outgrew her stutter. Early intervention likely could have helped, but May Beth never managed to convince Claire

to take action. School turned out to be a special sort of hell for Sadie. Children aren't kind about things they don't understand and, in May Beth's opinion, Sadie's teachers also lacked a certain understanding.

**MAY BETH FOSTER:**
Sadie turned out good in spite of them, not because of them. They thought that stutter meant she was stupid. That's all I'll say about that.

**WEST McCRAY:**
Forty-four-year-old Edward Colburn has never forgotten Sadie. He'd just started his career as a teacher at Parkdale Elementary when she came into his class. Parkdale, as I mentioned, is forty minutes away from Cold Creek, and buses in students from outside towns so they can go to school. This is how Edward remembers his former first grade student:

**EDWARD COLBURN:**
She was teased by her classmates because of the stutter and that caused her to withdraw. . . . We did our best to meet her needs, but you have to understand Parkdale has always been two things: underfunded and overcrowded. Add to that a mother who was largely unreceptive to any of our concerns and, well. It's not a recipe for a child's personal success. And it happens more often than you'd want to think, not only in economically depressed areas. Sadie was a very adrift, remote child. She didn't seem to have many, if any, interests of her own. She was reserved, but it was more than that . . . I'd almost say she was vacant.

**MAY BETH FOSTER:**
Then Mattie came along.

**WEST McCRAY:**
In May Beth's album, Mattie's arrival is marked with a Polaroid of a tiny, day-old bundle in six-year-old Sadie's arms. The way Sadie gazes at her newborn sister is almost impossible to describe. It's unbearably tender.

**WEST McCRAY *[TO MAY BETH]*:**
Just look at the way she's looking at Mattie . . . wow.

**MAY BETH FOSTER:**
Isn't it something? Sadie loved Mattie with her whole heart and that love for Mattie gave her a purpose. Sadie made it her life's work looking after her sister. Young as she was, she knew Claire wouldn't do it right.

**WEST McCRAY:**
Can you describe the girls' relationship with their mother?

**MAY BETH FOSTER:**
Claire enjoyed Mattie because they looked alike. She was Claire's little doll, not her child. She gave Mattie the Southern name. And Mattie thought Claire was the berries . . .

But that was Sadie's doing.

**WEST McCRAY:**
How do you mean?

**MAY BETH FOSTER:**
Sadie always covered for Claire, lied for her, even. Made sure Mattie understood Claire was sick . . . I think she thought if she did that, it'd hurt less for Mattie when Claire inevitably let her down. I don't know if that was the best thing for either of them. It cost Sadie a lot, especially after Claire left. I don't

know if Mattie ever fully appreciated what Sadie did for her, in that respect. If she'd lived long enough, maybe.

**WEST McCRAY:**
The pictures of Mattie are difficult to look at. She had shiny, stick-straight blond hair, sparkling blue eyes and Claire's heart-shaped face. It's nearly impossible to reconcile with that kind of vitality knowing how her story ends.

**WEST McCRAY [TO MAY BETH]:**
I can't help but notice Mattie doesn't look at Sadie with quite the same reverence.

**MAY BETH FOSTER:**
Mattie loved her big sister. Mattie *adored* Sadie but Sadie might as well have been Mattie's mother and that's a certain kind of dynamic. Throw in a six-year age gap, that's gonna add to it too. Looking after Mattie brought Sadie out of her shell and forced her to use her voice, no matter the stutter. But the times Sadie didn't feel like talkin' or couldn't get it out, Mattie would know what Sadie needed just by looking at her. So make no mistake, they were devoted to each other in their own ways. I don't know if all sisters are how the pair of them were. I have three of my own and I love them dearly, but we were never like that.

**WEST McCRAY:**
With each turn of the album's pages, May Beth's voice becomes less and less steady. As we reach the end of it, her eyes fill with tears.

**MAY BETH FOSTER:**
Oh.

**WEST McCRAY:**
What is it?

**WEST McCRAY [STUDIO]:**
She turns the album to me. On one side is a photo of the girls. They're sprawled on May Beth's plastic-covered couch, a red-and-orange knitted blanket shared between them. An oversized bowl of popcorn rests on Mattie's lap. They're absolutely entranced by whatever's on the TV in front of them; later May Beth tells me it was probably an old movie. The girls loved the classics. Sadie, in particular, was fond of anything with Bette Davis. But what's caught May Beth's attention at this particular moment is the page opposite. It's empty. There was a picture there, she insists, flipping frantically through the book to see if it somehow got loose and ended up somewhere where it shouldn't be. She checks the floor around us in case it fell out. It's nowhere to be found.

**MAY BETH FOSTER:**
But where did it—I don't know where it could have got to . . . it was a picture of . . . the girls were in it . . . it was . . . it was—I can't remember what, exactly, it was . . . but I *know* it had the girls in it. They were here. They were right here.

# sadie

I'm going to kill a man.

I'm going to steal the light from his eyes. I want to watch it go out. You aren't supposed to answer violence with more violence but sometimes I think violence is the only answer. It's no less than he did to Mattie, so it's no less than he deserves.

I don't expect it to bring her back. It won't bring her back. It's not about finding peace. There will never be peace.

I'm not under any illusion about how little of me will be left after I do this one thing. But imagine having to live every day knowing the person who killed your sister is breathing the air she can't, filling his lungs with it, tasting its sweetness. Imagine him knowing the feeling of the ground beneath his feet while her body is buried below it.

This is the furthest I've been from anything that I know.

I'm in the front seat, turning a switchblade over and over in my hand. There's a dirty water smell in the air. I close my eyes and open them and I'm still in the front seat, still turning the knife, air still heavy with the pond scum scent of it all. I close my eyes and open them again and it's like one of those running dreams where every impossible push forward is rewarded with the knowledge that you have to do it over and over again and there is no finish line and you don't know how to make yourself stop.

"Mattie."

The *M* of her name is an easy press. The double *t*s don't overstay their welcome.

When she was five and I was eleven, Mattie would crawl into my bed, terrified of the dark, desperate for me to say something that would make her feel safe. My fractured reassurances were never enough; all I could offer was my presence and she took what she could get, pressing her head against my shoulder and falling asleep like that. By morning, all my covers were tangled around her tiny body and my pillow always somehow ended up under her head. When I was eleven and Mattie was five, she wanted to talk like me, would storm around shattering her words until Keith smacked her on the butt for it and said, *Nobody talks like that who's got a choice,* and even though I hated him for it, I told Mattie he was right. When Mattie was five and I was eleven, I could no longer pretend each new sentence had a chance of coming out of me clean. I stopped talking for two weeks from the sheer grief of it until Mattie looked at me with her eyes impossibly wide and said, *Tell me what you want to say.*

Keith is not my father, but he sometimes pretended he was, would let people make the mistake and silently dared me to correct them. He would buy me candy at the gas station whether or not I was begging for it, then make a production of putting it in my palms just because he wanted to hear me force out a *thank you.* He would sit me at the table at night and have me memorize prayers to the utter delight of May Beth and Mattie was right to be afraid of the dark then because at night, he would come into my room and make me say them.

When I was nineteen and Mattie was thirteen, Keith came back.

I turn the switchblade one more time in my sweaty palm, feeling the weight of its neat black handle and the unforgiving blade tucked inside.

It was his, a long time ago.

It's mine now.

I'm going to carve my name into his soul.

# THE GIRLS

## EPISODE 2

**WEST McCRAY:**

In our last episode, I introduced you to the two girls at the center of this podcast, Mattie Southern and Sadie Hunter. Mattie was murdered, her body left just outside her hometown of Cold Creek, Colorado. Sadie is missing, her car found, abandoned, hundreds of miles away, with all her personal belongings still inside it. The girls' surrogate grandmother, May Beth Foster, has enlisted my help in finding Sadie and bringing her home.

For those of you just tuning in, this is a serialized podcast, so if you haven't listened to our first episode, you should do that now. We have more story than time to tell it—but I suppose that's true for all of us.

*[THE GIRLS THEME]*

**ANNOUNCER:**

*The Girls* is brought to you by Macmillan Publishers.

**WEST McCRAY:**
Claire left when Sadie was sixteen, which meant Mattie was ten. Their mother had wholly succumbed to her drug addiction by that point, and her exit was its most logical conclusion. May Beth's last conversation with Claire was two days before she abandoned her life and children in Cold Creek.

**MAY BETH FOSTER:**
She wanted money from me and I knew what she wanted it for. Said it was for the girls, for food, and I said *well, you tell me what you need and I'll pick it up at Stackett's for ya*, and she said *no, I need the money*. And we got into it worse than we ever had. I tried not to push her too much, because whenever I did, she'd keep the girls from me . . .

Anyway, I told her to get her shit together, that she was still young enough to turn it all around and God would reward her trouble, but she had to do her part too. She hung up the phone so hard, my ears were ringing all night.

**WEST McCRAY:**
The next day, May Beth went on a two-week vacation to visit her daughter in Florida. The day after that, Claire left.

Mattie had just entered fifth grade and was enjoying herself. Sadie had been dividing her time between high school—which, per May Beth, she didn't like at all—and working at the McKinnon Gas Station.

Her boss, Marty McKinnon, has lived in Cold Creek all forty-five years of his life and expects he'll live what years are left of it there too. He's an imposingly well-built, ruddy-faced guy but he's known around town as a gentle giant. He'd give you the shirt off his back, if you're not too afraid to ask for it.

**MARTY McKINNON:**
Sadie was a good kid, hard worker. I didn't need the help so much as she did, you catch my meaning. She'd uh, she tried all over town for a job before she ended up with me. They'd been talking about it at the bar, Joel's, you know. Makin' fun of her, like—

**WEST McCRAY:**
What did they say?

**MARTY McKINNON:**
They just thought it was funny she might be able to do anything worth paying for. She was a buck and change and she can't hardly talk, so how can you put her to work? That sorta thing . . . well, I thought that was damn unfair, so when she finally came my way, I offered her something. She was so grateful, that was the first and only time she ever hugged me. If you knew Sadie, you'd know she wasn't a . . . she didn't open up a lot. It was like pulling teeth just to get her to tell you how she was. I think that's because she was always terrified people would call CPS and she'd get separated from Mattie. But that was unlikely.

**WEST McCRAY:**
Why do you say that? It seems pretty obvious the girls needed help.

**MARTY McKINNON:**
Yeah, but everyone here does, you get me? We're not in the habit of borrowing trouble. Still, it worried Sadie and she thought Claire leaving would be the end of 'em—as if May

Beth would've *ever* let that happen—so she didn't say a word about it to anyone and made Mattie swear to do the same. Then, a week later, around four in the morning, I get a call. It's Mattie, frantic. She thought Sadie was dying. I drove over and Sadie was sick as a dog. It was bad enough I took her to the hospital. They hooked her up to some IVs and she was fine . . . just one of those freak things.

**MAY BETH FOSTER:**
I think it was the stress of Claire going, that's what caused it.

**MARTY McKINNON:**
Anyway, we were in the waiting room and Mattie just *lost* it, just started bawling her eyes out and Mattie's always been kind of dramatic, like Claire was, but this wasn't that. She was scared out of her mind. So I got her candy from the vending machine, tried to settle her down some, and she told me Claire had left and if anyone found out, she and Sadie would never see each other again. My God, the kid was so upset, she threw up all over me. It was a mess. First thing I did was call May Beth in Florida and she flew back that day. She really loves those girls. Sadie was so mad at Mattie tellin' me and at me tellin' May Beth, and at May Beth just for knowin', I don't think she talked to any of us for a week.

**MAY BETH FOSTER:**
It's funny, I always thought Claire would leave us one way or the other—but I still wasn't ready for it. Sadie never had her mother to begin with, so she didn't even know how to start losing her on this level. The only thing Sadie was afraid of was losing the family she had left and that was Mattie. And Mattie . . . Mattie was absolutely leveled by it.

**WEST McCRAY:**
Tell me more about that.

**MAY BETH FOSTER:**
I thought it was going to kill her. I well and truly did. Mattie got so depressed about it, she didn't want to eat. She lost weight she couldn't afford to lose. She barely slept . . . she'd have these waking nightmares about Claire leaving and open her eyes and realize that it wasn't just a dream. Sadie couldn't even calm her down. She was hysterical half the time, almost catatonic the rest of it. I told Sadie we needed to get Mattie to a doctor, but . . . Sadie wouldn't have it, and I didn't see it ending well if we did, to be honest. Sadie dropped out of high school instead. She thought maybe being at home would help.

**WEST McCRAY:**
And did it?

**MAY BETH FOSTER:**
No. Only one thing got through to Mattie.

**WEST McCRAY:**
About three months after Claire left, and for the first and only time, the girls received word from their mother. It arrived in the form of a postcard, which was later recovered with Sadie's belongings. On its front, a line of palm trees against a stark, beautiful blue sky. *Greetings from Sunny L.A.!* the card says. *Wish you were here!* It's addressed only to Mattie, and in Claire's messy scrawl it says, *Be my good girl, Mats.*

**MAY BETH FOSTER:**
Mattie came alive after that. From that point on, she was ab-solutely fixated on L.A.—they had to go there and find Claire,

they just *had* to, their mother wanted them to find her and start over . . .

I hate that it happened, as grateful as I was for it at the time. It put the color in Mattie's cheeks, it gave us our girl back, but my God, she and Sadie were never the same after that.

**WEST McCRAY:**
Sadie refused to look for Claire?

**MAY BETH FOSTER:**
It wasn't possible, for a lot of reasons. The money. They couldn't afford it. They didn't know where in the city she was . . . I mean come on. Claire probably wrote it when she was high. She didn't ask them to find her. That postcard was a good-bye. Mattie just didn't understand or accept it. And I guess . . . Sadie could've acted a little torn up about it for her sister's benefit, but she didn't . . .

**WEST McCRAY:**
Did Mattie blame Sadie for Claire leaving?

**MAY BETH FOSTER:**
No, but she blamed Sadie for not looking for her.

**WEST McCRAY:**
What did Claire mean when she told Mattie to be "*my* good girl"?

**MAY BETH FOSTER:**
When Mattie was being Claire's good girl, she was usually giving Sadie hell. I feel like I'm making Mattie sound terrible and that's not the case. She was just . . . young. Mattie loved Sadie but she worshipped Claire.

**WEST McCRAY:**
After the postcard, things slowly deteriorated between the girls.

**MAY BETH FOSTER:**
It was heartbreaking to see, the way Mattie would get with Sadie. Just vicious. Sadie forgave Mattie everything. She knew where that anger was coming from and bore it. That doesn't mean she was a saint—she wasn't. She'd get impatient, tell Mattie she was being stupid, that it was hopeless . . . it was the first real crack between them and it kept growing. It's amazing, really, when I think about how long and how hard Mattie held onto Claire while Sadie was just trying to hold onto Mattie.

The month before Mattie died, things were as bad between them as I'd ever seen. Mattie was becoming a woman and that's a dangerous time in any girl's life. She was her own person and that person had different ideas of how things should be than Sadie did. And she never said it, but I know Sadie was damn hurt about it.

I can't—if Claire hadn't sent that—if she coulda just made a clean break, I think eventually Mattie would've come to terms with it. But she had to screw things up all the way from L.A., and that's what Sadie and Mattie were fighting about the night Mattie disappeared.

**WEST McCRAY:**
That's the one thing everyone seems to agree was the catalyst for Mattie's disappearance: she attempted to leave Cold Creek in search of her mother. She got into a killer's truck for what she hoped would be the first leg on her long journey to L.A.

**MAY BETH FOSTER:**

Mattie never would've done something like that if she'd never got that postcard. I know it haunted Sadie and I know . . . I know if Sadie's out there right now, it's still haunting her.

# sadie

Something collides with my window.

*Thud.*

My eyes fly open and my head jerks up, my neck protesting the unholy angle it's been stuck in with a quick succession of alarming *crack*s. My body is halfway across the back seat before I've got a grasp of the situation. Two kids, boys—around ten or eleven years old—standing about five feet from the car. They're both so underfed May Beth would've declared them *ragamuffins*. One has a basketball in his hands. He's glaring at me. I glare back. He throws the basketball at my window. *Thud.* It bounces back in his hands. He takes aim again and anger surges through me. I reach across the front seat, my palm flying to the horn of the car. I press down and keep my hand there.

They run away.

I continue to let the nasal blare of the car horn fill this desolate section of neighborhood as I watch the boys' gangly legs propel them down the street. When they turn a corner, I let it go and it's completely silent and still. I'm parked in a cul-de-sac lined by houses in various stages of development, a large billboard advertising a community completion date that seems impossibly close. There's a swampy-looking pond just across the way from me, little ripples in the water made by hovering bugs.

I turn the car on briefly, just to get a look at the clock. Eight a.m. Jesus. May Beth says it's rude to bother anyone before nine a.m. and even then, dropping by at nine isn't all that decent either, unless it's an emergency. I rub the back of my neck and then I grab my backpack off the floor, rummaging around until I find a half-empty bottle of water, my toothbrush and toothpaste. I brush my teeth, throw open the car door, lean out and use what's left of the water to rinse and spit. My stomach growls. I could eat. I've got half a bag of salt and vinegar chips stuffed in the glove box. I've only just grabbed it before it's empty and I'm licking my fingers clean of the salty, sour dust. Mattie would be pissed if she saw me doing this, tell me I'd never let *her* get away with such an unbalanced breakfast because anything I did, she wanted to do on principle because little sisters are like that.

*It'd stunt your growth,* is what I'd tell her. *Don't want you to be a shrimp forever.*

But Mattie would've ended up taller than me. You could tell just by looking at her legs. They were so much longer than the rest of her and if you stared at them a while, the rest of her started looking really strange. Arms too skinny, waist too short, hands too big. She was always looking forward to the moment she'd finally get to stare me down and Mom always warned me it was coming, always said it when Mattie and I were giving each other grief because Mom always sided with Mattie about everything. We could've been fighting about whether or not the sky was blue and Mattie could've said it was purple and Mom would've told her she was right just for the look on my face when she did. I can't even put to words what it's like to swallow down a moment like that, but I can tell you exactly how bitter it tastes.

I get dressed, swapping out my stale Henley, underwear and jeans for a rumpled pair of black leggings, a fresh pair of underwear and a T-shirt that's clean enough. I'll have to find a place to do laundry soon, if I can bring myself to part with the cash. I grab my brush and run it through my knotty hair slowly, just trying to pass the time, and then I pull it into a ponytail. I lick my thumb and smooth my eyebrows down. I run my tongue over my teeth and pick a flake of dead skin off my bottom lip and then I start the car and make my way through Wagner.

Wagner reminds me of a phoenix just before it dies and is reborn. The developing subdivision I spent the night in speaks to the place it'll become after the rest of it bursts into flames; some quaint tourist hot spot rising from the ashes. For now, everywhere I look I see the kind of cracks that remind me of Cold Creek. People fighting to carve out a space for themselves that's a little better than the one beside it, but none of it's actually any good.

I park the car at a sorry-looking elementary school, wander across its lot and round the building to the playground at the back because across from the playground there's a house. I shove my hands in my pockets and brace myself as I move forward. There are people on the swings, their backs to me. A man and a girl, side by side. When the man reaches his arm around the swing's chain to put his hand on her small, bony shoulder, I slow my pace.

"You okay?" the man murmurs to her, his feet scraping across the ground from the slow drag of the swing. His voice is soft, silky with kindness. "I know it's an adjustment, but I'm an okay guy to have around . . . and if you ever need to talk, I'm right here for you."

The girl's shoulders tense, every one of her muscles

tightening at the feel of those calloused fingers against the barest parts of her body. She doesn't say anything and she won't say anything and I know why she won't, why her tongue keeps itself quiet. She doesn't trust him. His is a kindness that doesn't reach his eyes and she might only be a meatless eleven-year-old, but she's smart. She knows about the calm before a storm, a quiet building toward a greater chaos. Everything about this *okay* guy doesn't fit quite so well into the landscape of their lives. He's too sober, too concerned, too everywhere when she thinks she's alone. He's too many other things she can't put the words to, like the way he's touching her now, which is more familiar than it has any right to be and more intimate than should be allowed.

"It's gonna be fine, Sadie," the man says.


Marlee Singer.

That was the name Caddy gave me when my knife was pressed against his throat, his belt undone, hanging limply against his jeans. I felt his words against the blade. *Marlee Singer.* And more: *Lives in Wagner. She can tell you something about Darren Marshall.* I made him push his pants all the way down before I let up, just to give myself time to get away.

The gravel shifts beneath my feet as I walk the pathway leading to Marlee's front door. There are no signs of life beyond it, no curious fluttering of curtains in the window. I knock and wait. A car goes by. I run my hand through my hair and turn back toward the road. It was 9:45 last I looked but maybe she's still in bed. I turn back to the house, hoping for something from the second story, but there's nothing.

I creep around the side of the house and peer into the first window I see.

A living room. I lean closer, my hands gripping the edge of the windowsill. There's a couch. Coffee table. There are baby toys on the floor and . . . distantly, I hear the front door of the house open and moments after that, someone approaching. I feel the weight of their gaze on my body, sizing me up the closer they get. Sweat pearls against my forehead and under my hair, beginning its leisurely slide down the back of my neck and when I turn around, I face the woman I'm looking for.

Marlee.

"Who the hell are you?"

I'd put her close to forty, or maybe not quite. Her white-blond hair is pulled back into a tight ponytail, her mouth a gash of red lipstick. High cheekbones. Her eyebrows must be white too, either that or she doesn't have any. She's bony, almost in the way that Mattie was bony, but not because she's growing—from drugs or an eating disorder or not having enough money. I recognize all of these things, but I can't always tell them apart. She's wearing cutoffs and a T-shirt with vintage Mickey Mouse on the front and it's knotted just under her breasts. Silver stretch marks line her pink abdomen. I don't see any marks on her arms, not like Caddy.

"What the hell do you think you're doing?" She's got a flinty kind of voice, one I can't imagine as a whisper or a song.

"—"

A rope around my throat. I lock on nothing for far too long. She looks like she's a minute away from calling the police. *Spit it out,* I think. *Just spit it out.* Keith used to snap that at me when he got tired of waiting. If I was close enough, he'd grab me by the face with one hand, like he could force the words out of me if he just squeezed hard enough.

"*Hello?*" She waves a hand in front of my face. "What the

hell are you doing sneaking around my house? Give me one reason I shouldn't call the cops right now."

I exhale sharply. "I'm l-looking f-for s-someone."

Marlee puts her bony hands on her bony hips. I think I could wrap my fingers around her wrists once, twice, three times. Maybe I could break her in half, but there's something about her that makes me think I wouldn't get too far in the attempt, like my throat would be slit before I even knew what was happening. It's hard not to respect that.

"In my house?" She steps forward and I resist a step back. "Let's try this a question at a time, real slow: who the hell are you?"

"L-Lera."

Sometimes I wonder how my mother came to put *Sadie Lera* together. When I asked her she'd always say, *I had to call you something, didn't I?* But there has to be more to it than that. I want there to be. Even if it's just that she liked them both enough to mash them together, despite the fact they don't sound nice together at all.

"Lera . . . ?"

"C-Caddy Sinclair g-gave me your n-name," I tell her. Her eyes flash in a way I don't like. "He said you c-could help me."

"Did he now? Who is it you're looking for?"

"Darren M-Marshall."

She laughs, a brittle, unpleasant sound that makes my spine crawl.

"You're fucking kidding me," she says. It's not a question. She sniffs and runs an arm across her nose. The vaguely muted sound of a baby crying inside floats out onto the street. She spares me half a glance before making her way toward it.

"Go home, girl," she says and then she's gone.

I hear her front door slam shut.

But I didn't come this far to go home.

I round the house and I sit on her stoop, legs stretched in front of me and crossed at the ankles, my bag by my side. I stare at the sky and watch its forget-me-not blue deepen into something a little more, what's the word . . . *cerulean*. I stare until the sun puts itself directly in my line of vision and forces me to look away. I let my skin bake, then burn, let my mouth dry. Is this self-harm? Feeling the pain happening to you and letting it happen?

*I could die,* I think, and it feels like nothing.

It's just after three when Marlee's door creaks open, pulling me from a hazy stupor. I don't raise my head until she says, "Get your ass in here."

The door slams shut behind her and I begin the painful task of rising to my feet, my body stiff, my skin sore and sunburnt. I force myself to draw my shoulders back and walk into Marlee's place like I own it. The house smells stale and smoky, like someone made a point to close every window just before opening a pack of Lucky Strikes.

I stand in a dim hallway before the stairs leading to the second floor. It offshoots in two different directions, the living room—which I've already seen—and a kitchen. That's the room Marlee steps out of, wearing something different now, a pair of jeans with such artistic rips in the legs I can't tell if they're on purpose or not and a red tank top that grants a full view of her collarbone, where she has a tattoo of a knife surrounded by flowers, daring me to look at it.

"Didn't suppose there was any other way to get you off my stoop," Marlee says and I nod in agreement, crossing my arms. She crosses hers. "You're all sunburnt."

"Y-yeah."

"That's gonna hurt tomorrow."

It hurts now.

"L-likely, yeah."

She squints. "Why do you talk like that?"

"N-never heard a st-stutter before?"

"Course I have. I wanna know *why*, is all."

"Just l-lucky, I guess."

"And you're looking for . . . Darren," she says and I nod. She sighs and heads back into the kitchen. "Well, don't just fuckin' stand there."

I'm in pain, my skin too tight against me. I have to force myself to a mental place past the sun's sear just so I can move. When I finally get into the kitchen, Marlee's there, leaning against the counter. The place is a mess, but it's not disgusting. It just speaks to a woman who can't be expected to wash the dishes and look after the kid she's got at the same time. The sink is piled high with plates and bowls and glasses and sippy cups. Across from it, there's a small kitchen table against the wall underneath a window that gives a full view of the schoolyard across the street. There are two chairs on either side of it. The stuffing is coming out of one's seat. Everything's sort of retro, but not by choice. It's too hodge-podge for that. The floors are peeling laminate and the walls are beige. The window curtains are a deep forest green. It's ugly.

"N-nice p-place."

She knows I'm lying, but she doesn't care. Marlee scrutinizes all there is of me to scrutinize, from the tips of my toes to the top of my head. I dig into my bag for the photo and then I hand it to her. Her fingers are long and when the scene on the eight-by-six registers, her hands shake just slightly enough to leave me wondering if I imagined it.

"Jesus," she murmurs.

"I'm his d-daughter."

I don't know if I need the ruse, but I don't want to find out I did when it's too late. Marlee laughs, that same brittle sound I heard earlier. She hands the picture back to me and opens a drawer, pulls out a pack of smokes. She lights up, relishing that first hit of nicotine. When she inhales, all the lines around her mouth are cast in sharp relief.

"You're telling me *Darren Marshall*'s got a daughter." Her lipstick leaves a mark on the cigarette's filter. I see the struggle on her face, the words not sitting quite right. She takes two more puffs and then coughs and I swear I can hear whatever it is she can't shift out of her lungs settling there, accumulating. "And that's you."

"Sure."

"The little one too? She belong to him?"

"N-no."

"You want a drink or something?"

I nod. I want something to drink and more than that, something to eat. She opens her fridge and hands me a Coke. The shock of cold aluminum against my palm is the best thing I've felt for hours. I pop the tab open with a satisfying *hiss* and listen to the fizz.

"He must not have been in your life long," she says.

"L-long enough."

"He's really your father?" She waits until I'm mid-drink before she asks. I let the carbon bubble in my mouth, a nice, fleeting sensation. ". . . Darren."

"Why d-do you say his n-name like th-that?"

It sounds alien on her tongue, something her voice is fighting against.

Before she can answer, that soft child cry I heard earlier fills the house from upstairs. Marlee says *shit*, tosses her cigarette in the sink and runs the water over it. She points to one of the chairs. "Park your ass there. I'll be right back." And she doesn't move until I park my ass. She hurries out of the room and tells me *don't even think about taking anything* over her shoulder as she goes. That kind of warning is enough to make me want to reconsider the whole place because up until she said that, nothing here struck me as worth taking. There are bills on the table, though. Past-due notices. Seeing them puts a knot in my stomach the size of a grapefruit. That sort of dread you don't ever forget once you've known it. The crushing panic of needing money you don't have.

She comes back a few moments later with a baby boy on her hip. He's got the same white-blond hair as his mama, shaped into an unfortunate bowl cut. His eyes are bluer than the sky outside and he's got a button nose planted on the roundest face I've ever seen. Pudgy arms and legs. I guess he's where all the grocery money goes. He's squirming all over the place until he sees me and buries his head in Marlee's side, suddenly stranger-shy. Marlee points to the high chair folded in the corner.

"Unfold that for me?"

Five minutes later, the baby's in his chair and Marlee's rooting around her fridge again. Her son keeps his eyes on me and it's creepy in the same way those evil kids in *Village of the Damned* are creepy. The only baby I've ever really liked was Mattie. In all my days, I've never seen one as cute as she was. She was so round and soft and sweet. She had a little tuft of blond hair right at the center of her head, and that was all the hair she had for the longest time. It looked just like a toupee. Made me laugh. And her tiny hands were always in fists, like she was spoiling for a fight, waiting for the day she'd be old enough to hit something. She loved clutching each of my fingers in this surprisingly strong grip. She was so strong.

She was perfect.

"W-what's his n-name?"

"Breckin."

She gets him settled in and then grabs some applesauce and spoons it into his mouth. He burbles and half of it ends up down his shirt. This makes Marlee laugh, but it's different than the laughter I've heard so far. It's indulgent, kind.

It's the nicest her voice has sounded to me since I got here. She murmurs some nonsense at him.

"Where's D-Darren?"

May Beth said I can be off-putting sometimes, the way I cut straight through the bullshit and right to the bone when I've got my sights set on something—that I don't spend enough time on the lead-in to make things comfortable, I guess. I've decided the only thing someone can do about that is either love it or hate it because I'm not changing it. From the look on her face, I can't tell if Marlee hates it. Her smile fades, but she keeps her eyes on Breckin.

"Kid," she says, and I really wish people would stop calling me *kid*. "I don't know the first thing about you and you think I should tell you anything I know about him?"

"M-more or less."

She spoons more applesauce into Breckin's mouth.

"What you want him for?"

"I w-want to k-kill him."

The spoon freezes an inch from Breckin's face and his confusion is immediate. He slaps his hands on his high chair tray, calling Marlee's attention back to him. She dips the spoon into his mouth and then sets it all aside.

"It's a j-joke," I say.

"Right," she says back.

I pick at the tab of the Coke can, letting it catch under my nail before *ping*ing back into place. She says, "I want another cigarette."

"S-so have one."

"I don't smoke around the baby."

But in the end, she does. She moves herself to the corner of the kitchen and lights up again, carefully turning her face away from Breckin every time she exhales, like it will make a difference. She says, "He hasn't been around in a couple years. Used to always be around."

"At R—at Ray's."

"Sometimes." She fidgets, bites her lip. "Where are you from, anyway?"

"D-doesn't matter."

She rolls her eyes. "Come on, kid. Give me something."

"—" I set the Coke down. "I-I'm not a—I'm not a kid."

She brings the cigarette to her mouth, chewing on her knuckle while smoke drifts lazily around her face. Breckin doesn't seem put out over the impromptu end of snack time. He's babbling to himself, enthralled with the sound of his own voice.

"They're tearing this whole town down," she says after a minute. "They got this new development coming." She takes another drag, inhales so deeply, I fleetingly imagine her cancered future. "It's stupid. I don't know what they're trying at. This isn't like the rest of the state, you know? Fuckin' . . . Whole Foods and yoga . . . and if they pull it off, I can't afford to live here when it's a shithole. I don't know where I'd go."

"C-Cold Creek."

"What?"

"W-where I'm from."

"Never heard of it." She squints. "You know what he's about?"

"Y-yeah," I say. *I know it better than you.*

I take another sip of the Coke and it's starting to taste too sweet. I wish the air were moving around in here. Marlee takes another drag of her smoke and Breckin waves his hands around and I feel like this has happened a hundred times before me, that I've seen all there is to see of their lives. I look down at myself and the fire-red parts of my chest overwhelm me with the feeling that I want to be somewhere else. Anywhere else.

"You know his name's not Darren?" she asks. I nod. "I mean, that's what he went by when he was living here, but I never got used to sayin' it."

"W-what's h-his real name?"

"We'll just keep it Darren for now," she says.

"He was K-Keith w-when I knew him."

"Huh." She chews her lip. "That's not his name either."

"H-how d-d—how do you know?"

"Because my brother used to go to school with him. I was seven years behind them both. Time I finished, they were long gone. I moved out here, got hitched, got divorced and my brother, well. He was making a whole lot more of himself."

"H-how'd he d-do that?"

People around here hardly ever seem to do that.

"My parents had enough money for one kid and ended up with two." Marlee shrugs. "He was the boy. He was the one they pinned all their hopes on, so he got more. He got college."

"W-what was . . . he like?" I can't seem to resist asking. She knows I mean Keith. "B-back then?"

She looks away. "He was poor as most of the rest of us. But he was quiet. Sort of dirty too, like he didn't look after himself, like hygiene-wise. He was weird . . . he did some weird shit, and he got his ass kicked a lot for it. Bullied, I guess. And his parents—they were a mess. His dad would drink and go at him with a belt."

"Oh," I say.

She clears her throat. "By high school, my brother—thing you have to understand about my brother is he was a golden boy in every sense of the word—he took Darren under his wing, sort of, just started making a point of being nice to him. When I asked why, he said it was important to set that kind of example because *we're no better or worse than the people we walk amongst.*" She pauses. "He was a real asshole, my brother, in case that didn't make it obvious. Anyway, the other kids, they eased off and Darren and my brother became inseparable . . . it was sorta like—you're probably too young for that cartoon about the little dog chasin' after the big dog? Hell, I am too. But it was like that. Darren was always at my brother's heels. We'd have him at our house for dinner all the time . . ." She trails off. "He gave me my first kiss. I was ten and he was seventeen. That's what Darren was like back then."

"H-how'd he end up here in W-Wagner? How long ago was th-that?"

She shrugs. "It was a couple years. He was just passing through. He knew I lived here because he and my brother keep in touch. Anyway, he stopped by and he seemed different, little more put together, nothing like he was when he was . . ." She looks at the floor. "He was only supposed to be here for dinner and he ended up staying a lot longer."

"Mama," Breckin says plaintively, and Marlee moves to him, resting her hand on his head. She turns to me.

"Once he knew he was staying, he told me he was going by Darren Marshall now and if I could play along, that'd be swell."

"H-he say why?"

Breckin giggles. She shakes her head.

"And you st-still l-let him stay?"

I guess I don't do so well keeping the disgust out of my voice, because she tenses, raising her hand from her son's head. She waits a minute, like she expects me to push it, and part of me feels young enough to want to. I used to be an age where I believed I could talk my mother out of her worst decisions, the drinking, drugs, certain men she'd bring home to bed. Keith. Sometimes, I think about that Sadie, begging her mother to save her from . . . her mother.

I hate that version of myself.

"I don't gotta answer to you. But yeah, I did." She shakes her head a little, her brow furrowing. "You know, all the time I was with him, Darren never said he had a kid. My brother never mentioned it either. He would've known."

"I'm n-not lying t-to you," I lie. She just looks at me and I'm afraid if she does that for too long, she'll see the truth somehow. "So w-what h-happened?"

"We were together a few months. He'd sit right where you're sitting, every morning, and he'd have his coffee looking out that window."

I follow her gaze to the schoolyard. There are a couple of women at the playground now, pushing their kids, or their charges, on the swings. I imagine that place during the school year, the grounds teeming with children, running, playing, laughing, under the watchful eye of the man at the kitchen table.

"I was doing the laundry," Marlee says. "Cleaning out his jeans pockets before I threw 'em in the wash and I found this picture . . . this old, worn picture—an old Polaroid. It was . . ." She closes her eyes briefly and her forehead creases, like she can see it there, behind her eyes, and she wishes she could see anything else. "I don't want to get into it, but it was the kind of thing you can't explain or defend." She takes a shuddering breath out and opens her eyes. "People don't change. They just get better at hiding who they really are. I turned him out the same day. I wanted nothing to do with it then and I want nothing to do with it now."

She lifts Breckin from his high chair, pressing her face into his baby neck. I scratch at my chest and immediately regret the abuse of my own gentle touch. My skin is on fire.

"You h-hear of him since? Where he m-might be?"

"No."

"W-what about your b-brother?"

"I don't talk to my brother anymore," she says tightly. "He's of the opinion that how I treated Darren was wrong and we haven't spoken since."

"P-please—"

"Look, I'm sorry for whatever it is brought you here,"

Marlee says, "and I feel bad enough for you that I was will-ing to tell you that much. But I got a kid and I can't afford to get mixed up in whatever . . ." She waves her hands. "Whatever *this* is."

"—"

She watches me struggle.

"P-*please*," is all I finally manage.

She closes her eyes and Breckin sits between us, oblivi-ous.

"Jack Hersh. That's his real name. Do something with that."

"H-he d-doesn't go by it! That's n-not gonna get me any-where!"

"Maybe that's not the worst thing in the world," she snaps. "You shouldn't be chasing after someone that fuck-ing sick in the soul, father or not." Her eyes go wide. "Did he hurt you?"

"Yes," I say, flat and clean. "And m-my sister."

"Well, I'm sorry." She pauses. "But I can't help you."

It should earn me something but it doesn't. You can't buy people with your pain. They'll just want away from it. I pick up one of her past-due envelopes and turn it slowly in my hands.

"Hey—put that down," she says. "I *told* you. I don't know where he is now."

I slip the bill out, take a look at the number and she can't stop me because her arms are too full of baby. Not that one. Too high. I reach for another bill, this one outside of its envelope, and take a look at the number. That—that's a number I can do.

Just because you can't buy people with your pain—well. It doesn't mean you can't still buy them.

I hold it up and try again:

"W-what about y-your b-brother?"

# THE GIRLS

## S1E2

**WEST McCRAY:**
The ID tag on Sadie's green backpack lists May Beth Foster as her emergency contact. She collected it, and Sadie's belongings, from the Farfield Police Department in July.

**MAY BETH FOSTER:**
And let me tell you something about Farfield police: they don't give a good God damn.

**WEST McCRAY:**
Detective Sheila Gutierrez is a petite fifty-year-old mother of three who has worked at the Farfield Police Department for the last fifteen years. She is sympathetic to May Beth, but she'd argue her claim.

**DETECTIVE SHEILA GUTIERREZ:**
We've done everything within our power to find Ms. Hunter. We did a search, we talked to locals, we put out bulletins and alerted the press, as well as law enforcement in

surrounding areas. There was no evidence of foul play at the scene, and given the fact that Ms. Hunter left Cold Creek of her own volition as a response to a personal tragedy, we believe this could be an extension of that. The car sustained no damage. It's a very real possibility she left it there by choice. Regardless, there's no trace of her. That doesn't mean we'll be any less vigilant moving forward and if anyone has any information we encourage them to please call us at 555-3592.

**WEST McCRAY:**
May Beth keeps the car parked next to her place. The Chevy is old, but it still runs. She found a bill of sale in its trunk—not between Sadie and the Chevy's former owner, but the Chevy's former owner and the person who owned it before *them*. I got hold of the one who sold the car to Sadie, and she agreed to meet with me at a coffee shop in Milhaven, thirty miles outside of Cold Creek, to tell me about it.

**BECKI LANGDON:**
She was real strange, you know. *[BABY CRIES]* Oh hush, now. You hush . . . come on now, your mama's talking.

**WEST McCRAY:**
Becki Langdon—that's "Becki with an *i*," as she makes sure to point out in our email exchanges, despite the fact that it's written out for me to see—is a white, bubbly brunette and proud mother to a baby boy. Becki's time with Sadie was brief but she remembers her well.

**BECKI LANGDON:**
We—my ex-husband and I, that is—we were wanting to sell the car. It was mine, I'd had it for . . . God, since I was a teenager? But he had his own and we figured we could use the

money for the baby, so that's why we had it for sale. I really wish I'd kept it now because his sorry ass walked out right after Jamie was born and now my mom's driving me everywhere.

WEST McCRAY:
Can you tell me what Sadie was like? Or did she say or give any indication what she wanted the car for?

BECKI LANGDON:
I mean, it was a pretty standard exchange. No reason for it to get personal. Except she called herself Lera. I thought she was older too. She sounded older in her emails.

WEST McCRAY:
Do you have those emails? I'd love to see them.

BECKI LANGDON:
No, sorry. Cops asked me the same but I deleted 'em. Anyway, I met her and she was awfully twitchy, had a problem talking. I was worried because I didn't know if something wasn't right in her head. I must not've been very good at hiding it because she got bitchy with me.

WEST McCRAY:
What do you mean "bitchy"?

BECKI LANGDON:
Like she was gonna back out. I showed her the car, she gave me cash and we went our separate ways. You think I was the last person to ever see her?

WEST McCRAY:
I hope not.

**BECKI LANGDON:**
*[LAUGH]* Oh, God! I didn't mean it that way. My mouth, I swear. Sorry. *[PAUSE]* Hey, is that car—I mean, is anyone using it now? Like . . . do you think they'd be willing to sell it back?

**DANNY GILCHRIST** *[PHONE]*:
What do you got for me?

**WEST McCRAY** *[PHONE]*:
A lot of backstory and a girl that looks like she ran away after her sister was murdered. Honestly, I really don't think she wants to be found. And now I have to figure out a way to tell that to her surrogate grandmother.

**DANNY GILCHRIST** *[PHONE]*:
And then what?

**WEST McCRAY** *[PHONE]*:
And then . . . what?

**DANNY GILCHRIST** *[PHONE]*:
What's your deal with this?

**WEST McCRAY** *[PHONE]*:
I think Sadie ran away and I don't think that makes for much of a story.

**DANNY GILCHRIST** *[PHONE]*:
You know there's a real human element here, connecting a girl with the person who loves her and wants her home. After working with me on *AOT,* you should know that. So what's the real deal here, why don't you want to look for her?

**WEST McCRAY** *[PHONE]*:
I didn't say I didn't want to look for her.

**DANNY GILCHRIST** *[PHONE]:*
Okay, good.

So she ran away. What was she running from?

**WEST McCRAY** *[PHONE]:*
Trauma. Memories of her sister. Seems pretty obvious.

**DANNY GILCHRIST** *[PHONE]:*
What was she running to?

**WEST McCRAY** *[PHONE]:*
I'm all ears.

**DANNY GILCHRIST** *[PHONE]:*
You know where the trail goes cold. Farfield. All you've got is where she's been. So retrace those steps, that's all there is to it. *[PAUSE]* Maybe you find something, maybe you don't, and this isn't the show.

**WEST McCRAY** *[PHONE]:*
Yeah.

**DANNY GILCHRIST** *[PHONE]:*
Do your best. That's all we can ask.

**WEST McCRAY** *[STUDIO]:*
The name Sadie gave Becki is what sticks with me the most. When I ask May Beth about it, she tells me Lera is Sadie's middle name.

**WEST McCRAY** *[PHONE]:*
So she buys a car and assumes a different name . . . May Beth, it sounds like she doesn't want to be found.

**MAY BETH FOSTER** *[PHONE]*:
Even if that started out being the case, something has changed, you hear me? Something's not right. I feel it.

**WEST McCRAY** *[PHONE]*:
Well, I need more than a feeling to go on.

# sadie

I want to live my life on the internet. Everything is perfect there.

I found Kendall Baker on a computer in a library in some forgettable town along the way. She's beautiful. A girl with glow. Eighteen years old, but the kind of eighteen they write about in books. The kind of eighteen that lives faster than the speed of hurt.

A girl who has no reason at all to believe she isn't permanent.

As I scrolled through her Instagram feed, it struck me that all the curated snapshots of her existence would still look wonderful without all the filters she slaps on them. Kendall Baker has a hectic social life. Weekdays are spent being a perfect daughter and friend, but weekends are dedicated to blowing off the steam required to maintain that kind of facade. Through her feed and the comments on her pictures, I find out that most weekends, she and her brother, Noah, and their special chosen few leave the city where they live, Montgomery, and drive an hour away to slum it in a bar called Cooper's.

Cooper's is where I find myself now, Wagner hundreds of miles behind me. I arrive on a Thursday, park across the road and wait.

They don't show until Saturday.

Kendall Baker is my line to Silas Baker, Marlee's brother, and Marlee wasn't kidding when she said he got everything. *He got college.* He got college. He made a lot of good investments and reinvested back into his community. A lot of his money is tied to a lot of the businesses in the city. He got the Montgomery Good Citizenship award six years ago for his *outstanding contributions toward making Montgomery, CO, a city we're proud to call home!* In the accompanying photo in the newspaper article I found, Silas, radiant, white and blond, was surrounded by his wife and his children, and even though he's the one I want—the one who will lead me to Keith—his kids were the ones I lingered on.

And now Kendall Baker's life has a sick little hold on me.

Her feed led me to other feeds and soon, I could imagine her whole world. One of Kendall's friends, Javier Cruz—*Javi,* they call him, the *J* silent—the way he takes pictures of her makes me think he feels something for her. The way she is about him makes me think she doesn't feel it back. There was this one video—they were here, I think, Cooper's—and he had his phone's camera filming her and she was dancing like something out of a movie, her arms outstretched, her hands floating in front of her. I watched it over and over, entranced by his enchantment. I have never been kissed the way I want to be kissed and I have never been touched the way I want to be touched. I don't often let myself think of it, but ever since I saw that video, I can't seem to stop.

Cooper's is a two-story getup with a sleazy wooden exterior, the top half of it made up of rooms for rent. I've parked as close as I can to the front door. I leave my car and pass a line of motorcycles, following a gritty guitar riff inside. The walls are dark cherry awash in red light. There's a band at the opposite side of the room and stretched in front of them, the dance floor, where people are grinding against nothing or each other.

It's a hardscrabble crowd consisting of the middle-aged and the old-as-dirt and one anomalous group of perfect teen-agers who Definitely Don't Belong But Didn't Get the Memo. They're clustered together in a booth in the corner, hands wrapped around PBRs. It's strange, seeing them live and in the flesh, and I realize stalking their social media has given them the vague sheen of celebrity. Kendall and Noah Baker are as blond as their aunt Marlee, but they don't possess the same sallow complexion that speaks to hun-ger, sleeplessness and stress. They've been turned golden by the sun. Kendall's hair is in two loose pigtails and her lips are pouty and pink. She has an air of practiced bore-dom but I can tell there's nothing else she'd rather be doing. Noah has a tidy buzz cut and broad shoulders. Of the two of them, he looks more like their father. Javi has shaggy brown hair, light brown skin, a sharp nose and a lean body. A girl I recognize from their feeds but whose name I never caught sits next to him, her head tilted back, laughing at something Noah's said. She has beautiful brown curls that almost waterfall over her shoulders, her skin a warm brown with golden undertones. There's a diamond stud in her nose and it glints every time it catches the light. She's prettier than Kendall, but something about her makes me think she doesn't know it. That's a real tragedy and I mean it. It's sad when people don't realize their worth.

I make my way to the bar and ask for a shot of whiskey. The bartender is this built, white guy with long, greasy black hair that definitely needs a cut. He wipes his hands on the towel hooked into his belt loop and eyes me skeptically. Says, "Look a little young to me."

He sounds as gritty as the band.

I nod to the teens across the room.

"So d-do they."

He serves up a shot, tells me if I get sloppy and in trouble, it's on me but I don't think that's entirely true. I toss the shot back, grimacing at the kick, and wait for it to hit. There's this perfect line between sober and blurry that softens my stutter. When I drink myself to it, it's easier to talk. I scrub my hands through my hair and ask for one more and throw that down too, relishing the sting of it. Then I figure I've paid for the privilege of asking some questions.

Before I can start, I'm distracted by a man and woman, halfway down the bar. I can't see his face but I can see hers, the perfect cut of her pale cheeks, her thin blond hair pulled back with a pink clip. She's wasted. She can barely hold her head up. She reminds me of my mother. My mom met Keith in a bar. Joel's. She got drunk and he brought her home. I picture it sometimes, their meeting, her telling him, in her muddled voice, soured by drugs and booze, how hard she had it raising two little girls all on her own. Keith, suddenly interested, asking her their names. In my mind, she has to think about it, her glassy eyes fixed on nothing.

Then she offers us up.

The bartender swipes away my empty glasses before moving down the bar.

"H-hey." I call him back. "You know those k-kids?"

The bartender nods. "Sure."

"T-tell me what you know."

"Well, two of 'em belong to Si Baker. The two with 'em are their friends."

"You know S-Silas B-Baker?"

He laughs. "I know *of* him, sure. He owns this bar. But a guy like him don't hang around here. I don't deal with him direct. I wouldn't even know those were his kids if they weren't so set on telling everybody."

I make a noncommittal noise and turn back to the group

and watch them until Javi seems to sense it. He raises his head and starts scoping the room. I duck away, to the bathrooms, because I feel like this isn't how I want to be seen. I examine my reflection in the cracked mirrors over the sinks. It took me long enough to drive out here that my sunburn peeled into a tan that could almost look like it belongs with them. I find a rubber band in my pocket and knot my hair into a messy top bun. I roll the bottoms of my shorts until they're as far up my thighs as I can get them and then I knot my T-shirt at my waist, tight. I stretch my arms up and watch as the skin of my abdomen peeks through. My stomach gives a poorly timed gurgle, desperate for something to digest. I pinch at my cheeks and bite at my lips until I see color in both.

When I push back through the door, the band is taking fifteen and the sound system is filling in, the song over its speakers dreamy and slow. I guess it's not to the crowd's taste because they scatter back to the bar. I glance over at their booth and Kendall's eyeing the floor. Noah, Javi and the other girl all seem to be trying to push her out of the booth and maybe that video I saw, the one of Kendall dancing, wasn't just some wonderfully unexpected moment in time, but a moment she makes happen over and over again.

What would happen if I took that moment from her?

Kendall climbs over Noah but by then, I've already taken her place. I've moved myself to the middle of the floor. Kendall stops when she sees me. I don't think she's used to being stopped. I stand there long enough, with her eyes locked on me, and then *their* eyes locked on me.

I feel the heaviness of everyone's curiosity.

Kendall's perfect mouth forms a perfect *What the fuck?*

And this girl.

What's she going to do?

I hold my arms out to my sides and sway. I close my eyes

and I let the music own me, turning myself into the idea of a girl, or an idea of an idea—a Manic Pixie Dream, I guess, the kind everyone says they're tired of but I don't know that they really mean it. The girl nobody ends up loving long or loving well, but nobody wants to give up either.

I open my eyes and Kendall looks like murder. Noah and the brunette look uncertain. Javi takes a swig of his PBR and leans across the table, murmuring something to Kendall. She shrugs and he pushes himself out of the booth and makes his way over to me. My pulse quickens. *I know your name,* I think. *I know your name and you have no idea who I am.* He's taller than I thought he would be. He looks nervous. I reach my hand out to him and he swallows visibly before taking it. His palm is sweaty. I lead him farther out onto the floor and guide his hands to my hips and somehow they find the softest parts of me, parts I didn't realize were there to find. I bring my hand to the nape of his neck, the tips of my fingers teasing the edge of his hair, and wonder over the sensation because I've never touched anyone like this before. He smells sweaty, but it's nice, and when I meet his eyes, he's looking at me like he's thinking this is unreal, this is right out of a movie he made but never dreamed of starring in—except he did because who doesn't want to be the boy mysterious girls are made for?

Who doesn't want a love story?

I wish this was a love story. A love story about lovers whose mouths meet like two puzzle pieces fitting perfectly into place, about the electric feeling of one person's name on the other's tongue because no one has ever spoken them out loud like that before. About people who spend the night together looking at the stars until entire constellations exist within them. Everyone is perfect in that indistinct way most characters are and every perfectly constructed scene in their fictional lives is somehow more real than anything you've known or lived. Love stories, romances, leave a person secure in the knowledge they'll end Happily Ever After and who wouldn't want a story like that? I wish this was a love story because I know how it goes in one like mine, where the only moments of reprieve are the spaces between its lines. But here's the thing I tell myself to dull the sharp edges of everything that's surely left to come:

The worst has already happened.

The song ends.

"Hey," Javi says, and his voice is deep, soothing.

It makes me shiver.

*I know your name.*

"H-hi."

"Can I buy you a drink?"

"Y-yeah," I say, and then: "I st-stutter."

His mouth breaks into a warm smile.

"Cool," he says. "I'm Javi."


"So you're new," Kendall says, after we've all introduced ourselves.

Her voice is older than the rest of her, the kind of voice you earn by years of drinking whiskey and smoking unfiltered cigarettes. I don't know how that happens to some girls, but it just does. She's feeling me out in that pointed way girls do, but I'm used to people looking at me twice, from the stutter. I don't like it but it's something I know I can withstand. Kendall doesn't look like she's used to being withstood, and for now that's my advantage.

I've told them my name is Lera.

"Y-yeah," I say. I'm squished between Javi and the other girl, whose name is Carrie Sandoval. His thigh touches mine. Carrie's doesn't. I have to believe the contact, and the lack of it, is on purpose. "J-just m-moved in."

I take a swig of the Pabst Javi bought me and it tastes like piss, but between it and the shots, I'm humming and wondering why my mother couldn't have ever stopped at a feeling like this because this is when it's good and you still have control. I remember the first time I drank just to see if I could. May Beth tried to scare me away from it, told me that what Mom had was a catching thing, a passed-down thing, a sleeping disease that works its way through bloodlines and if you're lucky, it won't wake up, but why ever tempt it? I did. I had to. And guess what? I didn't turn into a junkie. Maybe that was the real reason May Beth never wanted me to try; it was just one more thing I'd never be able to forgive my mother for.

"And you just . . . ended up . . . here?" she asks. "Cooper's?"

"W-well." I pick at the label on my beer. "Your Instagram m-made it look like s-some kind of p-place to b-be."

Noah smirks. Javi's mouth drops open and he ducks his head. Kendall and Carrie share an incredulous look. Kendall says, "Did you just admit to Instagram stalking me?"

"W-wanted to see how you h-held up a-against your own hype."

Javi lets loose a peal of laughter then tries to take it back by covering his mouth with his fist. I stare at Kendall and wonder what it must be like to live a life so unchallenged that my unspectacular retort could make any kind of successful landing. There's a fire in her eyes that tells me maybe I need to walk this back if I want access to her father.

And that's what I'm here for, after all.

"How am I doing so far?" she asks coolly.

"T-too early to tell."

"I like you, Lera," Noah declares, tipping his bottle to me. I clink mine with his. Noah Baker has a TV news anchor's voice, if the news anchor was a little drunk. "You can stay."

"So where do you live?" Javi asks, and immediately flushes at the question, like it's somehow too personal, even though not that long ago his hands were on my hips. Kendall rolls her eyes but relaxes back into the booth.

Carrie snaps her fingers and says, voice sweet as a bell, "Hey, wait . . . did you move into the Cornells' place? You're the . . . Holdens, right?"

That's the gift of the city, I guess. The constant flow of it. I can't remember people coming in and out of Cold Creek the same kind of way, the kind of leaving and arriving with the energy of a promise behind it. In Cold Creek, it's only birth and death, that kind of coming and going. The Cornells' place. The Holdens. It's too good for me not to take.

"Yeah," I say.

"That's like three streets away from me," Javi says.

"My sister-in-law sold that place," Carrie says. "It's real fucking cherry. There's a sauna and like, some kind of tree-house in the back?"

I nod. Sure.

Noah eyes me. "Parents got it good, huh?"

"G-good as yours."

"And what do you know about them?" Kendall asks.

"Your d-dad seems like a b-big shot," I say, meeting her eyes. Noah knocks his fist against the table in affirmation, and then takes a swig of his beer.

"You g-guys." I nod at the four of them. "You g-grow up t-together?"

"You tell us," Kendall says. "Since you know everything."

"My family moved to Montgomery around third grade," Carrie says. She gestures to Javi, Noah and Kendall. "These three are lifers, though."

"Their dad was my T-ball coach," Javi says, nodding at

Noah, who polishes off the rest of his bottle in one impressive swig. He reaches across the table to thump Javi on the arm.

"Come on, dude. 'Nother round. On me." He flashes me a bright white smile. "In celebration of our new friend."

"I'm g-good, thanks."

I tap my nail against my mostly full bottle. Any more than this and I don't think it would be good. The boys leave. I turn to Kendall. "You know a g-guy named J-Jack Hersh?"

She raises an eyebrow. "Who?"

"N-no one." I pause. "Or D-Darren M-Marshall?"

"What the fuck are you talking about?"

We sit there in silence. I never know what to do with girls. Pretty girls. I want them to like me. It's a strange, almost visceral *need* that settles itself inside and it makes me feel stupid and weak because I know it's a fault line I can trace all the way back to my mother. Worse than that is the fact that I can recognize this need inside me and yet never work myself right enough to satisfy it. Ask me how many friends I've had, even before Mattie was killed.

"That was quite the entrance," Carrie says and I don't know if that's a compliment or insult.

Kendall's lip curls. She says, "I dunno. It seemed kinda familiar."

A weird sense of pride rushes through me. It was ridiculous—so brazen.

But it was good because it got me here.

"Javi was pretty into it," Carrie says.

Kendall stares at me from under her long eyelashes. "He's such a pussy, it's kind of amazing he made a move. You better be nice to him."

"He's c-cute." I glance at the boys, still at the bar. "What about Noah?"

"He has a boyfriend."

I finish off my PBR and Kendall's phone chimes. She digs it out of her pocket and the screen lights her face. She says, "It's from Matt."

"Don't answer him," Carrie says.

"I *have* to," Kendall snaps. "You told me not to answer him the last time and I didn't, so this time, I have to or else he'll—"

"What, be even more of an asshole to you?"

"Who?" I ask.

"Matt Brennan. Kendall's asshole boyfriend." Carrie stares Kendall down. Kendall lets it roll off her back. "You'll meet him at MHS, if Kendall hasn't pulled her head out of her ass and dumped him like she *should* by then—"

"M-MHS?"

This draws Kendall's eyes from her phone.

"Montgomery High?" *You fucking idiot* seems implied.

I force a laugh. "H-haven't made the mental t-transition yet."

"What was your old school like?" Carrie asks.

I give her a tight smile and try to remember high school. I never liked school; no one was interested in knowing me beyond making fun of my mouth and by the time my classmates were past the point of caring, so was I. High school always felt like an elaborate lie to me, some made-up fantasyland I was locked in for a set number of hours a day and just beyond its doors was the trailer my mother walked out of and inside that, my sister—and my sister needed me. So what was the point of algebra? Has there ever been one?

Kendall's phone goes off again, saving me.

Carrie groans. "*Fuck* him."

"Fuck who?" Javi asks, sliding back in the booth beside me, Noah just behind him.

"Matt," Carrie answers, despite the warning glare Kendall shoots her.

Noah reaches over and snatches Kendall's phone from her hands. She tells him to *give it back, you motherfucker, give it back,* but Carrie says, "You'll thank us for this later," and Noah says, "Jesus, Kendall, if you're not going to drop him at least make him beg."

"Give me my fucking phone," she says.

"You promised." Noah waves the phone in front of her face before shoving it into his pocket. "You promised you'd leave this bullshit at home tonight and I promised you I'd do this if you didn't." He reaches across the booth and covers Kendall's mouth with his hand when she starts to protest and I think if any boy did that to me, even if he was my brother, I'd rip his arm out of its socket. "So shut the fuck up about Matt and drink your stupid drink that I bought you."

Kendall scowls, but she takes a mutinous swig of her new beer, giving Noah the finger with her free hand while she does.

"Hey," Javi says to me.

"Hi."

"Didn't stutter that time," he says and I vow to let it be the only time he makes me blush for however long I'm around him. "My cousin used to stutter but he could sing, though. Like, he didn't stutter when he sang. Is it like that for you?"

I shake my head, even though I actually *don't* stutter when I sing—but I can't sing worth a damn and I'm not in the mood to become some party trick.

"I don't st-stutter when I'm a-alone."

"Cool," Javi says, even though that's not the word I'd use. "My cousin grew out of it."

"Lucky h-him."

Kendall squints at me. "So do you do it because you're nervous? I don't get it."

I bite back the urge to tell her it doesn't matter if she fucking gets it.

Javi laces his fingers behind is head. "So what do you think of Montgomery so far? Why'd your family move out here?"

"We . . ." I stare at the table for a long moment and then I decide maybe it's easier to tell a lie steeped in just enough truth because it won't be as hard to lose track of. "M-my little s-sister d-died. We needed a ch-change of scenery." It quiets them the way it should. When I look up, Kendall's expression has softened because she's not a monster. "But you c-can't really get away from s-something like that."

"I bet you can't," Javi says.

"Th-thought I'd try, though," I say, brightly as I can muster. I give Kendall a small smile. "Hence, c-crashing your party."

"Well. I'm sorry about why you're here, but . . . I'm glad you're here," Javi says and it still doesn't sound right. "Because Montgomery's fucking boring. It needs someone new."

"It's not that bad," Carrie says.

"No, it *is* that bad," Javi replies. "It's the same old shit, every day . . ."

Noah wads up a napkin and tosses it at Javi's head. "If the same old shit is you not *doing* shit, then I'll bite, you goddamn benchwarmer." Noah looks at me and points to Javi. "*He* needs someone new. You into guys, Lera?"

"Shut the fuck up," Javi says.

I shrug. "S-sometimes."

"You, buy this girl a drink," Noah tells Javi, and then to me, "You, get this boy laid."

Javi's face is a shade of red I didn't think could exist in the natural world.

"You're such an asshole," he mutters.

Noah gives Javi the biggest, assholiest grin. "Hey, if you're not gonna buy *her* a drink, you can at least buy me one."

"We just went up there!"

Noah turns his bottle upside down. "And I'm out."

"I'll g-go with you," I tell Javi, and that's all it takes.

"I'm sorry," Javi says after we climb out of the booth. He half-turns to give me the full force of his sincerity and ends up tripping over his own feet. "He's really—"

"It's f-fine."

When we reach the bar, the bartender sets us up with a line of shots but instead of walking them back, Javi knocks one down and texts Noah, flashing the screen at me before he hits send: *You want em come and get em*. Javi picks up another shot and nudges one my way.

"To your sister," he tells me.

I find myself blinking back tears at the unexpectedness of it, his kindness stealing some part of me away. I grab the shot with a shaking hand. I say, "T-to her," and I barely manage to swallow the fiery alcohol down. I cough into my palm. "W-what was that?"

"Jäger," he says and I know I'll never be able to drink Jäger again. It will remind me of this moment, of her, of choking on my own grief in front of a boy whose name I knew before he knew mine.

"You're, uh." He pauses. "When I saw you dancing, I was like, *wow*."

The liquor has loosened his tongue.

"Y-you act like a g-girl's a brand-new thing."

"I'm just telling you you're interesting," he mumbles.

I notice Noah crossing the room toward us and I want . . . space. I want to take this moment alone with Javi and I want it to last longer. Something about that makes me ashamed. This isn't what I'm here for. And maybe I'm a little wasted, thinking that it could be.

"You w-wanna get s-some air?"

"Yeah." Javi nods eagerly. "Yeah, I'd like that."

Leaving the bar is a truly wonderful feeling; I didn't realize how stale the air was in Cooper's until I take a deep, clean breath.

"N-Noah gives you a lot of sh-shit, doesn't he?"

"That obvious, huh?" He shoves his hands in his pockets.

"W-what'd he call you? B-benchwarmer?"

Javi blushes. "Yeah . . . I've just never been that guy, you know? I mean, it's not easy for me to . . ." He fumbles for the words but can't seem to find them. "It's kind of why I fell in with Noah and Kendall. They at least try to make things happen. But that's the big joke—because I just sit on the sidelines and pretend to be part of it."

"D-didn't see them d-dancing with me."

He smiles such a small, earnest smile. I can't think of the last time I made someone so pleased with themselves. It makes me want to cry.

"I guess not," he agrees quietly, like it means something.

"I'm g-glad you did."

"I'll be hanging at Noah and Kendall's place tomorrow," he says. "You should come."

"Th-think *she'd* like that?"

"Kendall needs a shake-up." He shrugs. "I see the way she looks at you. She knows she needs one. I told you, Montgomery's a . . . it's one of those cities that feels like a town. That's why we end up here every week, just to get away from it."

"W-will their parents b-be home?"

"Yeah, they might be around."

"W-where do th-they live?"

"Two-twelve Young Street."

A soft *click* inside me. A piece locked into place. This *will* lead me to Silas, who will lead me to Keith and in the meantime . . .

Maybe I could let myself have whatever this turns out to be.

"S-sounds like it could be fun."

"Great," he says.

We walk the edges of the parking lot. I stare at the stars dotting the ink-black sky. The farther we get from the bar, the more stars there are to see and it's beautiful and the beauty makes me ache. I didn't tell Mattie enough about this kind of thing, I don't think. About small miracles, like the stars at night and how much brighter they seem in wintertime. The sun rising and setting and rising again. I decide to share the thought with Javi, just to release myself from it, and he gives a small smile and says, "Small miracles. I like that."

I think he'd like anything I said.

That's new to me.

I point. We're in front of my car.

"Th-that's where I l-live."

"What?"

"K-kidding. But it's m-mine."

I unlock the door and open it before I really know what I'm doing.

He climbs into the back and says, "Cozy," and I follow in after him and stare at his profile and he shifts uncomfortably under my gaze. I imagine pressing my palm against his chest, pressing my body against his. I imagine feeling his heartbeat under my palm. I imagine kissing him and his mouth is as soft and tender as the rest of him. I would let his gentleness take me somewhere else, let myself pretend what it might be like to belong to someone. I would let myself push his hair out of his eyes so I could see them seeing me and this is not a love story . . . but in this small space, the sound of our breathing between us, I wonder what it would take to make it one.

I swallow hard, lick my lips, the ghost taste of the shot still on them.

*To your sister.*

I lean forward and reach across the front seat, open the glove box and grab a marker. I hand it to him and he stares at me, confused.

"I l-left my cell at h-home," I tell him and stretch my arm out. "R-write your number and I'll c-call you f-first th-thing."

Javi opens the marker and worries the cap between his teeth. He scrawls his number up my wrist and the light, careful graze of his touch makes me believe being with him would have been exactly how I imagined it. He asks me if he can have my number and because he can't, and because I don't know what else to do, and because maybe I want to do it, I kiss him on the cheek. I don't think I'm very good at it, the clumsy meeting of my mouth against his lightly stubbled chin, but he doesn't seem to mind.

"Y-you c-can have that," I say. "I h-have to go n-now."

"Already?"

"Yeah, b-but I'll c-call you t-tomorrow."

"Okay," he says. He gives me a shy smile, and gets out of my car. Then, after a second, he turns back to lean in and say, "It was really, *really* good meeting you," and I promise I'll call him again because I don't know how else to respond. I watch him walk back to the bar and then I stare at his number on my arm and repeat it softly to myself, until it's stuck in my head, like how any other girl might do.

Then I climb into the front seat, put the key in the ignition and head to the city.

# THE GIRLS

## S1E2

**WEST McCRAY:**
May Beth lets me look through the personal possessions left behind in Sadie's car. I'm hoping to glean a greater understanding of where she's been, where she was headed and if she ever got there. And—if we're lucky—where she still might be.

There were clothes, nothing trendy. Everything seems geared toward comfort, functionality and compactness. T-shirts and jeggings, leggings, sweaters, underwear, a couple of bras. There's a green canvas backpack, something Sadie was rarely seen without in Cold Creek, and inside it, her wallet—empty; a half-eaten protein bar; a crushed, empty bottle of water and a take-out menu for a place called Ray's Diner, located at a truck stop just outside a town called Wagner. This is the only thing I have to go on. I ask Detective Gutierrez if the Farfield PD looked into it.

**DETECTIVE SHEILA GUTIERREZ [PHONE]:**
A cursory investigation into Ray's yielded no new information. It was a long shot; it's a truck-stop diner, people are constantly coming and going. Add to the fact Ray's distributes its menus to surrounding areas, it was only ever going to be a long shot. Our time and resources were more effectively spent concentrated on the area the car was found.

*[SOUND OF ENGINE BRAKING]*

**WEST McCRAY:**
The truck stop is called Whittler's and I arrive there on a Tuesday evening, after taking a plane out from New York. I'm staying in a motel in the nearest town, Wagner.

If I accept Detective Sheila Gutierrez's words at face value, this can only prove to be a waste of my time. On the other hand, May Beth's general distrust of the Farfield Police Department's efficacy is never far from my mind. Basically: I have to find out for myself.

How Sadie ended up at this particular spot—if she ended up here at all—is as much a mystery as everything else surrounding her disappearance. Was there something in particular she was looking for or was this just some random stop along the way?

*[SOUNDS OF A DINER, MURMURED CONVERSATION, FOOD COOKING, THE CLATTER OF PLATES]*

**RUBY LOCKWOOD:**
What can I get ya?

**WEST McCRAY:**
Ruby Lockwood is a formidable woman with pitch-black curls piled high on top of her head. The lines on her face suggest she's a little older than she actually is—she's in her mid-sixties. She's worked at Ray's Diner for thirty years and spent twenty of them married to its owner, Ray.

**RUBY LOCKWOOD:**
Ray was fifteen years my senior. When I started here, it was a dive, but I was just a waitress, so I kept my mouth shut. Then he falls in love with me, I get around to falling in love with him, we tied the knot and I worked on turning this place into something special. Just ask anyone—here, ask Lenny! Lenny Henderson. Lenny, this guy's with the radio.

**LENNY HENDERSON:**
Is that right? People still listen to that?

**RUBY LOCKWOOD:**
Tell him how special it is here.

**LENNY HENDERSON:**
I always like coming to Ray's, it's real homey. Ruby treats her regulars like the family she never wanted. *[RUBY LAUGHS]* And the meatloaf's better than my mama makes, but don't go telling her I said that.

**WEST McCRAY:**
Well, I've got it on the record here but no one listens to the radio.

*[THEY LAUGH]*

**WEST McCRAY:**
I don't know what Ray's was like before Ruby fixed the place up, but I can tell you what she turned it into. There's something immediately nostalgic about it when you step through its doors, or rather—it's the *idea* of nostalgia. Ray's Diner plays to that fifties Americana feel, with its Formica countertops, red vinyl seats and turquoise accents. It smells like how a Thanksgiving meal looks in the movies. I'm hungry, so I order the meatloaf and Lenny's right; it's better than my mama makes.

Ray died a few years ago of throat cancer.

**RUBY LOCKWOOD:**
We were gonna rename this place Ruby & Ray's. We were gonna have a grand reopening for it and everything. Then he got sick and after he died, it didn't feel right calling it anything else. I miss him every day of my life. He was my soul mate and now this diner is the closest I'll ever be to him, 'til it's my turn to come home.

I got no plans to retire.

**WEST McCRAY:**
Ruby says she never talked to the Farfield PD about Sadie.

**RUBY LOCKWOOD:**
You had me convinced my memory was shot—I wouldn't forget talking to the police, if they came around here. And then I thought: Saul.

**WEST McCRAY:**
Saul is Ruby's brother-in-law, the late Ray Lockwood's youngest brother. He's a bald man, who just entered his forties, with colorful tattoo sleeves on both arms. He's in charge when

Ruby's not around. And Ruby wasn't around the day the Farfield PD came to visit to ask about our missing girl.

**SAUL LOCKWOOD:**
It was a young guy, I think, the cop who came. He asked me if I saw her and he showed me a picture. Didn't look familiar—

**RUBY LOCKWOOD:**
But you're horrible with faces.

**SAUL LOCKWOOD:**
Then he questioned some of the waitstaff, and showed *them* the picture, and they didn't remember seeing her. He left the picture with me, if I remember right, and told me to follow up with anyone that was on shift at the time . . .

**RUBY LOCKWOOD:**
You didn't follow up with me. I don't remember ever seeing a picture of this girl. I bet you threw it out, didn't you, Saul?

**SAUL LOCKWOOD:**
Maybe? I wasn't keeping track of it, at least. I mean, come on. A missing girl? Around here? Take a look at the girls working the parking lot! They're all missing. We got a business to run. Lots of people come through here. I can't keep track of every single one.

**RUBY LOCKWOOD:**
He's not wrong. It's true we got less regulars than passersby, but unlike *some* people, I never forget a face.

**WEST McCRAY:**
Well, I have a picture right here, so let's find out if you saw this one.

**RUBY LOCKWOOD:**
All right, give it here and—oh.

**WEST McCRAY:**
Ruby was telling the truth. She never forgets a face.

# sadie

Even in the dark, Montgomery is beautiful.

I have no choice but to hate it. It's the set of a movie brought to life. The houses here are gorgeous, lined neatly along each street, all of them tastefully decorated and immaculately landscaped. American flags hung with quiet pride. Cars in driveways that probably cost as much as much less impressive houses. On the main street, it's shop after shop boasting an earthy, artisanal aesthetic that screams *we're local!* Local or organic or both. Craft beer. A yoga studio. A weed dispensary. A little café hawking wheatgrass shots. There's a poster for an outdoor concert in the park come weekend; some band I've never heard of. One of the streets is closed off, filled with stalls for a farmer's market in the morning. I pass the empty high school awaiting fall term and imagine a bunch of white-teethed teenagers— Kendall, Noah, Carrie and Javi among them—pouring out of its doors and they're all in school colors because what else would they be wearing? On one side of town, there's a playground with a climbing wall and a splash pad and the slides and swings look so . . . *new.*

I know better than to let myself want, but whenever I got weak and gave in to the urge, the trailer I grew up in turned into a house, the lot turned into a backyard with more than enough room to lie in the sun without witness of creepy neighbors. An empty fridge turned itself full. In the summer, every sweltering room was suddenly cool and in the winter you didn't need to bury yourself under a hundred blankets for warmth. Cold Creek's main street would transform into a street lined with store after store after store where everything was in the miraculous price range of You Can Afford All This and More. Montgomery is almost more than I can understand because it's so much more than it ever occurred to me to want. I hate it. I hate the people who live here. May Beth always told me I can't do that; I can't hate people for having more than me, but she's wrong. I can. I do. It's the perfect wall between myself and the kind of longing that poisons your guts and turns your insides right out.

Silas Baker lives in a house on a hill, of course. I wouldn't believe he was Marlee's brother if she hadn't told me herself. I guess there's no straight line from one person to another, no matter what you think you can or can't tell just by looking at them and least of all by whatever comes out of their mouth. It's strange to think of Silas choosing Keith over his sister. I can't imagine choosing anyone over Mattie. Ever. I wonder how much Marlee told Silas about Keith. Either way, there's no suggestion of her kind of poverty here. Sometimes, no matter how successful you get, it leaves a stain on you that you can't get out but Silas Baker scrubbed it good, covered it in his wealth. His house is a large two-story, all modern angles, with huge windows allowing for a view inside if you can get close enough to look. The roof slopes down and is covered in solar panels. There's a smart-looking blue Mercedes in the driveway.

I drive slowly past, parking far enough away to be invisible but close enough for a view of the driveway and front

door in my rearview. I rest my head against the window.
About an hour later, a behemoth of a red truck—the kind
you'd need a stepladder just to get a foot on the running
board—drives past on the wrong side of the road. It pulls
into the Bakers' driveway, narrowly missing the Mercedes.
After a long minute, Noah stumbles out. He rounds the
truck and drags his sister from the passenger's side. They're
a lot drunker than they were when I left them. I wonder if
Javi's as bad, if he stupidly drove himself home. They make
an ugly lurching walk to the front door and it's painful,
watching the ten-minute attempt to get their key in the lock.
And the whole time they're doing this, my sister is dead.

"She's dead," I whisper and I don't know why this is the
thing I choose to say out loud because it hurts to say it, to
feel the truth of those words pass my lips, to have them be
real in this world. But *She's dead* is the reason I'm still alive.

*She's dead* is the reason I'm going to kill a man.

How many people live with that kind of knowledge inside them?

But I wish Mattie was next to me instead. I wish she was
gazing bored out the window, looking so perfect and still it'd
steal my breath away. I'd do something like muss up her hair
because it drove her crazy. Mattie could never stand when
the fine, stringy strands got tangled because it would take
every single one of a comb's teeth and thirteen Hail Marys
to get it straightened out again. She'd push at my hands and
I'd grab her by the wrists and marvel at how small she was
and how much smaller she used to be. When she was little,
I loved taking her tiny fists and cupping them into my palms
and that only felt like it was yesterday. I don't know where
the time went between then and now. Thirteen years. That's
a long time and I lived it.

Thirteen, Mattie.

I kept you alive for thirteen years.

Waking her up in the morning, making her meals, walking

her to the school bus, waiting for her at its stop when the day was over, grinding my bones to dust just to keep us holding on and when I lay it out like that, I don't know how I did it. I don't know where, underneath it all, you'd find my body. And I don't care. I'd do it all again and again for eternity if I had to.

I don't know why that's not enough to bring her back.

I remember when she was born. Mom never looked better than when she was carrying Mattie. Not healthy—she still had that junkie's pall—but Mattie made her seem like she could amount to something. When she started having contractions, she sent me over to May Beth's and I stayed there until she came back with a baby in her arms. She handed Mattie to me first, then locked herself in May Beth's bedroom for three hours because she needed to "rest." I was so happy. I wanted to be a big sister so bad, I didn't even need to be sold on it. May Beth was scared I wouldn't like the interloper because most kids hate that sudden division of parental attention, but Mattie couldn't take away what I didn't already have. Here was the promise of *something*. I knew that I could be her world. I knew she was definitely going to be mine.

I just wanted to matter to someone.

I roll the window down and keep my eyes on the Bakers' house. The first signs of life arrive with the break of dawn, which is still far earlier in the morning than I expect anything to happen. The sky is barely pale with the thought of sun and I'm half-dozing, a trickle of drool trailing from my chin to my shirt collar, when I hear the chirp of a car door being unlocked. I jerk awake, the blurry scene before me slowly coming into focus.

Silas Baker is more than the picture online made him out to be. Blond as Marlee, but healthier, clearly not held back by little things like oh, rent. Food. Raising a family on noth-

ing. He's big. He has broad shoulders and the kind of
business-casual style that's dressing down the muscles that
are surely underneath. There's something distractingly pol-
ished about him. He's almost a Ken doll and I feel if I were
close to him, I wouldn't see a line on his face.

He takes a look around the quiet street and then gets into
the Mercedes and there's no question of whether or not to
follow him because whatever's happening here has created
a surplus of questions in me, the primary one being *what
the fuck?* I bring my hand to the keys but then I worry that
would be too obvious. He doesn't seem to have noticed me
yet. My fingers hover over the ignition while I try to figure
out how to do this. Didn't think I'd be tailing anyone today.
Also, I've never tailed anyone before. I mean, I've seen it
done—in the movies.

The Mercedes pulls out of the driveway and there's no
way around starting my own car if I want to follow his. The
clock on the dash says it's a quarter to seven. My palms sweat
as the two of us drive down the road. When he makes a turn
that puts us on the main street, there's a small amount of
congestion that takes some of the heat off me. Vendors arriving for the farmer's market. Two cars end up between
mine and his and that makes it even better. By the time we're
on the highway leading out of town, I feel less conspicuous,
even though the sun's fully out now, and there are no places to
hide. We drive another five miles or so when Silas makes an
abrupt turn onto a dirt road that seems to stretch forever
to nowhere. I stop at the turn, count to sixty, and follow. The
gap between us makes me worry I might lose him, so I press
my foot on the gas but then I worry that's going to call too
much attention to myself. I ease off.

Farmland surrounds me; untended fields on either side. A
world at the end of the world. That's what this feels like, driving into nothing. I don't know what the hell he could possibly

be doing out here. His car turns left and seems to just disappear, and I almost make that same left, but I get this feeling in the pit of my stomach and I slow down just a little instead. The Mercedes is parked on a side road that's leading to—a house. From the brief glimpse I get, I can tell it's abandoned.

Silas is waiting for me to pass.

Fuck.

It's a mile before I find a spot to park, a small clearing in front of a gate with a NO TRESPASSING sign leading to who knows where. If Silas Baker passes this way, he'll see my car, but it's a gamble I have to take. I pull the keys out of the ignition, shove them in my pocket and let myself out, hastily locking the doors. It's already warm out, one of those days you can tell is going to end in air thick enough to choke on. I take a deep breath and then I run, I run the mile back to Silas's turnoff. By the time I'm just about there, my shirt is soaked through with sweat and I can smell myself. I need a shower. I've *needed* one, but I'll figure that out later. I creep up the lane, where the Mercedes is in the distance, parked next to the house. Silas isn't in the driver's side anymore. My heart beats warily. I don't know what this is. It's an easy path up to the house, but I stumble into the long grass and crouch there. Bugs hover at my face, arms and legs before landing on my skin and taking a bite. The grass tickles and scratches my shins. I start forward, my feet moving clumsily along ground that feels as dry as my throat. I keep my ear out for sounds of him, but there are none.

I move so slowly it's an eternity before I'm at the house and the best word I could use to describe the place is *rotten*. It's got to be over fifty years old. It's a two-story with a screened-in porch that's ready to fall in on itself. The front door is barely hanging on its rusty hinges and most of the first-story windows have been covered in particle board, save for one that's empty, offering a clear view in. The windows on the second story are all uncovered and broken. The house has long been tagged with beautiful and ugly graffiti. *Joey loves Andy.* A naked woman stretched across the space between two windows. Painted ivy along the bottom of the foundation climbing as far as it can reach. Satan and his forked tongue. A series of watchful eyes. *Carrie hates Leanne. Cocksucker.*

I reach the broken window and peer in. It's worse inside than outside, giving way to nature, weeds poking through the floorboards. There's a hint of a threshold to another room full of garbage creeping out. I don't see Silas but if he comes through the front door, he'll only have to turn his head to have a clear view of me.

I listen. Nothing. I move from the window and look for the best place to position myself. I strain my neck upward to the second story and realize that just because I can't see Silas doesn't mean he can't see me. Shit. I shouldn't stay in one place long.

I'm slowly making my way to the side of the house and I'm almost there when I hear the front door open. I lose all sense of self, safety, and throw myself around it, hear my body collide with the corner of the house at the same time the door falls back into place. I bite my lip, feeling the splintered wood siding dig into my shoulders. He's there. I know he's there. The heaviness of the pause that follows lets me know he knows he's not alone. And then:

"Who's there?"

His voice is deep, a cool authority running through it, and I wait, my palms pressed against the ground. His footsteps sound into all this emptiness—one step, two steps, three steps—and I realize how alone I really am. That if Silas Baker found me here, he could make me scream and only the two of us would hear it.

Mattie, in that orchard, screaming.

A light breeze moves through the grass. It almost sounds like the ocean. If I closed my eyes I could see myself there. I won't close my eyes.

"Hello?" he asks again. Quieter now.

The wind just—stops.

And then it's too still.

Footsteps again. The soft crunch of his shoes . . . working their way toward his car. I don't exhale until I hear the engine and I don't move until long after I'm sure he's gone to wherever it is he goes after this. I stand slowly, the blood rushing back to my numb joints. I lean against the house for a long moment before facing it.

What were you doing here, Silas?

I make my way to the front of the house and carefully climb onto the porch, sidestepping the most rotted-looking parts of it. I hesitate before gripping the door handle, imagining it still hot from his touch even though I know that won't be the case. I pull it open and step into the house, startling as it rattles closed behind me. I press my fist to my chest, willing myself to calm down.

Only a little daylight manages to reach the first floor, from that one broken window I was looking through. The place is musty, dusty and smells of decay. I sneeze eight times in a row, which makes my eyes water more than I can see through. I wipe them and squint into the darkness and begin my trek from room to room, stepping around and through the garbage and debris, some of it recognizable, most of it not. I'm tense. The small noises I'm making seem too loud and I keep glancing over my shoulder, worried he'll reappear. But he doesn't.

So far.

I spot a Coke can that looks like it could've been from the eighties by the design. If not then, at least some time before mine. I float through the ghosts of a kitchen, a dining room and a living room before I find myself in front of a mostly intact set of stairs leading to the second floor. Sunlight pours through the broken window at the top and highlights a palm print in the dust on the old wooden banister.

*This way,* it whispers.

The stairs have collapsed halfway up, leaving a gap wide enough it'll be tricky getting across it. It was probably easy for a guy as tall as Silas, who looked to be over six feet. I stretch my right leg across the gap, get my foot on the closest remaining step and use the banister to hoist myself onto it. It shakes back and forth alarmingly and the small effort takes more out of me than it should, leaves me feeling nauseous and shaky. I better get a decent meal in me soon. I know what it's like to be hungry and I'm better at it than most people, but I'm tapping into the last of my reserves. I'm not in the habit of making myself useless.

The stairs make disconcerting noises as I trudge up the last of them, finally getting two feet on the landing. It's much smaller up here than it looks on the outside, and a little cleaner than downstairs. The collapsed stairway is too much of a deterrent to vandals, I guess.

I look around. I don't know where Silas would have gone from here; there are no tells like the palm print. In one bedroom there's an empty brass bedframe and moldy sheets, broken pieces of furniture. The other looks empty but for a wall where a small painting of a forest hangs. It's somehow survived being in this place for who knows how long. In the bathroom, the sink has been ripped out of the wall and there's shattered glass from the mirror of a broken medicine cabinet all over the floor. A stained, cracked porcelain tub with no feet holds a broken toilet inside it. The floor looks like it's absorbed years of water damage. I'm afraid to step on it. I rub my sweaty forehead because it's hot in here, stifling. I pull at my shirt collar.

Why the hell would someone like Silas Baker be out here?

The painting.

I go back to the empty bedroom and stand in front of it. It's an oil painting, unsigned, and it looks wrong. It's too . . . intentional. I press my finger against the canvas's bumpy surface and then trace it along the frame's immaculate edge.

It's not even dusty.

I grab the picture by its corners and set it on the floor. Behind the picture, there's a perfect hole dug out of the wall and in the hole, there's a small metal box with a padlock on it. I reach inside and it surprises me, how light it is. I shake it and the rustling sound my ears are met with puts me in mind of money. Is that what this is?

Silas Baker, squirreling away cash . . . for what?

Does it matter?

I'd take his money. I always need that.

I leave the house with the box in my hands, making that perilous jump over the gap in the stairs, and step outside. When I'm outside, I search for a rock to bust the lock with because anything is breakable if you put enough force behind it. I finally find a nice, gray, jagged one with some heft, curl my hand around it and give the box a good *thwack*. The rock hits the lock, then hits the ground. The impact tears the skin away from my knuckles and brings tears to my eyes. I clutch it against my chest and it takes everything not to cry out.

I try again.

And again.

And again.

The sun gets farther and farther up the sky. My stomach turns, sick from the heat. The heat makes my head feel foggy. My shirt dries of sweat and soaks itself through again. The lock never breaks, but the hinge holding the lock does, and when it happens, when it tears off, I don't even realize it. I hit the metal box again and it flips on its side, its contents spilling out.

# THE GIRLS

## EPISODE 3

**ANNOUNCER:**
*The Girls* is brought to you by Macmillan Publishers.

**RUBY LOCKWOOD:**
Yeah, I saw her. She was blond, though.

**WEST McCRAY** *[PHONE]*:
So . . . I think I might actually have a bead on this girl. I don't know what exactly it's going to lead me to—but it's more than I started with.

**DANNY GILCHRIST** *[PHONE]*:
Don't sound so excited.

**WEST McCRAY** *[PHONE]*:
I'm going to find Sadie and all she's gonna want is to be left alone. You do realize that, don't you?

*[THE GIRLS THEME]*

**WEST McCRAY [DINER]:**
You're telling me she had a different hair color than she does in this photograph? She was blond instead of brunette?

**RUBY LOCKWOOD:**
Yeah, and by the looks of it, she'd done it herself. And she was rail thin, a wisp of a thing, not much to her. Didn't talk right either. That stood out more than anything else. She had a stutter.

**SAUL LOCKWOOD:**
Oh! Yeah . . . I remember her now. She ordered a . . . coffee. I thought she was a runaway. She pissed you off some, didn't she, Roo?

**WEST McCRAY:**
So you *did* talk to her?

**RUBY LOCKWOOD:**
She talked to *me*. She wasn't just passing through. She was looking for someone, so she made a point to ask.

**WEST McCRAY:**
Who was she looking for?

**RUBY LOCKWOOD:**
Her father.

**WEST McCRAY:**
What?

**RUBY LOCKWOOD:**
She was looking for her father, so she said. She had a picture of him and everything. Knew his name, she knew he'd been a

regular down here at the diner a couple years back. She
wanted to get in touch with him and she wanted to know anything I could tell her.

**WEST McCRAY:**
What did you say?

**RUBY LOCKWOOD:**
I told her I'd never seen the guy. But she seemed pretty desperate and I felt sorry enough for her I asked for her phone
number and said I'd call her if I ever saw him.

**WEST McCRAY:**
Do you still have that number?

**RUBY LOCKWOOD:**
Well, get this—she said she didn't have a phone and that was
the second weird thing about her, because every kid and
their granny has a cell phone these days, right? I got one—
hell, my ninety-year-old mother has one. I ended up giving her
a menu and told her she could call the diner and check in with
me to see if he'd been around.

**WEST McCRAY:**
Back up—you said that was the *second* weird thing about
her. What was the first?

**RUBY LOCKWOOD:**
I knew the man she was asking after and he didn't have any kids.

**WEST McCRAY *[STUDIO]*:**
His name is Darren M. I'll omit his last name until I track him
down. I searched him online and got a lot a results but every
Darren I made contact with wasn't the one I was looking for.

**WEST McCRAY** *[TO RUBY]*:
And you knew him.

**RUBY LOCKWOOD:**
I sure did. Actually, he told me he'd been a regular through
the years. When he was passing through, I guess he made a
point to stop for the apple pie—but it wasn't until he lived in
Wagner that *I* considered him a regular. He shacked up with
some woman in town for a few months and he'd have lunch
here by himself every day. Real good guy. Kept to himself.
Never caused trouble.

**WEST McCRAY:**
Do you have the name of the woman he was with?

**RUBY LOCKWOOD:**
It was Marlee Singer.

**WEST McCRAY:**
Are you still in contact with Darren?

**RUBY LOCKWOOD:**
No. Once he ended it with Marlee, he was gone from here. I
didn't even see him every now and then. I used to have a
phone number, because Ray was alive at the time, he was getting toward the end, and Darren asked me to tell him when
Ray passed. Darren sent the most beautiful flowers when it
happened, they were white roses and baby's breath. I thought
that was such a thoughtful thing to do. But I don't have that
number anymore.

**WEST McCRAY:**
Could you look for it, maybe, and tell me if you find it? If I can
get ahold of him, it would be really helpful.

**RUBY LOCKWOOD:**
I doubt I'll find it and I'm telling you, Darren doesn't have kids.

**WEST McCRAY:**
You sound so certain of that but if he only lived here briefly, it seems fair to assume there's a lot about him that you never got around to knowing.

**RUBY LOCKWOOD:**
I'm certain because I *asked.* He sat where you're sitting now, shooting the shit, and I asked him if he had kids and he said no. What do I care if he has kids? What's he got to gain by lying to me? Nothing.

**WEST McCRAY:**
What's Sadie got to gain by lying to you?

**RUBY LOCKWOOD:**
*[LAUGHS]* Come on. You think she's the first girl trying to put the screws to some man she calls daddy? I'll tell you what else, she was damn rude.

**WEST McCRAY:**
Rude how?

**RUBY LOCKWOOD:**
When I said I hadn't seen Darren before, she called me a liar. Take my word—I'm *telling* you, she was running some kind of con. She didn't like that I saw through her.

**WEST McCRAY** *[STUDIO]***:**
When I'm done talking to Ruby, and before I search online for Darren, I try to get in touch with Marlee Singer, but she doesn't pick up the phone. Then I call May Beth. When I tell her the news, she's absolutely stunned.

**MAY BETH FOSTER** *[PHONE]*:
No. No, that can't be right. Sadie didn't know who her father was. She always told me she didn't give a damn.

**WEST McCRAY** *[PHONE]*:
Well, his last name isn't Hunter, if it is this guy.

**MAY BETH FOSTER** *[PHONE]*:
Darren . . .

I'm telling you, I never heard that name in my life. *[PAUSE]* But I guess that doesn't mean anything. Claire had a lot of men in and out, before and after Irene died . . . God. She's really looking for her father? That's what she said?

**WEST McCRAY** *[TO RUBY, IN DINER]*:
There a chance anyone else in the diner was in contact with Sadie?

**RUBY LOCKWOOD:**
Anyone other than Saul and me, I got no clue. She was only here for . . . couldn't have been an hour.

**WEST McCRAY:**
If I leave a photo of Sadie with you, you think you can put it up? Ask around?

**RUBY LOCKWOOD:**
Sure thing.

**WEST McCRAY** *[STUDIO]*:
A day later, I get a phone call from a man named Caddy Sinclair.

# sadie

The café is called Lili's.

I duck inside and navigate past the ridiculous line at the register, trying not to breathe in the scent of food, of caffeine. I feel like I never want to eat again. I feel like if I don't eat something soon, I won't make it much further. My body is trembling, tremoring, and I'm freezing, even though it's hot, my teeth chattering. I don't know how to make this go away. I need to make it go away. I slip into the bathroom and sink-wash myself in frustrating stop-starts as women filter in and out. I just. Want to be clean. I use the cheap floral soap and gritty paper towels to rub a weak lather over my arms and legs with my shaking hands. The dirt from the house washes away, leaving a mishmash of tiny cuts on my shins that I didn't notice from my trek through the grass. I slip my hand up my shirt, cleaning the sweat from under my breasts. My hair has about another day left in it before I have to find some way to wash it. I twist it into a tight bun. I lean forward against the sink and let out a sob, whispering *okay, okay, okay,* until I feel its cold porcelain beneath my fingers.

*He took Darren under his wing, sort of, just made a point of being nice to him.* Fucking Marlee. *He took Darren under his—*

*Fucking* Marlee. Silas could sense it, I bet, that same sick soul lurking underneath, someone he could share himself with. He was just better at hiding it than Keith was. But Marlee had to have known it, she had to. *I don't talk to my brother anymore.* Why else would she give up the only relationship she had with the one person who could bankroll her? I pound my fist against the sink because there's nothing else in here I can hit. *She. Knew.*

And now I know.

I run my hand over my mouth. My eyes are wide and wild and I can't see myself beyond them. I can only see what they've seen.

Do I kill him?

Do I kill Silas Baker?


I stole Keith's switchblade the night Mom kicked him out.

That night didn't end how it was supposed to, in a lot of ways, but I thought I could kill him when I was half the girl I am now, a coltish thing. Or maybe I didn't think I would kill him—maybe I was too young to imagine anything so final, so irreversible—but I wanted to hurt him badly enough to make him afraid of me the way I needed.

The way he should be afraid of me now.

He kept the blade on the nightstand in Mom's bedroom next to his Bible. Once, a few weeks after he moved in, he called me in and sat me on his lap and showed it to me. *Sadie, look at this,* he'd said, and I watched the blade flick out of its handle before I realized it was a knife. *That's the business end,* he'd said, and pointed to its tip. *I don't wanna ever see this in your hands, you hear me?*

I dip my hand into my pocket, letting my fingertips drift

over its contours, and remember how it looked in my grasp when my hands were much smaller. It almost didn't make sense. I was surprised, when I pulled it on Caddy, how much it belonged.

I can't move through this town and leave it the way I found it.

I press my fingers to my forehead.

I have to stop it.

But Keith.

But wait.

A woman comes in. I turn to her, my mind racing. She's middle-aged, with dark black skin. She very sweetly asks me if I'm okay. I tell her I'm fine and ask if I can use her phone. It comes out of my mouth more fractured than usual, the stress of everything worsening my stutter. She says, "Of course," in the softest voice and something about it further breaks me and I don't know if it's the relief that kindness can exist in this world or the guilt of kindness existing in a world that doesn't deserve it. I call Javi. He picks up on the third ring, his voice thick with sleep, and I ask him to meet me here and he says quickly, excitedly, *yeah, yeah, I'll be right there, don't go anywhere.* The woman smiles at me as I pass the phone back to her.

I step back into the café, waiting near the door, picking at one of my fingernails until it bleeds. Javi arrives eight minutes later, trying for all the world to look casual, but I can tell by his heaving chest he must have run here. There's a vaguely sick pall to his skin and a vaguely boozy scent to his sweat. Remains of last night.

Last night feels so far from me now.

"Hi," he says and I can't bring myself to return his smile. He doesn't notice. He leans back on his heels, eyes drifting to the registers before clapping his hands together. Everything he says next comes out rushed, nervous: "It's still kind

of early to head over to Noah's. We could give 'em a minute
to wake up, that sound okay? I haven't even eaten breakfast.
You hungry? Let's eat. It's on me. What'll you have?"

I don't want to eat.

I have to eat.

If this were a normal situation, I wonder if I'd try to be
delicate about it, if I'd pretend to be a girl with a dainty appetite, or more appealing, none at all. I tell him I want their
protein snack box and their most calorie-laden smoothie in
its largest size and he can't mask the surprise on his face,
but he recovers quickly and makes the order. Soon enough,
we have our food and wedge ourselves into a table in the
back corner of the café, as far from the bustle as possible, at
my request. Javi matches my appetite with his order, but eats
in a way that suggests he wasn't that hungry. He's even shyer,
more uncertain than he was, now that he's sober.

I stare at my meal, my stomach turning at the thought of
it, but I have to eat.

I have to eat if I want to do anything next.

I close my eyes briefly, and then I slip a piece of apple
into my mouth and carefully chew it into a paste and then I
realize that I can't taste it. It's nothing on my tongue. I ignore my rising panic and take another bite of apple, trying
to force myself to reach past everything that's wrong to
something crisp, sweet and fresh.

After an agonizing moment, its flavor seeps into my taste
buds and then it's *too* sweet.

I never used to like apples.

May Beth said when I was little, an only child, I was always hungry, starving, arms reaching for food and even
then, I was still picky. She said I only understood sugar and
grease and if she tried to give me anything good enough to
grow bones, I'd cry until my eyes were so swollen, I couldn't
see. In those moments, she'd trick me; put pieces of apple

on my tongue and call them candy. It wasn't long before
I caught on and bit her hard enough to draw blood. But
then Mattie came along and May Beth said she'd end up
pickier than me if I didn't set a better example and did I
want to see my little sister aching for food?

I couldn't think of anything I wanted less.

"Can I ask you something?"

I place a piece of cheese on my tongue and it sits in my
mouth. I have to take a long drink of the smoothie to force
it down.

"S-sure."

He leans forward, his eyes searching my face.

"What's wrong, Lera?"

"L-let me eat," I tell him. "L-let me f-finish eating f-
first."

He sits there awkwardly, patiently, while I work through
the breakfast he's bought me. It's an awful, absurd exercise
in self-preservation, putting the food in my mouth, con-
sciously instructing myself to *swallow*, because if I don't it
will just sit there. All this production just to make it to the
next moment. Javi gives me a small smile and I hear his
voice, last night, over the din in the bar: *Their dad was my
T-ball coach.*

Sometimes, I feel made of Mattie's absence, this complete emptiness inside me and the only thing that makes it
bearable, that quiets it, is moving, is putting distance between her murder and pushing myself closer to the promise
of taking Keith's life. It still hurts, though. It always hurts.
Other times, I can only feel the weight of it, all of it, of every
Sadie I've been, every choice that she's made, and everything she could have possibly gotten so wrong that she'd
end up here. Now. Like this. Alone.

I get halfway through the smoothie before my stomach
finally says *no more* and then I grasp the edge of the table,

fighting the utter rejection my body wants to do of normal, automatic things. I remember the last time I felt this way. After Mattie died.

"Lera." Javi reaches across the table and puts his hand on my arm. "What is it?"

# THE GIRLS

## S1E3

**WEST McCRAY:**
Caddy Sinclair is a tall, skinny white guy in his midthirties. He lives in Wagner and shares an apartment with his brother. He spends most days at Whittler's Truck Stop, hanging around outside, or—when he can afford it—eating one of Ruby's famous specials. He's a local legend; everyone knows his name and that, he tells me, is precisely his problem.

**CADDY SINCLAIR:**
I wouldn't mind being left the fuck alone.

**WEST McCRAY:**
Well then, I really appreciate you talking to me.

**CADDY SINCLAIR:**
Whatever. It's not like I'm doing you some big favor. If you find this girl, I want to know.

**WEST McCRAY** *[STUDIO]*:
Caddy's an interesting contradiction; before he wanted to be left alone, a quick Google search of his name reveals a teenager who desperately wanted to be the next Eminem. If you head on over to musiccamp.com and search for the user "Sick Caddy," you can listen to six demos he recorded in a friend's basement. If you're streaming from our podcast's official website, you'll find an embedded player on this episode's page. But do me a favor before you check it out: read the content warnings.

**CADDY SINCLAIR:**
That was a different . . . stupid time in my life. I'm not going to talk about it. Every kid thinks they got the makings of something great when they ain't shit. Then you learn it's better being nothing, anyway. *[COUGHS]* So you want to know about this girl, huh? She's missing?

**WEST McCRAY:**
Yeah, she's missing. I'm trying to help her family locate her.

**CADDY SINCLAIR:**
She's probably dead.

**WEST McCRAY:**
Would you know something about that if she is?

**CADDY SINCLAIR:**
Nope. Mind if I smoke? *[PAUSE, LIGHTER SOUND]* The last time *I* saw her she was alive, but if she's as out of her mind as she was when I met her, and if she comes at the wrong people like she came at me . . . well, you could lose your life for a lot less in this world.

**WEST McCRAY:**
Let's back up a little here. You told me when we talked on the phone that Sadie came to you for information about Darren. She'd never been to Wagner before from what I can tell, so how did she know she needed to talk to you?

**CADDY SINCLAIR:**
Figure someone inside told her about me. Damned if I know. That part's not real important, though; it could've been anyone. I'm the go-to guy around here. People want something—I mean, people want to know something, they're going to come to me. I always know what the fuck's going on because I just . . . I just do.

**WEST McCRAY:**
Did you know Darren?

**CADDY SINCLAIR:**
We weren't friends, but if he saw me at the diner, we'd talk. Ruby knew him better. I didn't know he had a daughter.

**WEST McCRAY:**
And that *is* who Sadie told you she was—Darren's daughter.

**CADDY SINCLAIR:**
Yeah, she showed me his picture and it was Darren, all right.

**WEST McCRAY:**
Do you happen to have a picture of him?

**CADDY SINCLAIR:**
No, but I can tell you what he looked like: white, tall, broad. Dark hair. He was just a guy. Nothing in particular really stood out.

**WEST McCRAY:**
Tell me what happened next.

**CADDY SINCLAIR:**
She pulled a knife on me.

**WEST McCRAY:**
Really? Just like that?

**CADDY SINCLAIR:**
Yeah. She told me to tell her everything I knew about Darren or else.

**WEST McCRAY:**
And did you?

**CADDY SINCLAIR:**
Do I look alive to you?

**WEST McCRAY:**
What did you tell her?

**CADDY SINCLAIR:**
I told her the truth. I told her the most I knew about Darren was that a few years back, he was with Marlee Singer and she'd probably know more about him than I did. I told her Marlee lived in Wagner. Kid took off. Didn't seem right in the head to me. If you *do* find her, let me know. I want this on record because I'm gonna charge that bitch with assault. Switchblades are illegal too.

**WEST McCRAY:**
Thanks for your time, Caddy.

**WEST McCRAY** *[PHONE]*:
Was Sadie a violent person, May Beth?

**MAY BETH FOSTER** *[PHONE]*:
No. No! Never. I mean . . . she could've been, but in the way we all could be. It wasn't something that she *was*. It wasn't in her nature, if that's what you mean.

**WEST McCRAY** *[PHONE]*:
Caddy said Sadie had a switchblade. She pulled it on him. There wasn't a switchblade in her belongings.

**MAY BETH FOSTER** *[PHONE]*:
Then he's lying. Sadie wouldn't—she wouldn't . . . if it's not in her things, he's lying.

**WEST McCRAY** *[PHONE]*:
Or she could still have it.

**WEST McCRAY** *[STUDIO]*:
Whether or not she still does, I think the real question is why she felt she needed it.

# sadie

I'm outside Silas Baker's house again.

A cold sweat breaks out on the back of my neck as I pull up behind his Mercedes. That must mean he's home. The food from Lili's does an uneasy turn in my gut. I get out of the car, pocketing my keys, and make my way to the front door when I hear the laughter—what sounds like Kendall and Noah—coming from the back of the house. I round it slowly, until I reach the backyard and find them there, lounging by a pool.

The private side of the Bakers' property is no less impressive than its public-facing one. Their pool is inground, long, wide and deep with a diving board. There are four chaise longues, two on either side, fancy metal tables between them.

The backyard is lush; the grass is jewel green with thriving vegetable and flower gardens taking up opposite sides. A pine deck leads to a sliding glass door to the inside of the house. Noah drifts on a float in the water. Kendall is resplendent in a tiny red bikini, sunning herself on a soft monogrammed towel. Everything around us seems blessed to be here, and I try to process the luxury of it, of everything I'm seeing against everything else I've seen today. The only thing my head is able to arrive at is, *this isn't real . . .*

"Where's Javi?" Noah asks, tilting his head at me.

"I d-don't know." I shrug. "He s-said he'd m-meet me h-here."

"Huh." Noah grabs his phone, which is resting on his abdomen, and thumbs out a text. He waits a minute and says, "Not answering. Maybe on his way."

"Weren't you wearing that yesterday?" Kendall asks me. Noah laughs.

"D-didn't go home last n-night."

Kendall leans up on her elbows, the action pushing her impressive chest out in a way I think is meant to intimidate me. "How come?"

"T-too hard to b-be there."

"Well, hope you don't mind doing this all morning," Noah says. "We're on lockdown because when we came home last night *someone*"—he points an accusatory finger at his sister—"didn't have the decency to fake sober. Grounded for a goddamn month."

I look around. "What a p-p-punishment."

Noah smiles. "I don't know you all that well yet, Lera, but I detect a hint of sarcasm."

"Only a h-hint," I return. "W-where're your p-parents?"

I look up at the house, half-expecting to see Silas Baker's face in the window, gazing down at this poolside scene. *Where are you, Silas . . .*

"Dad went over to the florist's," Kendall informs us.

"What?" Noah raises an eyebrow. "He in shit again?"

Kendall stretches languidly, arms over her head, toes pointing to nothing. "Mom heard him get up at the asscrack of dawn today to go into the office. And she told me he was late as hell getting home from T-ball last night. He promised he'd be here all weekend, no work, and he lied. Now she's pissed, so she went out with Jean and she's not picking up the phone. Sunday family dinner is going to be *great*."

"K-Kendall," I say abruptly. "C-can I b-borrow a swimsuit?"

"They won't fit you." She nods to her chest.

"Jesus," Noah says, because I guess he's got limits. "You could lend her a tank or shorts or something." He kicks his legs, pushing the float to the edge of the pool, and climbs out. "I'm gonna try Javi again. Not like him not to answer."

"Whatever," Kendall says. She groans, getting to her feet like it's the last thing in the world she wants to be doing and it sends a flare of anger through me that is almost immediately put out for something that feels so much worse.

She doesn't know her father is a monster.

"Come on," she mutters and I follow her inside. "You can borrow some of Noah's trunks and one of his old shirts . . ."

"D-don't like sh-sharing, huh?"

"No offense, but you look like you need a shower."

"N-no offense, b-but you look like a bitch."

She stops in her tracks and turns to me, smiles nice.

"You can always leave," she says.

I don't say anything. She shakes her head like that's the end of it and we step through the back door. I imagine what it must be like to step through it every day just because it's your home and you live here. I get that feeling I got when I first saw Montgomery, that if I can't have any of this for myself all I really want is to see it ruined.

Inside, it's incredibly stark, monochromatic. The family photos on the wall are professionally shot, black-and-white, all of them taken next to the flower beds outside. I study each one as I pass, following Noah's and Kendall's progression from babies to toddlers to awkward tweens, to now. Their mother, a lithe blond with curly hair that keeps getting shorter. Silas and the way he doesn't change. The most offensive part about him is how inoffensive he looks. Anyone would look at him and think he was safe.

The family portraits suddenly shift to Silas, his T-ball teams.

"There's Javi," Kendall says, startling me.

She points him out in a picture. I can't make myself look.

"What's wrong with you?" she asks.

"J-just a little h-hungover."

"I'm not." She sounds pleased.

I follow her past the living room where there's a white sofa and just looking at it makes me nervous, the thought of it. When she was nine, Mattie went through a clumsy phase. In fact, I don't think she ever entirely grew out of it, but when she was nine, it was at its worst. There's not an inch of our trailer she hasn't spilled something on.

Kendall leads me into the kitchen. It's all gray-and-white marble countertops, stainless steel appliances. The table sits in front of a window overlooking the garden side of the house and I can just see the edge of the deck. The rest of the room stretches toward the front door.

"Hold on a sec," she says, opening the fridge. "I'm starving."

The front door opens.

"Kendall, whose car is that out there?"

My body turns to ice.

Silas's back is to us as he shuts the door. He has a bouquet of white roses and baby's breath in one hand. He scrubs the other through the back of his short blond hair before facing us and when he does, his eyes immediately fall on me.

"Who's this?" he asks.

"Dad, this is Lera Holden," Kendall says. "She's new in town. Did I tell you about her last night? I can't remember."

"I'm sure you can't," he says drily. He tilts his head back and sizes me up and my fingers twitch. "Holdens . . . you just moved into the Cornells' place, right?" I manage a nod. "I heard they had a daughter. That's your car out there?"

He asks the question with a smile and his smile is all teeth.

I look at Kendall. Her body is half in the fridge.

"C-can I use your b-bathroom?"

Silas reacts to my stutter, a near imperceptible grimace.

"Sure," he says. "It's upstairs. Third door on the right."

I duck past him without thanks and turn a corner that leads to a staircase, my body weak with relief once I'm finally outside his line of vision. It takes a conscious effort to move one foot in front of the other to get me to the top of the landing. There, I listen.

A low murmur. His voice. Kendall's throaty responses. I creep down the hall and find the bathroom. I push the door open and take a shocked step back.

"G-get out!" a girl yells. "I w-want y-you t-to g-get out of h-here!"

She's eleven, naked in the tub. Her knees are curled up to her chest and her arms are crossed around them, trying hard to cover her rosebud breasts. When she leans forward, she bares her back, the knots of her spine painfully visible. She presses her head to her knees and turns a hateful gaze to her left, to the man leaning against the sink. He's taking up the whole bathroom. His arms are crossed, but he's not moving. She desperately wants him gone, she's said it out loud and everything, but he's not moving.

"There's no need," he says slowly, "to be like this."

"G-go a-away! W-where's M-Mom? *Mom!*"

"What do you think she's going to do?"

The girl opens her mouth and closes it and he smiles a little, sort of sadly, like he's just admitted something to her that they both don't like hearing. She turns her head away from him and I watch the small rise and fall of her shoulders as she breathes in and out, that rapid pulse revealing how angry she is. The water is cooling. She's not going to get out until he leaves.

But he's not going to leave.

"Sadie," he says to her. "We're family now."

A peal of laughter floats upstairs. I turn to it, then back to the empty bathroom, my heart thrumming. Ever since Mattie died, it's been like this, this surfacing of ugly things, forcing me to witness them because living through it all wasn't enough. When Mattie was alive, I could push it down inside me because I had things to do, I had to look after her.

And now . . .

I still have things to do.

I press my hands over my eyes and then I lower them and take a look around. This room is, of course, no less spectacular than any other part of the house. It's so much bigger than any room with a toilet in it has a right to be. There's a separate shower and a bathtub. The towels over the towel rack look softer than anything I've ever dried my hands with. The expanse of mirror over the side-by-side sinks is surrounded by lights.

I close the door loudly, just in case they're listening downstairs, and then I move farther along the hallway, until I find the room that must be Silas and his wife's. There's a king-size bed in the middle of it, covered in a clean, white comforter. The door to a walk-in closet is half open. There's a vanity in one corner of the room, and a mahogany desk with a laptop on it in the other. I tiptoe over to it and move the cursor. The screen lights, prompting a password for desktop access. Shit . . . there's a color photo on the desk, him and his kids. I pick it up and turn it over but there's nothing on the back of it. I lift the laptop up. Nothing.

I open every drawer, riffling through them, shifting through papers and junk for anything that could be a book or a notepad with a goddamn list of passwords in it—people are still stupid enough to do that, aren't they?—and find nothing. I fight the urge to slam the last drawer shut and push my hair from my face, frustrated. I've been up here too long.

I've got to get back.

I slink out of the bedroom, go into the bathroom and flush the toilet before I make my way downstairs.

I find Silas still in the kitchen, leaning on the island, scrolling through his phone.

His phone.

Kendall's gone. I turn my face to the window. I can hear Noah and his sister talking faintly through the glass.

"Can I get you a drink or something, Lera?"

I nod without looking at him and he sets his phone down and goes into the fridge. I reach out quickly to touch the screen so it stays unlocked, but I don't have time to pocket it.

Silas doesn't ask me what I want, just sets a bottle of water between us. He gets one for himself and I watch him twist the cap off. His hands are big, veins snaking along the tops of them, his fingers thick.

They look . . . strong.

"Welcome to the neighborhood." Silas nods at the water and I open it. "I think my wife made a gift basket for your mom and dad. We were going to run it to you this weekend but you can just take it home. How are you liking Montgomery so far?"

I shrug and take a sip of the water and it is ice cold relief against my parched throat. My eyes drift to the still un-locked screen of his phone. I don't know how long before it'll turn off on its own. A few minutes, five, ten if I'm lucky . . .

"The Cornells' house is pretty nice."

"Y-yeah."

Because I have to speak sometime, don't I.

"What do you like most about it?"

"F-four w-walls and a roof."

"It's a real boon to Montgomery, having your parents in the community. I know it's no fun having to uproot your life especially during your senior year. Your father's research in . . ." He trails off, frowning. "What was it, again?"

"S-something . . ." *Fuck*. "Important."

He laughs softly, the lines beside his eyes crinkling. "Okay." Then all the laughter is gone, just like that and it's awful when someone can do that, turn it on and off in less than the time it takes to blink. "Your car—I thought I saw it earlier."

I set the water down.

"W-where?"

The silence between us is heavy and all I can think is I want away from him. I want away from him, *I want away from him now . . .*

He pauses. "Never mind."

The back door slides open and Noah leans his head in, dripping water all over the hardwood floor. "Hey, Dad, you wanna grab me a drink and that leftover roast beef sandwich in the fridge? Lera, you coming back out?"

"Sure," Silas says.

"Noah—"

Noah turns at Kendall's voice. Silas puts his back to me as he opens the fridge. I grab his phone and slip it into my pocket and then I just—

I don't remember the hurried trip down the front hall. I don't remember opening or closing the front door. I'm outside and I'm breathing hard, like I've run some kind of marathon as I fumble my car door open, getting myself half inside the driver's seat. I swipe through Silas's contacts with sweaty hands. Keith isn't in there. Darren isn't. But Jack—*Jack H* is. Langford. Place called Langford, at *451 Twining Street, Langford . . . 451*—

"I'll take my phone back now."

# THE GIRLS

## S1E3

**WEST McCRAY:**
In some ways, the town of Wagner reminds me of Cold Creek.

There are fewer businesses on the main street than there should be, and the houses look kind of . . . defeated. But it has one thing going for it Cold Creek doesn't: a sense of promise.

Suburbia is taking root. A new development will hopefully inspire an economic upswing—though that might price some of its longtime residents out. Marlee Singer is one of those residents. She's in her late thirties, with white-blond hair. She's mother to a one-and-a-half-year-old boy. She lives across from a schoolyard playground and in the afternoons, during the school year, it teems with children sliding down the slides and fighting for turns on the swings.

She finally answers one of my calls the day I'm set to fly back to New York. When I tell her I'd like to talk about Sadie and

Darren, Marlee only agrees to go on record to tell me that she's got absolutely nothing to say. She and Darren were together briefly, it didn't work out and no, they don't keep in contact anymore. She doesn't have his number and she doesn't have any pictures either. It's not a time she cares to remember, which begs even more questions she's equally unwilling to answer.

**MARLEE SINGER** *[PHONE]*:
Lasted three months. He never said anything about a daughter. We're not in touch anymore. I got no way to reach him. I like it that way. I don't even think about him unless someone else brings him up—so thanks for that.

**WEST McCRAY** *[PHONE]*:
Caddy Sinclair said he directed Sadie Hunter to you, to ask about Darren, though. It seemed pretty clear she was headed your way. I'm just trying to figure out what happened.

**MARLEE SINGER** *[PHONE]*:
I'm telling you I never met her and if she was around here looking for me, I don't know a goddamn thing about it.

**WEST McCRAY** *[STUDIO]*:
I'm forced to take Marlee Singer at her word—even though I'm not sure I should. I've postponed my flight for her though, so I sit in a motel and review everything I know about Sadie's disappearance so far. There's nothing I've overlooked that will turn itself into my next lead. What's particularly frustrating is that outside of dyeing her hair blond, and giving people her middle name, Sadie didn't seem like she was going to any greater lengths to cover her tracks. It doesn't feel like it should be this hard to find her. I express as much to May Beth.

**MAY BETH FOSTER** *[PHONE]*:
I was thinking . . . Claire had a lot of men, but there were only a couple who stuck around for longer than usual. They might know something. There was Keith—he was there when the girls were little. Arthur McQuarry, but he's dead now. And Paul. Paul was the last man Claire had around before she walked out. If any of them got close enough, Claire might've let something slip about this Darren guy.

**WEST McCRAY** *[PHONE]*:
I'll see if the living two will talk to me.

**MAY BETH FOSTER** *[PHONE]*:
Her father, though . . . I just can't wrap my head around it. I don't even know what Sadie would need from this man. Help? Money? I would've given her anything she asked for, didn't she know that? I spent my whole life helping those girls. I wasn't about to stop.

**WEST McCRAY** *[PHONE]*:
I know, May Beth.

**MAY BETH FOSTER** *[PHONE]*:
Just—look into those men I told you about.

# sadie

I thought Keith was nightmare enough.

I didn't count on the way his violence would tendril out and lead me to other nightmares. Silas Baker is very angry. He's angry in a way that's trying to pretend he's not, but I see him. I'm the only person in this city who sees him. His hand is out and my hand is holding his phone. *451 Twining Street, Langford. 451 Twining Street*—he rips it from my grasp and I don't even flinch. *Langford. 451 Twining Street.*

"Who are you?" His voice is low and dangerous.

"—"

"Who are you?"

"I'm L-Lera. H—"

"No. You're not." He looks out onto the empty street. "Because I met the Holdens this morning. They have a daughter but she's not you." He turns back to me. One of his hands grips the frame of my car, the other the top of its open door. "You followed me."

I shake my head.

"You followed me this morning. I saw your car."

"I d-don't know w-what you're t-talking about."

His grip on the door tightens. I watch his knuckles go white. His gaze travels over my body, to my eyes, trying to figure me out; if he actually knows me, has ever known me, if he *should* know me. His attention shifts beyond me, inside my car. The dirty clothes tossed in the backseat, crumpled food wrappers. My green bag in the passenger's side. He reaches across me for it and I push back at him hard enough to make him stumble. I make a frantic reach for the door to close it, but he recovers too quickly and jerks it all the way open, making it groan.

"You took my phone. What else did you take?"

"G-get the f-fuck—get the *fuck* away!"

He pushes me back against the seat, his hand pressed against my throat to keep me there. He leans inside and makes that same reach for my bag and I choke against the pressure. My fingers fumble into my pocket for the switchblade. I get it out and push the release and the sharp tip of the blade pokes against his abdomen. He stares in bewilderment at the knife and then slowly raises his eyes to meet mine and I think, *yes*.

This is where I kill Silas Baker.

I push the knife forward at the same time his hand comes behind my neck. He slams my face into the steering wheel. The shock of it, the pain of it, overloads my senses and my body goes limp. The switchblade slips from my fingers and drops into the footwell. He pulls me bodily out of the car and I realize, dully, there's blood on me, but it's not his.

It's supposed to be his.

And—*oh,* there it is, the belated, dizzying pain of impact. *Did he break my fucking nose?* His hold on me is bruising. Blood is pouring out of my nostrils and now it's on him too.

"Who are you?"

My eyes roll side to side, hoping to glimpse someone pressed against the window of one of the houses surrounding us, readying to call the police, but there's no one. The only sound I can hear is his labored breathing. His chest heaves. I lick my lips. They taste like copper.

"You know how much trouble you're in? I'll call the po-lice."

"You w-won't," I say thickly and then, "Y-you *can't.*"

What little pretense left between us disappears.

"What do you think you know?" he hisses. His breath is hot on my face, unbearably close. When I don't answer, he grabs me by the cheeks, squeezes them like Keith. "What do you think you know, huh? You want money, is that it? What do you think—"

It takes both of my hands to get him off me. He pushes me to the ground and my chin connects with the driveway before the rest of me does, my skin wearing against the pave-ment. I spit, roll onto my back and stare up at him and then I scream. He jerks toward me and I scramble back, dirt and pebbles tearing into my elbows. I yell louder, letting my voice become one clear, ugly note across his perfect life.

"Dad, what the hell—"

Silas takes several steps back at the sound of his son.

"Oh my God, Daddy—"

Kendall.

Noah and Kendall stare stupidly at the scene in front of them, not knowing what to make of it. They see blood, they see me on the ground, they see their father standing over me and they don't move. Neither of them move to help me.

"She's not who she says she is." Silas points at me and I get to my feet slowly, watching the blood from my nose pat-tern the pavement. "I met the Holdens—I met them this morning and this is *not* their daughter. She's some kind of . . . drifter. Some thief! She tried to steal my phone, she pulled a knife on me—"

"Oh my God." Kendall moves to the house. "I'm calling the police—"

"*No!*" Silas bellows and she stops in her tracks. He points to me. "You—get the hell out, get the hell off my property—*get out of here!*"

I take halting, dazed steps to the car. Silas moves away from me and Kendall rushes forward and grabs at his arm, pulling him to her. I sniff and immediately regret it, the taste of blood thick and metallic at the back of my throat. I ease into my car slowly and pull out of the driveway. By the time I'm at the end of the street, I'm shaking so hard, I don't know how I'm driving and in my head, three, no four words:

*451 Twining Street, Langford . . . 451 Twining Street . . . Langford.*

When Silas Baker's house feels far enough away, I pull over.

A long, long time ago, when Mom had just left, I ran a fever of 105. May Beth was too many states away, visiting family, and I was so sick, I didn't know my own name, no matter how many times Mattie called me by it.

*Sadie, I think you're sick.*

*Sadie, you gotta tell me what to do . . .*

*Sadie, I think you're dying.*

She ended up phoning my boss, Marty, who bundled me into his pickup and took me to the hospital an hour away, where they stuck an IV in my arm and waited for the numbers on the thermometer to go down. May Beth cut her family vacation short just to look after me and I was so mad at everyone I didn't speak to any of them for a week.

Whole thing ended up costing us too much.

I stare down at myself. My shirt is soaked in my own blood, my nose still bleeding. I'm glad Mattie isn't alive to see this because I can just imagine her hands fluttering uselessly beside me because she never knew what to do when I needed something, when I needed help. Never. You can't blame her for it, though. She was just a kid.

Kids shouldn't have to worry about that kind of stuff.

It's not right any other way.

# THE GIRLS

## EPISODE 4

*[THE GIRLS THEME]*

**ANNOUNCER:**
*The Girls* is brought to you by Macmillan Publishers.

**WEST McCRAY:**
Arthur, Keith and Paul.

These are the names May Beth Foster gave me. Men who were with Claire long enough they might know something about Darren M., the man Sadie claims is her father.

Arthur is dead, like May Beth told me he would be. He lived with Claire and the girls for six months, when Sadie was thirteen and Mattie was seven, and overdosed two years later. May Beth doesn't have much to say about him. He was a dealer. Keith, there's no record of anywhere. I put a team on finding him. By May Beth's accounts, Keith lasted longest. He came into the girls' lives when Mattie was five and Sadie was eleven.

**MAY BETH FOSTER:**
He was the one who really tried. He looked after those girls as best as Claire would let him. Keith was my favorite.

**WEST McCRAY:**
Why is that?

**MAY BETH FOSTER:**
Well, whenever Claire brought a man home, it was like . . . my heart would just sink because it always ended worse than it started. And it always started bad. Keith didn't start bad. He picked Claire up at the bar, Joel's, found her there—she was often there . . . and he brought her home. And he was stone-cold sober. That stood out to me. Not as a bad thing, mind, but Claire usually had men as wrecked as she was. That first night, he put her to bed, and then he introduced himself to me.

Right away, I liked him. He treated me like . . . he treated me with *respect*. He treated me like I was the girls' flesh-and-blood grandmother. That meant something to me. Then I come to find out he was a God-fearing man, and I believe in the power of prayer myself. He taught the girls a little religion. So that was—I liked that a lot. He was only supposed to stay the weekend. He stayed a year instead, and if I'd had it my way, it would've been forever.

**WEST McCRAY:**
Describe his relationship with the girls.

**MAY BETH FOSTER:**
He told me he'd always wanted kids and this was the closest he'd ever got, would probably ever get to having them. Mattie thought he was wonderful . . . he had a sort of juvenile

sense of humor, and she was young enough to enjoy it. Sadie—well, she never liked Keith.

**WEST McCRAY:**
Why's that?

**MAY BETH FOSTER:**
He was sober, like I said. I know how that sounds but . . . he didn't use. He didn't get in the way of Claire using, but he was clean himself. He just accepted Claire for what she was, and wanted to be part of their lives. Maybe that's a sickness in itself, enabling . . . but he tried to create structure for the girls and up until that point, Sadie felt that was her job. He was an interloper, in her eyes.

**WEST McCRAY:**
You'd think she'd want a little of that stability for herself—that an actual adult in her life would let her be a kid again.

**MAY BETH FOSTER:**
She didn't know how to be a kid. Mattie was so wound up in Sadie's purpose, Sadie was terrified of losing that.

**WEST McCRAY:**
How did it end between Claire and Keith?

**MAY BETH FOSTER:**
Terribly. That much followed the pattern. She kicked him out in the middle of the night. I could hear her screaming at him from across the lot. Damn miracle nobody called the police. I looked out the window and she had all his things on the lawn and he was shouting back at her.

Claire just got tired of them, you know. Once she felt she got all she could from them, they had to go. This was no different.

He grabbed all his things and left. He walked past and saw me watching from my window. He waved good-bye. I never saw him again.

Tell you the truth, I cried over that one.

**WEST McCRAY:**
Paul Good works for a logging company in the Northwest. He looks it too; he's a tall, muscular guy, with red hair, a beard and a tanned, sun-worn face. He's not a particularly hard man to get ahold of, but it does take him the better part of a week to decide whether or not he wants to speak on the record. He was with Claire Southern for eight months, sure, but it was a difficult time in his life. He was using. He was depressed. Four years clean, he wasn't sure he wanted to revisit it.

**PAUL GOOD** *[PHONE]:*
I don't know I got a lot to say . . . or what exactly it is you want me to say.

I look back at that time and I think . . . I was a *kid*. I was a mess. I mean, I got a family now. I got a wife, I got a little girl of my own. I don't know what I thought I was doing then. No . . . that's a lie. *[LAUGHS]* I thought I loved Claire.

**WEST McCRAY** *[PHONE]:*
How did you two meet?

**PAUL GOOD** *[PHONE]:*
Oh, Jesus. I was driving home—Abernathy was home, then—from the bar. I was drunk too. I shouldn't be saying that. It was stupid, but that's not my life anymore. Anyway, she was walking. She was walking in the dark, on the wrong side of the road. *[LAUGHS]* It's amazing I didn't kill her. I pulled over and

asked her if she needed a lift and she said yes, and soon as she got in that car, she starts crying. She'd been having a rough night, drinking for some of it—but she was more sober than I was. Talked my ear off on the way to her place. When I got her there, she told me I was a good listener and maybe I could, you know, do that for her again. She didn't invite me in that night, but man . . . she got me.

The first part of our relationship was on the phone. And I fell in love with the life she sold me, which was a lot different than what it actually was . . . the way Claire told it, her mom was sick and she cared for her. Then she got pregnant. Then her mom died and then she got pregnant again and she was look-ing after two girls alone. She sounded so devoted to 'em and I'd always wanted kids myself.

I moved in with the three of them and then the truth really come out. I mean, there were signs that she had some prob-lems . . . she drank too much—on the phone, I could tell when she'd been drinking. She'd nod off. That was the heroin. By the time I realized the extent of it, she was my heart. I didn't mind the kids but I *loved* Claire. So I started using too. I made myself sick for her.

**WEST McCRAY** *[PHONE]*:
Paul entered the girls' lives when Sadie was fifteen and Mat-tie was nine.

**PAUL GOOD** *[PHONE]*:
They didn't hate me or nothing, they just didn't *want* me. So I stayed out of their way and they stayed out of mine. They probably deserved better from me, though. There wasn't a whole lot of consistency in their lives and I could see Sadie was trying to give that to Mattie. I left her to it.

**WEST McCRAY** *[PHONE]*:
What was Sadie like?

**PAUL GOOD** *[PHONE]*:
Stubborn as hell. Hated her mother. Sadie thought she knew better'n Claire so far as Mattie was concerned and she probably did, if you want the truth. But her and Claire were always at each other's throats . . . and Claire favored Mattie, so it got ugly sometimes. I don't know. Like I said, we stayed out of each other's way and if I sensed a screaming match coming on, I ducked. Only thing I cared about was Claire and crack.

**WEST McCRAY** *[PHONE]*:
Tell me how it ended.

**PAUL GOOD** *[PHONE]*:
She got tired of me and I was running out of money. One day, I come home and found her with another guy. That was it. She didn't respect me. Dumb thing is, I still loved her, but I couldn't stay with her after that. Damnedest thing, though . . .

**WEST McCRAY** *[PHONE]*:
What?

**PAUL GOOD** *[PHONE]*:
After I left, it was like a fog cleared in my mind. I realized I wasn't living the life I was supposed to, that I didn't actually *want* to be an addict. So I packed it up and I just left town . . . ended up here, got clean. It sounds simple when I put it like that. There wasn't anything simple about it. But getting out of Claire's orbit was the first step. That place— those girls . . . it just had this feeling . . . I don't know if I should say it.

**WEST McCRAY [PHONE]:**
I'd like to hear it.

**PAUL GOOD [PHONE]:**
Like the three of them were doomed. I guess I always knew there wasn't going to be a happy ending for 'em. When you called me, caught me up on what happened to all of them . . . I don't know. I want to say I was surprised but I'm not. But it's sad. It's damn sad.

**WEST McCRAY [PHONE]:**
Paul, in all the time you were with Claire, she ever mention a Darren?

**PAUL GOOD [PHONE]:**
Can't say she did.

**WEST McCRAY [PHONE]:**
So you've never heard that name before?

**PAUL GOOD [PHONE]:**
That's right.

**WEST McCRAY:**
When I'm done talking to Paul, I give May Beth a call.

**WEST McCRAY [PHONE]:**
We're kind of at a standstill in terms of what more I can do right now.

**MAY BETH FOSTER [PHONE]:**
What does that mean? You're giving up?

**WEST McCRAY** *[PHONE]*:
No, it just means I've got to dig in and try to find a new lead.
If I don't find one, we've got to hope some new develop-
ments occur in the meantime.

**MAY BETH FOSTER** *[PHONE]*:
Well, that sounds like giving up to me. We don't have that kind
of time. Sadie's out there, and anything could be—anything
could be happening to her—

**WEST McCRAY** *[PHONE]*:
It can take a long time to work a story like this, May Beth. I
know that's not what you want to hear but you've got to be
patient, okay? You've got to be patient.

*[LONG PAUSE]*

**MAY BETH FOSTER** *[PHONE]*:
I might have something.

**WEST McCRAY** *[PHONE]*:
What?

**MAY BETH FOSTER** *[PHONE]*:
I might . . . I might have something that you can use. I don't
know. *[PAUSE]* I just don't want to get her in trouble but . . .
but then, if she's—if she's already *in* trouble, and this helps
you find her . . .

**WEST McCRAY** *[PHONE]*:
What is it? What do you know?

**MAY BETH FOSTER** *[PHONE]*:
I don't know. I don't know what to do. I don't want her to get
into trouble over this, I just—I want her to be safe. I want her

to be *here*. *[PAUSE]* But I don't want her to get in trouble. She's had it hard enough.

**WEST McCRAY** *[PHONE]*:
Okay . . . okay, May Beth, do you remember what you said, the very first time you called me?

**MAY BETH FOSTER** *[PHONE]*:
I wanted you to help me.

**WEST McCRAY** *[PHONE]*:
Yeah, that's right, but do you remember how you put it? You told me you didn't want . . .

*[LONG PAUSE]*

**MAY BETH FOSTER** *[PHONE]*:
I don't want another dead girl.

**WEST McCRAY** *[PHONE]*:
So whatever information you've been holding on to . . . you don't want that to be the difference, between finding her alive and not, do you? If Sadie's alive, and you think what you know could get her into some kind of trouble, you have to look at it like she's alive to fix it, you understand? As long as she's alive, she can fix it. *We* can fix it.

**MAY BETH FOSTER** *[PHONE]*:
I know, but . . .

**WEST McCRAY** *[PHONE]*:
I can't find Sadie, let alone help her, if I don't have all the information. And I have to be able to trust you as I move forward with this. We can take it off the record, if that helps. Do you want to do that?

**MAY BETH FOSTER** *[PHONE]*:
Yes. Please.

**WEST McCRAY** *[PHONE]*:
Okay, then that's what we'll do.

# sadie

*Greetings from Sunny L.A.! Wish you were here!*
I'm parked on the shoulder, almost clear of Montgomery.
I just needed to stop a minute.
I stare at the postcard, palm trees lining its front.
I turn it over slowly.
*Be my good girl, Mats.*
The night before Mom left, I was sleeping on the couch.
I can't remember why I wasn't in my bed, but I wasn't,
and I couldn't have been waiting up for her because I never
did. I was just there, stretched out all wrong, my feet
hanging over the arm, my head sunk in the middle of the
cushions. She'd been out with one of those men she liked to
keep in her back pocket, the kind she could get a drink or a
dime from, but didn't necessarily have to bring home. I
woke up to the feel of her fingers lightly petting my hair
and I felt so small, like I never did, like I imagine Mattie
must have often felt having always been Mom's favorite.

She reached for the remote and turned the TV on low,
going through the channels until she finally gave up. She

bent her head close to mine and twisted a strand of my hair around her finger, tucking it absently behind my ear. I remember my muscles tensing at her touch, giving me away, and being so afraid she would stop because of it. She didn't; we continued the charade. Me, pretending to sleep. Her hands against my forehead, then the soothing carefulness of her fingers combing through my hair. We stayed like that for . . . it must have been an hour, maybe a little less.

I thought, *This is what it feels like to be a daughter.*

I thought, *God, no wonder Mattie loves Mom.*

Then she brought her face close to mine and whispered, "I made you," in my ear.

That's when I realized she was sober. My mother wasted was the default. Her sobriety was like a punch in the stomach in the rare event I witnessed it. I wanted her sober all the time, even if she didn't like me better for it. We stayed like that until I fell asleep for real and in the morning she was gone and I knew. I knew it was forever and I knew there was no way I could explain it to Mattie. She almost didn't survive it.

But then this . . . I trace the edges of the postcard.

Just delayed the inevitable.

I was sixteen. I dropped out of high school, which was a lot less complicated than I thought it would be. I remember standing outside of Parkdale, waiting for someone to stop me, to tell me I was throwing my future away, but I didn't live in a place that possessed that kind of imagination. For some people, the future ahead is opportunity. For others, it's only time you haven't met and where I lived, it was only time. You don't waste your breath trying to protect it. You just try to survive it until one day, you don't.

I rest my head against the seat and breathe. I slip out of my shirt and the air turns my skin to gooseflesh. The front of my shirt looks like a crime scene. I grab a bottle of water from my bag and wet the clean back of the shirt. I use it to wipe off my face, my beat-up elbows. I go through my things again, grab the cleanest shirt I can find and put it on. I shove the bloodstained one under the backseat so I don't have to look at it and check my face in the mirror. The scrape on my chin looks ugly. My nose is swollen, achy and tender to the touch. I don't know if it's broken. I don't know what I'd do if it was.

At least I have somewhere new to go, so it wasn't for nothing. I drag my hand across my face and it fucking *hurts*, and it feels . . . heavy. I'm so tired. I need to really stop. I need to get farther away before I think about doing that. I lean forward, peering out the windshield. The sky has gone gray, a thunderstorm on the horizon. It's already raining by the time I pull away from the shoulder. I watch the road disappear under the car. I feel like I'm teetering on some kind of edge I can't see over.

*451 Twining Street, Langford.*

If I had a phone, I could figure out where the fuck that is and how far away. Next town . . . next town I'll find another library. I glance at the gas gauge. Half empty. My eyes close. No. I rub them open, blinking against the flare of oncoming headlights.

Javi. I make myself think of him because thinking of him makes my blood burn hot enough to wake me up a little. I was weak about Javi, too desperate for a taste of some other life. Too hungry and too tired to think it through clearly. *I tried,* I tell myself. *At least I tried.* As if it counts for anything when Silas Baker is still out there, still alive. *Fuck you, Javi.* I squeeze my eyes shut briefly and what I found in that house—

My knife against Silas Baker's abdomen.

*I tried.*

What good is trying when you fail.

I push it all from my mind and ease the car to a stop because there's a red light in front of me. I stare at it, watch as it blurs around the edges before turning green. A moment later, I finally pass the YOU ARE NOW LEAVING MONTGOMERY sign.

It rains harder and the rain turns the world into a gloomy watercolor. Every so often, sheet lightning flashes across the sky. It's just the start of the weather, I can feel it. There's an electricity in the air and it's making my skin hum, tells me it's going to get worse. The highway stretches endlessly nowhere, but then—a shape of someone on the side of the road. I squint past the rain. They have their thumb out. I didn't know people still did that. I slow as I pass, so I can get a look at them. It's hard to see clearly but . . .

A girl.

I pull over carefully. It takes her a full minute to register it, like she can't believe someone actually stopped for her and it makes my heart hurt a little. But just because I can be soft doesn't mean I'm stupid. I roll the passenger's side window down. She leans in. She's wearing a jacket with a hood that's done little to protect her from the elements. She could be blond or brunette. I won't know until her hair dries. Her white skin looks irritated from the rain, blotchy and red, but that still leaves it looking a sight better than mine.

"Y-you're n-not a psycho, are you?"

She blinks against the rain. "Not last time I checked. You?" I can't get a sense of her voice over the car's idling engine and the weather.

"M-maybe. W-where you headed?"

"Markette." She points ahead. "It's about forty miles that way. Straight through."

"D-do you know where L-Langford is? I n-need to g-get there."

"Nope, but I could probably look it up on my phone."

"Then I could p-probably give you a r-ride."

"I'd sure appreciate it."

She waits for me to let her in. I hesitate.

"I've never d-done th-this before."

"I can pay you," she says. "Cash or gas, next station."

I unlock the door.

The girl hasn't stopped apologizing to me since she climbed in the car because, thanks to her, the seat got all wet. She peels out of her jacket and reveals a slightly drier tank top underneath. Her jeans look like they've been painted on. It's got to be uncomfortable and I feel bad for her but I don't know what I could do to make it better.

She squishes back against the seat, stretching out her legs, and wrangles her wallet from her pocket. She opens it to show me the bills and credit cards inside. I can't imagine her doing something so stupid if a guy had picked her up. It's vaguely insulting.

*I'm dangerous,* I want to tell her.

But after today, I believe it less and less.

"Just so you know I'm good for it," she tells me and now that I can hear her, her words kind of run together, sort of the way actresses talked in old movies, and I think if I sounded like that, I'd talk all the time.

"Okay."

Then, she gets her phone out and asks me what's the name of the place I'm looking for again. *451 Twining Street, Langford.* She taps it out and a moment later informs me it's four hundred miles away. I tell her to get a pen and a piece of paper out of the glove box and write all the directions down, exactly how to get there. It goes quiet while she scribbles. The scratch of the pen and her breathing lulls me into that hazy space again. I turn the radio on. The sound of some man's voice fills the car.

"This is West McCray with WNRK and I'm here today with . . ."

The voice is distractingly clean and gentle, sort of smooth in the exact same way Silas Baker's was, and the way my stomach lurches tells me I don't want to hear any man's voice right now. I turn the radio off. The girl gives me a crooked smile and finishes writing the directions, handing them over. I half-glance at the paper before setting it on the dash.

"W-what's your name?"

"Cat."

"S-Sadie."

I close my eyes briefly. That wasn't the name I meant to give her.

"Thanks for the lift, Sadie."

"No p-problem, Cat."

"Looks like we were both leaving Montgomery," she tells me. "And I've been on the road for . . . I don't know. But I'm telling you, it's always the nicest places that are the worst. They got all there probably is to give and they won't. You can't bleed 'em, not even a little."

"You b-bleed p-people a lot?"

She rolls her head toward me and some of her hair is starting to dry into ratty blond tangles. All she does is smile, then asks me, "So what happened to your face?"

I sniff and immediately regret it. "F-fell on it."

"Ouch."

"A l-little."

"You mind if I change my jeans? They feel gross."

I shrug and she grabs at her soaking wet bag and rummages through it. Doesn't look like much inside it escaped the rain either, judging by all the muttered cursing that follows. After a long minute, she triumphantly declares, *"Aha!"* and pulls out a pair of black leggings, which are so knotted up in her bag, as soon as they come out, the rest of everything else she's got does too, spilling all over the car.

"Oh, fuck."

She spends the next few minutes feeling around, between and under the seats, to make sure she has everything and she does it in a way that tells me she can't afford to lose anything.

Once she's done that and she's satisfied, she peels out of her stiff jeans and underwear—leaving her naked from the waist down—and gets into the dry pants.

After she's redressed, she sighs contentedly. "Better."

This is survival, what she's doing right now. I recognize it. A girl who bulldozes a person by being ten times herself in front of them. I want to tell Cat she doesn't have to do this in front of me, but there's no point.

"So what are you doing?" she asks and I tell her I'm driving. She laughs. "I mean, why are you headed to 451 Twining Street, Langford, Colorado?" It's startling, hearing it repeated so perfectly by a perfect stranger, but I guess after writing it all down, it would be stuck in her head.

"Road t-trip," I say. "W-with my s-sister."

"Cool." She looks around the car, the empty backseat. "Where is she?"

"P-picking h-her up there."

"At 451 Twining Street, Langford?"

"Th-that's the p-plan."

"But you didn't know how to get there?" she asks. I swallow, but I don't know what to say. I feel her studying me. She lets it slide. "I don't have any siblings. I think I like it better that way, though. How old is she?" She taps her fingers along the door handle and that's when I realize I've made her nervous. "Younger or older?"

"Thirteen. I'm n—I'm nineteen."

She whistles. "Man. Thirteen. That was nearly a decade ago for me. You remember that age? You just think you know everything."

"Y-yeah."

"God," she murmurs, but I have a feeling whatever she's remembering about thirteen is probably different from what I'm remembering about thirteen. Mom was still around with some guy, Arthur . . . lasted about half a year. Arthur something. I don't remember him so well. Everything after Keith felt like a dream but Arthur had . . . slick black hair, a big nose. His voice was off-puttingly high. I couldn't understand what Mom saw in him until I realized he always had money and he always had drugs. He was a dealer. Mom broke him in the end, got him dipping into his own supply. By the time they were done, he had nothing.

Then he was gone.

Mattie was eight and that was about the time she started figuring out something was wrong with Mom. She was making friends with kids at school at that point and it was hard not to notice that the other kids' mothers didn't medicate at the breakfast table, didn't lose the ability to string a sentence together by noon and weren't blacked out by dinner. I remember sitting outside the trailer with her and reciting May Beth's greatest hits because May Beth told me I had to look out for Mattie that way, make sure Mattie loved the mother she had instead of wasting her life wishing for another, like me. And I love May Beth, but I hate that she did that to me. To this day, she still acts like it was my idea.

*Mom's sick, Mattie, do you understand? It's not her fault. You wouldn't blame someone for getting cancer.*

". . . I was such a bitch." Cat's midsentence. She's been talking this whole time. "I couldn't even imagine twenty, but I thought I had it all figured out, you know? I wanted to be like . . ." She pauses. "Like *this,* actually, I wanted to do whatever the fuck I wanted. Hitching on the side of the road." She laughs. "It was a lot less ugly in my head." Before I can ask her how ugly it's been, she asks, "What about you?"

"—" She stares at me while I block. After the moment passes, I feel a heat in my face and do something I never do. I apologize for it. "S-sorry."

"It's okay."

"It h-happens when I'm t-tired." I scratch my forehead and I wish I hadn't said that either. "Uh. I d-don't know. I had to l-look after my sister a lot. My mom w-wasn't really . . ." I wave a hand feebly. "A mom."

"That's rough. What's her name?"

"M-Mattie."

It's unbearable, saying her name out loud to someone else. I didn't even say it to Javi. It's the first time I've let another person hear me say it in a long, long time. There was a point with May Beth, where Mattie became *her. She.* Because I couldn't—

I couldn't.

"What's wrong?" Cat asks because it's all over my face.

"Nothing."

"Sorry if I . . ."

"It's nothing. I j-just h-haven't seen her in a while."

I exhale shakily. I don't feel well, I guess. I feel like I'm surfacing from some sort of fever dream. I think of myself in Silas's driveway. The blood I only just cleaned off my body. It feels like years ago now, but when I look at the clock, it hasn't been hours.

"What's she like?"

"Who?"

"Your sister."

I stare out at the road, trying to see at what point the rain might end but, if anything, it's gotten worse. What little visibility there was has gone all to shit. The sky is almost black now. I'm just thinking how maybe we should pull over when the Chevy starts hydroplaning.

I lose control.

Cat's hand flies to the door handle as my car swerves into the opposite lane. I hear her whisper *oh shit* as I jerk the wheel in the opposite direction, which is the wrong thing to do. I try, frantically, to remember what the right thing is. I slam my foot on the brakes. Not the right thing. By the time the car stops spinning, we're sideways in the middle of the road and I feel like I'm dying. A car in the oncoming lane blares its horn and swerves around us, somehow managing not to skid across the water itself. And then it's silent, except for the sounds of both of us panting with the shock and relief of a near miss.

After an eternity, Cat says, "Maybe we should stop for a while."

"Y-yeah," I say, when I can finally unclench my teeth. I straighten the car and get us back on the right side of the road, facing the right direction.

We find a place to park about ten miles away and even if I don't know how to handle a car when it skids, I'm at least smart enough to know not to park on the shoulder with my lights off. We end up next to a field that's turning into a lake. Cat's calmed some and she's trying to explain to me what to do if I ever find myself in that kind of situation again and it's pissing me off because *I know*. I know about easing on the brakes and turning with the swerve. I just didn't remember it in the moment because it's different in the moment. I close my eyes to her and she finally senses she's pushing it because she says so: "I'm not helping."

I open my eyes. "Yeah."

She leans into her window, nose to glass.

"I wonder when it'll stop."

"D-dunno."

"You can let go of the wheel, you know."

I flush and uncurl my fingers from their death grip on the wheel and then I try to rub some life back into them.

Cat leans forward and grabs her bag from the floor. She pulls out some of her things—a wet map, a roll of plastic bags and a swollen notebook and sets them on the dash. Says, "Might as well dry some of my shit out."

I point at the notebook. "What's th-that?"

"Journal." She flashes a smile at me and then grabs it, flips it open and offers me the briefest glimpse. All I see is ink, a lot of it bleeding now. Some of the pages have scrap paper, tickets and other things taped to them.

"I keep records. Places I've been, people I've met. What I think of them."

"What are y-you g-gonna p-put in there for me?"

"Haven't decided yet." She opens the book and lays it out on the dash, cover side up. "I'm a runaway, I guess. Been one for a couple of years now."

"I can s-see it."

"What's it look like?"

I shrug. "Y-you."

She smiles a small smile. She turns back to the window, looking out at the field. There's a barn in the distance. It looks like it's dissolving. I blink heavily, shake my head.

I say, "M-my sister ran away once."

"Yeah?"

"J-just once."

The skin prickles on the back of my neck and I glance over my shoulder just to make sure the backseat is empty.

"Little hell-raiser, huh?"

"Yep."

"Teenagers."

"She w-was an ingrate, actually," I say. "Sh-she always p-pulled all k-kinds of shit. Never once c-cut me a break. She was always t-trying to get away from m-me."

Being tired is worse than being drunk. Things you never wanted to say coming out of your mouth and you can't stop it and by the time you realize you shouldn't have said it, it's too late. It feels like a betrayal. I want to take every word of it back, even if it's true, because I don't talk about Mattie like this to anyone else. I might think it but you *don't* talk about your family like that to anyone. *I would die for Mattie,* I want to say, because that's the part I want Cat to know, if she has to know anything. Not all the times Mattie pissed me off because she was thirteen years old and that's what thirteen-year-olds are supposed to do.

"Maybe you two can talk it out."

"Don't y-you have anyone?" I ask her, because I want something from her for everything of mine I didn't mean to give her.

"What do you mean?"

"P-parents?"

"Well, yeah."

"You like th-them?"

"They're fine."

"Th-then why r-run away?"

"Because it was the right thing to do."

"Why?"

"My dad's an asshole."

"Y-you j-just said they were fine."

"Yeah, well." She laughs. "I don't owe everybody my life story . . . then again, what are you gonna do with it? My dad's a corporate asshole and I got tired of being his punching bag, that's all. It got ugly. My mom picked the wrong side. Blah, blah."

"Th-that's sad," I say and she shrugs. "I d-don't have a dad."

"No?"

"My m-mom had a lot of sh-shitty boyfriends."

"At least that way you get breaks in between 'em."

"N-not the way she slept around."

"*Respect,* Sadie's mom. A woman's got needs." Cat cackles. I don't. She searches my face. "How many boyfriends? Who was the worst?"

I shrug.

"Come on."

"—" I don't owe anybody my life story but like she said, what's she going to do with it? I keep one hand on the wheel and lift my hair from the back of my neck with the other, trying to feel out the cigarette scar. Once I have it, I tell Cat to look. I say, "Th-that one."

"Shit. He just put it on you?"

"S-something l-like that."

She reaches over, running her fingertip on the raised, puckered skin, and leaves it there a long time. I shiver at that pinprick of warmth. It's the only time I'll ever like the way that scar feels.

"What happened?"

*Look at me when I'm talking to you.*

It's not a memory worth chasing, here in this car.

I push it away.

"I d-don't want to t-talk about it."

"Okay," she says.

"W-what's it like? D-doing th-this?"

She shrugs. "When I get in a car with most men, they just wanna fuck. When I get in a car with women, they just wanna talk. Not always, though. Sometimes it's the opposite."

"You're p-pretty," I say, like that's a reason. I feel my face turn a deep, deep shade of red and try to redeem myself. "I mean, it's easy t-to talk to a p-pretty f-face. I don't know."

She turns to me. "How long you had that stutter, anyway?"

"All my l-life."

"It's kinda cute."

I look at the car ceiling because there's something about

it that's vaguely insulting and weirdly flattering at the same time. My stutter is not cute unless I say it is, and I'll never say it is. Mostly, it's exhausting. Still, there's something nice about being worth the effort of Cat's lie. It's nice enough it makes me feel everything that's hurting a little less. Mattie once asked me . . . she'd just come home flush from a crush on Jonah Sweeten and asked me how you know when you like someone, and if I liked any boys like she did, and I didn't know what to tell her. That I tried not to think about that kind of stuff, because it was painful, because I thought I could never have it, but when I did end up liking someone, it always made me ache right down to my core. I realized pretty early on that the *who* didn't really matter so much.

That anybody who listens to me, I end up loving them just a little.

I turn my head to Cat and she stares at me and I stare back until I can't take it anymore and look away. I turn the radio on and a song is playing. It's the one that played at the bar yesterday night. That was only yesterday . . . my eyes drift closed and I don't know how long they stay that way when I jerk back awake. Breathe in.

"S-sorry," I say, embarrassed.

"You look beat," she says. "Literally and figuratively."

I look in the mirror, and the side of my nose, underneath my eye, is a little more swollen and bruised than it was before. The tired, dark circles I have are just enhancing the damage.

"Does it hurt?"

I shrug, but yes, it hurts. It hurts worse than it did before I got in the car and it'll hurt worse than that tomorrow, but more than that I'm just—tired.

She reaches over, her hand skimming my face and I flinch back away from her and she says, "Sorry, I don't know why I did that." And I want to say, *Sorry, I don't know how to let you.* Why don't I know how to let her? I think of Javi in the backseat of my car, and everything I didn't let myself do in there with him, and for what? So maybe it's not a love story, but why can't I let myself be worth a moment's tenderness?

Why?

"It's o-okay," I say and then, gathering all my courage: "Y-you could . . . it's okay if y-you want t-to d-do that."

She reaches over and cups my face softly in her hands and gives me a sad sort of smile that tells me I've given even more of myself away. I've put my weak, wanting heart into the universe. I close my eyes and let myself feel it, the heat of her palms against my cheeks. Then she kisses me. Her lips are soft and unexpected and right. I open my eyes.

"Thanks for picking me up," she says.

"I d-didn't d-do it for that."

"I know. I just wanted to thank you."

I lean my head against the steering wheel and wait for the rain to let up, and my eyes slip closed and I open them again. I'm fucked. I know if I close them one more time, that'll be it. Every good thing her kiss made me feel is fading, my sad reality kicking back in. I pinch the bridge of my nose and hiss, and the pain doesn't even sharpen the dullest parts of me.

"If you want to sleep you can."

I lower my hand.

"I d-don't," I say stubbornly.

"Doesn't seem like you got a choice," she returns. Then, "It's okay, Sadie."

But it isn't.

I stare out the window and think of my mother's finger-tips pressed lightly against my forehead. *I made you.* I wonder if she knows about Mattie, wherever she is.

I wonder if she knows I'm all that's left.

# THE GIRLS

## S1E4

**WEST McCRAY:**
The day Mattie disappeared started like any other. May Beth remembers it vividly; she dreams of it every night.

**MAY BETH FOSTER:**
She came by that morning. I have a rule: it's not decent to bother a person before nine. So Mattie's favorite thing, if she was up and around before then, was to come pounding on my door at nine-oh-one, fling it open and shout, "Good morning!" into my trailer. Shout it right in my face, really, because the door opens up to my kitchen. *[CHUCKLES]*

So that's what she did. She flung the door wide, I was at the table, having my coffee and she *screamed*, "Good morning, May Beth!" And I wanted to throttle her because I loved her that much, but I just smiled at her and I asked her, "Where're you off to today, Mats?" like I always did and she said, "Everywhere," like she always did.

I told her to figure things out with her sister and stay out of trouble in the meantime.

**WEST McCRAY:**
Mattie and Sadie had been fighting that week.

**MAY BETH FOSTER:**
It was about Claire, of course.

Mattie wanted to go to L.A. but she knew they didn't have the money, so whenever she'd pick a fight about it, deep down she understood—or at least, I think she understood—that it was impossible. Mattie would have her moment, let it die a while, then have another.

But somehow, she'd found out Sadie had been squirrelling away cash in case of an emergency. If they didn't end up needing it, Sadie told me Mattie would take it to college. Now that Mattie knew about this money, she decided that meant they could hop a plane to L.A. and look for Claire. Of course Sadie told her that wasn't happening.

I had them over for an early dinner that afternoon and they weren't talking. It was awful. Usually, Sadie would try to smooth things over, but not this time. When I asked her about it afterward, she said, and I'll never forget it—she said, "I don't think I'll ever be enough for Mattie."

Mattie was never content with just having her sister.

**WEST McCRAY:**
Sadie worked the gas station that night.

**MARTY McKINNON:**
Sadie might not have been the most forthcoming girl, but it was clear she was upset about something. Find out later, it was that fight.

**WEST McCRAY:**
The fight was brought to the Abernathy Police Department's attention by Sadie herself, but played no significant part in their investigation into Mattie's murder. It's just another layer of tragedy in a story that's already seen more than its fair share.

**MARTY McKINNON:**
It was a long shift, I remember. Sadie said she really needed the money, so I gave her a few more hours. She clocked off pretty late and—

**MAY BETH FOSTER:**
She came back to my place. She didn't do that all the time, only when she was real worn out and maybe . . . maybe looking for a bit of mothering. I was glad to do it, because the opportunity didn't come along too often with Sadie. Anyway, she fell asleep on my couch and she looked so peaceful, I didn't want to wake her. I should have. I can't help but wonder what might've happened if I had. Maybe she and Mattie would've crossed paths before Mattie ever got in that truck . . . because that's the thing—no matter what happened between them, Sadie always checked in on Mattie for whatever she might need. She always had a meal on the table or in the fridge, ready to heat up. No matter how frustrated Sadie got with her sister, she never stopped looking after her.

But that night, I wouldn't let her. I didn't wake her up. I thought it would be good for Mattie—for Mattie to stand back and notice that absence, to realize how much Sadie did for her even if Mattie thought Sadie didn't get it right enough of the time. So I texted Mattie and I let her know Sadie was with me and she wasn't going to be home.

**WEST McCRAY:**
Mattie never got it. She'd left her phone in the trailer. Sadie discovered this when, the next day, she sent a string of frantic texts to her little sister, demanding to know where she was. They read as follows:

*SORRY, MATTIE. FELL ASLEEP.*

*WHERE ARE YOU?*

*I DIDN'T DO IT TO BE A BITCH, I PROMISE.*

*I'M FREAKING OUT—JUST TELL ME WHERE YOU ARE.*

*DON'T DO THIS TO ME.*

**MAY BETH FOSTER:**
I'll never forget it. Sadie came back to my place and told me Mattie was gone. I said, "I'm sure she's somewhere around town, just being a little bitch about it." That's exactly what I said. I've never forgiven myself. And Sadie just looked at me and said, "This feels different." She was right.

**WEST McCRAY:**
I don't need to paint you a picture of what this retelling does to May Beth because you can hear the utter agony in her voice. Still, I want you to know she sits across from me at her table the entire time, her gaze fixed on something I can't see, her hands twisting the tablecloth. She's not

shying from her hurt, and it's a true privilege that she'd share it with me, but her desperate attempt to control it tells me the pain I'm witness to is barely scratching the surface. I don't know how she survives it, frankly. She doesn't seem to either.

**MAY BETH FOSTER:**
It's killing me a little more every day. And if that's what it's doing to me, you can't imagine what it did to Sadie. She . . . became a shell of who she used to be. I lost her a little more each day.

**WEST McCRAY:**
It's understandable, then, that May Beth wants to protect Sadie from further hurt. She's so afraid of the information she's been keeping from me she makes me fly back to Cold Creek just to get it. It's not that she doesn't trust me, she says, but she'd feel better saying it to my face.

When I get there, I turn the microphone off and she tells me what she knows. Five days later, I have a new lead, and once she's been reassured that what she's told me won't cause any kind of problems for Sadie should we find her, May Beth agrees to tell me again for the podcast.

**MAY BETH FOSTER:**
Once I say it, everyone's going to understand why I don't think much of the Farfield Police Department, because if they were as thorough as they claim they were, if they did everything in their power to figure out what happened to Sadie, they would've found this and they would've followed through on it. It was under the passenger's seat of her car.

**WEST McCRAY:**
It's a credit card. Sadie didn't have any credit cards when she lived in Cold Creek. And this one doesn't belong to her. It belongs to a woman named Cat Mather.

She's an easy enough person to track down.

# sadie

I dream of small, broken bodies.

Prone and hurt, catalogued and kept sacred in dark spaces. The look in their eyes is one of utter incomprehension giving way to pain, to emptiness. Sometimes they stare right at me. Other times, the middle distance. There's nothing I can do. It's too late.

I dream of Mattie's face.

I jerk awake, the side of my head knocking against the windshield. The throbbing in my nose is near unbearable— but survivable.

*It's survivable,* I tell myself.

I turn the car on and glance at the clock only to discover I wasn't out for more than an hour. I feel more tired than I did before I gave in to sleep and my bones are aching in a way that makes me miss my bed, makes me miss the idea of a home. The trailer's not even that, anymore, though. It wasn't when I left it. It's not home if I'm the only person in it.

I yawn. It was the shuffling and shifting beside me that

woke me up. Cat rummaging around, I think, but by the time my eyes were open, she was sitting very still beside me, staring out at the road. I follow her gaze. The rain has stopped. Must have just stopped. The midafternoon sun is out, making the pavement gleam.

Cat doesn't look right. Everything she laid out on the dashboard is gone, back in her bag, I guess. An hour doesn't seem like it would be enough time for it all to dry.

"What's w-wrong w-with you?" I ask.

"What? Nothing. I was just waiting for you to wake up."

"I-I'm awake." I clear my throat. "You wanna g-get outta here?"

"Sounds like a plan."

I pull back onto the road while Cat sits rigid beside me. We drive the next hour in silence. She's different now. I can't put my finger on why—all I did was sleep. I roll the window down and take a deep breath. I can see the air, thick with post-rain haze.

"Hey, hey." Cat taps me on the arm with one hand and points left with the other. The road reveals a small gas station and we must be between nowhere and somewhere, because it's surprisingly busy. It's got two pumps out front and probably the world's grimiest bathrooms out back. I pull in. The sign next to the pumps says SELF SERVE (CASH ONLY, PAY INSIDE).

It's the best of the worst available options, just slightly less talking involved than if an attendant shows, expecting you to tell them what you need. But I'm not feeling up to it. If Mattie were here, I'd let her do the talking. She liked doing her best impression of a person in charge to save me from The Look, or worse. Because there are worse people than *Becki with an i*—Becki, imagine her, the tip of an iceberg— and I swear I've met them all. There's a lot of folks out there willing to pay for their comfort with someone else's voice.

Cat unbuckles her seat belt and shoves some crumpled money into my hands.

"Should be enough," she says quickly. A yellow truck pulls up behind us. "Uh, I'm just gonna stretch my legs . . . go to the bathroom."

"Okay."

She gets out of the car.

I watch her round the station and sit there for another minute, or maybe much more than a minute, because the next thing I know an older man raps his knuckles against my window, startling me so bad I near hit the roof. I roll the window down and stare. He's all silver hair and bushy eyebrows, the skin of his deeply tanned face sun-leathered enough to make it hard to guess how long he's actually been on this earth. Forty. Sixty. I don't know.

"Whoa! Didn't mean ta scare ya." His voice has a faint withering of age about it. "But it's self-serve and you've been sittin' out here so long, I thought you didn't see the sign. We got a line happening behind you, so . . ."

"—" I block, of course. I can feel the word in my mouth, trying desperately to free itself. When it finally does, it comes out, "Sssssssorry."

I sound drunk.

"You been drinking?" the man asks.

I'm never sure if being asked if I'm drunk is a step up from the suggestion I'm stupid, but it all points to the same thing, I guess—that there's something fundamentally not right about me and once you feel that on you, you want to get away from it.

"If you been drinking, you know I can't just let you drive outta here."

"C-couldn't st-stop me. I got a"—I flash a smile—"got a g-good head st-start."

I keep that smile plastered on even as I feel heat creep

past my neck, to my ears, and bloom across my cheeks until my whole face is tomato red. The hard lines around the man's brown eyes soften. He either feels sorry for me or he's embarrassed for himself. I won't know which until he opens *his* mouth.

He clears his throat and makes it a peace offering: "How about I fill it up for ya."

"I'll pay i-i-i—"

I give up and nod toward the building.

*I'll pay inside.*

The air-conditioning gives the station a bite, raises the hairs on my arms and legs. I need to restock a little—food and water—but doing it at a place like this, where anything remotely healthy is too expensive to look at and the shit food is at a premium too, isn't very smart of me. I grab a bottle of water from the fridge and a dusty jar of peanut butter from a shelf near the back. I pick up a plastic spoon at the coffee counter where I contemplate a seventy-five-cent coffee from an old metal percolator and decide that money's better spent on food. So no coffee, but my metal-warped reflection is how I want people to picture me: the skin of my face stretched upward and downward at impossible lengths, my eyes dozing somewhere near the middle, my nose a long sliver with two pinprick nostrils, all of me blurring oddly together like watercolors poured down a canvas that can't keep hold of its art.

The bells over the door spastically announce the old man's entrance and I expect Cat to be behind him, maybe, but she's not. I follow him to the counter with my peanut butter and water and that, combined with the gas—even with Cat's contribution—lightens my wallet too much.

Money burns fast. Knowing that doesn't get easier with age and it's worse when you learn it young. The beauty of childhood is not entirely grasping the cost of living; food just appears in the fridge, you have a roof over your head because everyone does and electricity must be some kind of sorcery, like right out of *Harry Potter* or something, because who could ever put a price on light? Maybe it's not even that you believe in magic. It's that you never really had to think about any of it before. Then one day you find out you've been walking the razor's edge all along.

"Th-thanks," I tell him.

When I get back outside, Cat is nowhere to be found but the line that's formed behind my car is looking more than a little pissed off. I get inside it and pull forward into a parking spot and that's when I notice all her stuff is gone from the front seat.

"What the fuck," I murmur. I get back out of the car. The place seems busier than it did a second go, people moving in and out of the store.

I cup my hands around my mouth. "C-Cat?"

A few heads turn my way, but none of them are her. I jog around the building to the bathrooms and a sign on the door says to ask for the key inside—but Cat didn't do that. She got out of the car, walked behind the building and now she's . . . she's gone.

The back of the station faces a steep incline toward a field of wildflowers. It stretches about a mile before it meets highway. There's no one I can see. My chest gets tight. Did something happen? Did someone . . .

Did someone take her?

I look back, my heart thrumming, skin buzzing. I picture Cat, this girl I don't even know, finding herself here, trying to open the door. She sees she needs the key. She needs the key, and she'd go get it, but there's someone behind her, someone comes around from behind her—

No.

Stop.

I remember my fumbling search through the loneliest, emptiest places in Cold Creek, shouting Mattie's name perfectly, solidly, holding out for that moment my voice would fracture because the fracture would mean I wasn't alone, that she had come back.

It was the only time in my life I wanted to stutter.

I kept calling for her, kept searching. I couldn't let myself stop looking, couldn't let myself cry either, because never in my life would I risk crying where Mattie could see because for Mattie, I was supposed to be strong.

I remember the moment when I finally gave in, when I no longer had the strength to push against reality. I let the tears come and as soon as I did, I got a text from May Beth.

*The police are here. You need to get back.*

A woman brushes past, startling me.

"'Scuse me," she mumbles as she opens the bathroom door. She has a key in her hand.

Where the *fuck* is Cat? I run to the front of the station and push through the doors harder than I can keep myself from doing. The bells go crazy. The old man's head jerks up in alarm.

"D-did you see a g-girl?" I ask. "She was w-with me. I c-can't f-find her." He frowns. "She was b-blond, c-curly hair . . . ?"

He snaps his fingers. "Didn't know she was with you. I saw her. She hitched a ride with some fella in a yellow truck. They pulled out while you were in here."

I take a step back.

"O-okay. Thanks."

"You bet."

I walk back to the car and the panic inside me fades into confused embarrassment.

I bring my fingers to my lips.

Cat ditched me.

I mean, I don't care.

It wasn't like we were—

It's not like . . .

When I get back to the car, I realize the backseat is a different kind of messy than it was before I picked her up . . .

She was going through my things, looking for—what?

I pull the door open and see blood. My stained shirt unearthed from where I stuffed it under the seat, now crumpled in a heap on the floor mat, the switchblade beside it. I slam the door shut and get back in the driver's side.

I hope whoever she ended up with wasn't a worse person than me.

# THE GIRLS

## S1E4

**WEST McCRAY:**
Cat Mather lives in Topeka, Kansas.

She was once a missing girl.

The first things I find when I Google her name are desperate, public Facebook posts from her maternal aunt, Sally Quinn, asking after her niece's whereabouts. Those posts are nearly two years old. Shortly after she put them up, Sally informs her friends to cease all searching; Cat has essentially divorced herself from her family and wants nothing to do with anyone and that's that. She's just a runaway.

Cat, in a lot of ways, is what I expected Sadie to be. Restless, reckless, dramatic. Her own Facebook profile is full of pictures with her tongue sticking out, her hair dyed bright, bold colors. She's often wearing shirts with the anarchy logo on them. At least, she was then. That was when she was around to share status updates with not-so-subtle allusions to personal unhappiness. *Fuck this family*, one says. *Stop the planet, I want off*, says another. She was gone not long after that last one and spent the next two years moving from place to place, until just a few months ago, when she got caught behind the wheel of a stolen car.

Now she's living with Sally and awaiting her court date.

At first, Cat doesn't want anything to do with me. Her privacy is important to her, and she wasn't thrilled with the idea of her criminal history being shared with the world. When I explained to Cat about Sadie, and how we found Cat's credit card in her car, she's more willing to talk.

**CAT MATHER:**
Yeah, I was with her, just for a little while. She gave me a ride. She scared me, kind of. I don't know.

**WEST McCRAY:**
This is what Cat Mather looks like now: she's a white, twenty-three-year-old woman with a plain, unassuming face that almost belies the actions that have gotten her into this mess. Her aunt, Sally, greets me at the front door. Sally is a friendly, middle-aged brunette, who gives me a brief primer on the Mather family on our short trip to the living room, where her niece awaits.

**SALLY QUINN:**
She's my sister's daughter. They've been estranged for a long time. Family problems. It's terrible. Cat disappeared when she was nineteen. I've been hoping this whole . . . unpleasantness would help them reconcile somehow, but it hasn't happened. Maybe it will, though. I really hope it does, because Cat's father—

**CAT MATHER:**
Hey, Sal. Maybe leave something for me to talk about?

**SALLY QUINN:**
[LAUGHS] Anyway, here she is.

Good luck.

**WEST McCRAY:**
As soon as Sally's gone, Cat quickly makes one thing clear:

**CAT MATHER:**
We're here to talk about Sadie, and that's all. Got it?

**WEST McCRAY:**
Fair enough. One thing that stood out to me when I got ahold of you was when I asked if you knew Sadie, you said *yes* right away. She's been giving other people an alias, but she was up front with you when you met. She told you her real name.

**CAT MATHER:**
What name was she giving people?

**WEST McCRAY:**
Lera. How did she end up with your credit card?

**CAT MATHER:**
It was in my bag. I had it for emergencies, but I preferred dealing with cash. I must have dropped it when I was with her.

**WEST McCRAY:**
She didn't use it.

**CAT MATHER:**
She wouldn't have been able to. I realized pretty quick it was gone. Canceled it.

**WEST McCRAY:**
Tell me about how you two met.

**CAT MATHER:**
We were both leaving this place, Montgomery, at the same time. I was hitching and she picked me up.

**WEST McCRAY:**
Do you know what she was doing in Montgomery?

**CAT MATHER:**
Nope.

**WEST McCRAY [STUDIO]:**
Montgomery is a postcard town.

Actually, it's a city, but that's what Danny likes to call a particular kind of place. You know—the kinds that make you wish you were there. Remember when I said Cold Creek wasn't the dream Americans aspired to? Well, Montgomery *is*. It's a beautiful, picturesque college town with a thriving economy, driven in large part by its student population and the wealthy baby boomers who want to live out their retirement basking in the glow of the young. If you haven't been, you simply must. If it's too far out of your way, check out the movies *Love the One You're With*, *A Fine Autumn Day* and *Our Last Dance*. They were filmed there.

**CAT MATHER:**
She wanted to get out of there. I could tell because I did too. Places like that, places that look so nice they don't seem real?

The worst shit you can imagine happens in them. And I'm not wrong. You seen the news?

**WEST McCRAY** *[STUDIO]*:
Recently, Montgomery has been devastated by a grotesque scandal involving one of the pillars of its community.

Silas Baker is—or at least he *was*—a well-regarded local businessman, who played a part in Montgomery's economic success. He invested in the legalized recreational marijuana boom, made a fortune and then reinvested back into his home city. He owns a few department stores; a local bar, Cooper's; the grocer's; and has a financial stake in several other popular businesses within the city. For this, he was awarded Montgomery's Good Citizenship Award six years ago.

A few months ago, he was arrested for sexually abusing the young children he's coached in T-ball over the last seven years. They ranged in age from five to eight years old.

**CAT MATHER:**
. . . I think she felt sorry for me because it was raining like you wouldn't believe. I could barely see two feet in front of my face and I was soaked clean through. She sort of slowed as she passed me, then she pulled over. It was a black car—a Chevy, I think?

**WEST McCRAY:**
Yeah, that's what she was driving.

**CAT MATHER:**
Anyway, she asked me if I was a psycho and I asked her if she was one and once we got that outta the way, I got in the car. She had this stutter. She was kind of messed up. Not because of the stutter, though, that's not what I mean.

**WEST McCRAY:**
What do you mean?

**CAT MATHER:**
She looked like someone clocked her in the face. Her nose was swollen, bit of a black eye, scraped chin. I think it must've happened that day because it just got worse looking the longer I was with her.

**WEST McCRAY:**
Did she tell you what happened?

**CAT MATHER:**
She said she fell but that was clearly bullshit.

**WEST McCRAY:**
So you guys talked.

**CAT MATHER:**
Well, yeah. It's awkward enough getting in a car with a stranger. You have to fill the silence somehow. She said she was on a road trip and she was picking up her little sister to go with her.

**WEST McCRAY:**
Her sister, Mattie, who had been murdered eight months earlier.

**CAT MATHER:**
And if I'd known that, maybe I wouldn't have gotten in the car because that does sound kinda psycho to me. Not that I stuck around with her that long in the end, anyway.

**WEST McCRAY:**
What did she say about Mattie?

**CAT MATHER:**
Just . . . she told me they were sisters and that she was the oldest, and Mattie was a pain in the ass, and that was about it. I could tell talking about it upset her, though. It made me think they were estranged and trying to make up. I never once guessed the kid was *dead*, though.

**MAY BETH FOSTER** *[PHONE]*:
She was talking like Mattie was alive?

**WEST McCRAY** *[PHONE]*:
That's what Cat told me.

**MAY BETH FOSTER** *[PHONE]*:
Are you sure? That's what this girl said? That Sadie was talking about Mattie like she was alive? Did she mean it? Did Sadie actually believe that?

**WEST McCRAY** *[PHONE]*:
Maybe, maybe not. It could've been something she was telling everyone. Not everyone shares their life story with strangers, May Beth.

**MAY BETH FOSTER** *[PHONE]*:
But what if that's what she believes?

**CAT MATHER:**
We were driving, and the weather kept getting worse and then we spun out—

**WEST McCRAY:**
You spun out?

**CAT MATHER:**
We hit some rain and the car ended up in the middle of the road. We were fine, but the weather wasn't getting better, so we decided to pull over until it cleared up and uh, she couldn't keep her eyes open after that. Like—it was almost instantaneous. *Wham*, hit her. I thought maybe she was on drugs or something.

**WEST McCRAY:**
Okay, so you said she looked like she got punched in the face, she loses control of the car, then she couldn't keep her eyes open—it didn't cross your mind she might've been injured? Concussed?

**CAT MATHER:**
No, it didn't. I just . . . I thought she was on drugs. Soon as she passed out, I started looking around the car to be sure, you know—

**WEST McCRAY:**
For drugs?

**CAT MATHER:**
Yeah, I was looking for drugs. I wanted to know what I was maybe getting myself into. Don't look at me like that.

**WEST McCRAY:**
I'm not looking at you like anything, Cat.

**CAT MATHER:**
I wasn't going to steal from her, okay? I've hitched *a lot*. You have to be prepared for anything. You just have to.

Once I ended up with this guy, I got these vibes. He made a stop, and I looked through his car and I found a rope and a screwdriver under his seat and I shit you not, that screwdriver looked like it had dried blood on it. I can't tell what a person's about when I get in their car, but if I have a chance to find out, I'll take it.

WEST McCRAY:
What did you find?

CAT MATHER:
She had a shirt and it was fucking *covered* in blood. It was stuffed in the backseat. There was also a switchblade on the floor, must've been forced out from under the front seat when we spun out.

WEST McCRAY:
Are you sure what you saw on that shirt was blood?

CAT MATHER:
I know what blood looks like! It was just—it might've been hers, it might've been someone else's. But the knife too? She had it stashed, like she was hiding it, was the thing. So I started thinking I was in trouble.

WEST McCRAY:
You didn't ask her about it?

CAT MATHER:
That's a really stupid question.

It was . . . she seemed really *nice*, you know? I didn't get vibes from her like I did that guy—but that *shirt* . . . if you'd seen it, you'd get it. It was completely covered in blood.

I stayed in the car, thinking I should leave the whole time, like I just went back and forth over and over, until she finally woke up. That was about an hour from when she fell asleep. Then I drove with her until we hit a gas station. I was headed for this town called Markette, still a ways off, but I couldn't—even if she *was* nice, I couldn't risk not knowing for sure. So I ditched her at the gas station. I felt a little bad about it, but you gotta do what you gotta do to stay alive.

**WEST McCRAY:**
Is it too much to hope you know where she was headed?

**CAT MATHER:**
Actually, yeah, I do. She needed me to look up directions on my phone. I wrote 'em down for her and I never got it out of my head.

**WEST McCRAY** *[PHONE]:*
She's looking for her father.

**DANNY GILCHRIST** *[PHONE]:*
Right.

**WEST McCRAY** *[PHONE]:*
And I have two separate witness accounts who say she had a switchblade. Caddy said Sadie threatened him with it. Cat found it in her car.

**DANNY GILCHRIST** *[PHONE]:*
You mentioned she was hurt.

**WEST McCRAY** *[PHONE]:*
Yeah, she got hurt in Montgomery. So what happened there? What is it about her father that's taking her to these places,

and why is she arming herself? And how'd she end up with what sounds like a broken nose and a black eye? *[PAUSE]*

There was something about meeting Cat . . .

**DANNY GILCHRIST** *[PHONE]*:
What?

**WEST McCRAY** *[STUDIO]*:
It was hard to articulate to Danny, what I was feeling at the time. I couldn't stop thinking about Cat—that if I had been looking for *her*, if her aunt had tracked me down for help, that's where the story would have ended: sitting across from her in a living room with her refusing to talk. But it wouldn't have ended there, not really, because it was also Cat, ending up in cars with strange men and bloody screwdrivers, all to get away from whatever was haunting her at home. And then there's Sadie in her car, her own face bruised and battered. It all suddenly, and belatedly, felt too real, the things these girls had gone through, what can happen to missing girls. I didn't like that. But I couldn't say it out loud to him then. I changed the subject instead.

**WEST McCRAY** *[PHONE]*:
Never mind.

Okay, so I know she didn't stay in Montgomery and I know where she ended up. Where do you think I should head first? Montgomery or Langford— Hang on, I got another call.

Hello?

**MAY BETH FOSTER** *[PHONE]*:
Claire's back.

# sadie

I get to Langford.

Four in the morning.

First thing I see is a twenty-four-hour Laundromat, and I decide that's got to be a sign. I pull in. I'm about ready to drop, but I need this, some step toward feeling more human. My face has turned into the kind of pain that's almost sickening in its persistence, and when I look in the mirror, I wonder if I should go to a drugstore and buy some kind of makeup to put on top of the damage so I can keep from scaring people away. Mattie knew more about makeup than I did. Once, when she was eleven, I caught her in the bathroom with black liquid eyeliner making a perfect kitten eye. I told her I didn't ever want to see that shit on her face until she turned thirteen and I don't know why I made that rule. Was it so bad of her? It just seemed like something a parent would say so I made myself say it, when what I really wanted was to ask her how she did it and if she could make those same perfect lines across my own eyelids.

I step inside the Laundromat. Behind a counter is an old

woman who looks like she's keeping herself alive through sheer force of will. I hand her a bill and she hacks up a lung into the same hand that passes me change and detergent.

The machines are old. I put the quarters in the slots and don't even bother sorting my clothes. I sit in one of the hard plastic chairs, listening to the spin, then glance at the old woman, who still has her eyes on me. Can't blame her for it, given how I look.

"C-can you t-tell me what's at 451 Tw-Twining Street?"

She tilts her head to the side, thinking, then she says, "That's not the Bluebird, is it?" I don't know what the Bluebird is until she gets out her cell phone and gestures me over to show me a blurry photo of a motel with a bunch of middling reviews beneath it.

One of my mother's last boyfriends was Paul.

He was six foot six, thick inside and out. Arms and legs like old-growth tree stumps and hands too big to hold. I didn't mind Paul because he didn't give a damn about Mattie or me. If we had to occupy the same cramped trailer together, so be it. He didn't act like we were in his way and even when we were, it didn't matter. Not a lot got under Paul's skin, which is why I think he lasted so long. Anyway, Paul—he didn't talk a lot. Not because he couldn't, but because he didn't want to. When I was around Paul, I'd watch, rapt, as the people he surrounded himself with led one-sided conversations without ever expecting anything in return. It was unmistakable, the way they looked at him. They *respected* him. Paul taught me a person committed to silence can suggest importance, strength. So long as they're a man, I mean. It's not an option when you're a girl, not unless you want people to think you're a bitch.

I wish I could do this next part without talking.

I sit in my car outside the Bluebird, a few miles from the Laundromat, my load of laundry cooling in the backseat. I tap my fingers against the wheel. The Bluebird. Not a single bird in sight, but there's a FOR SALE sign out front: $39.99 A NIGHT, WI-FI NOT INCLUDED.

It's run-down, badly in need of new siding, a new roof . . . new everything. I'm parked across from the front office, and I can see through its picture window. An old man is watching a TV mounted to the wall, his back to me. A black-and-white movie.

I rest my head against the wheel.

*Where are you, Keith?*

I get out of the car with my bag slung over my shoulder and when I face the Bluebird, the man at the desk is no longer mesmerized by the television. He's turned toward the window and he's watching me in such a way, I wonder if he recognizes me, if, maybe one day, so many months ago, he looked for something to watch on TV and my face flitted past him on the news, never leaving his head. And now: here I am.

I cross the lot. Soon as I step inside, he says, "Took your time about it."

He looks much younger up close. Grayed prematurely, I guess. But he can't be more than fifty. He has light brown skin and tattoos up and down his arms and his legs that disappear under the edges of his blue shorts. His voice is put-on, a kind of put-on that pretends we're friends.

"I w-want two nights."

He yawns. "Sure."

I look away from him, to the TV behind his head. It's so old it has dials. It's playing a Bette Davis movie. Her beautiful small face and big round eyes command the screen. *Dark Victory*, I think. I liked that one. Now and again, me and Mattie used to spend weekends with May Beth and we'd watch the classics on one of the three channels she got. The Bette Davis ones were my favorite. Bette Davis *is* my favorite.

On her gravestone, it says: *She did it the hard way.*

"Just need some ID and we'll get you set up."

I blink away from the movie, turning my attention back to him.

"W-what?"

"Age. Can't rent you a room if you're underage."

"B-but I'm n—"

"Just let the ID do the talking." He smiles. "Otherwise we could be here all night."

I hate him.

"It's policy," he adds at the same time the television *pop*s. Its screen turns to snow and static blizzards through the speakers, painfully loud. "Oh, shi—"

He catches himself before he lands the *t* and turns, hand raised, to fix the set with his open palm. I stare at the back of his head and try to figure out if he might know Keith. If this is a place where Keith is *Keith* at all. Maybe he's Darren, here. Or maybe this is one of the places he feels safe enough to call himself by his real name. Maybe he's Jack.

"Y-you know D-Darren M-Marshall?"

He turns, surprised. "I do."

Sometimes I'm lucky.

"C-cool." I pause. "He's a friend of my f-family's. T-told me I should st-stop by if I was ever in th—in the area."

"Well, how about that . . . yeah, Darren's a real good pal of mine. What did you say you wanted?" he asks. "You said two nights? Single or double?"

"Single."

"I'll give you five percent off. Any friend of Darren's . . ."

"H-he around? H-haven't seen him in a while."

"Nah, not right now. Sure it won't be long before I'm

seeing him again, though," he says. "You know how it is."
But I don't. He yawns again, makes me sign for the room—
*Lera Holden* it is—takes my money and tosses me a key card.

"Room twelve," he says. "Second to last down the strip."

"Th-thanks."

"Y'know, in my granddad's day, the nuns thought they
could beat that outta you."

He laughs. He's talking about my stutter. I stare at him
until he turns bright red and fumbles for something to say,
but there's really nothing he could say to turn it around.

He settles on, "Have a good night."

It's the kind of motel that makes you feel every one of
your secrets. The cost of the stay is only how much you're
willing to live with yourself. That, and almost eighty dol-
lars. I close the door behind me, draw the curtain, lock the
door and once I do that last thing, I lean my head against it
because having four walls around me allows for the tension
to release itself from my spent, sore muscles. I let myself get
lost in my own hurt. But only for a second.

Then I turn, absorbing my new setting.

There's a chemical smell in the air that can't mask the
stuffiness of the room. A dull beige, stained wallpaper with
a repeating flower print attempts something reaching for
sweetness and fails. The bed is covered in a lifeless green
comforter. There's an old TV set—dials on this one too—
on top of a wooden bureau with noticeably chipped edges.
There's a tiny red table and plastic chairs. The carpet is a
deep wine red with flecks of electric purple in it, fuzzy in
some spots, threadbare in others. I slip out of my sneakers
and curl my socked feet into the gritty carpet. From here, I
can see the pale aquamarine tiles in the bathroom and a bit
of the shower.

Still no bluebirds.

But a shower would be nice.

I take a change of clean clothes with me into the tiny bathroom where I strip naked and run the water, which doesn't get as warm as I need; I spend the whole time shivering but it's so much better, being clean. Or as clean as I can get here. There's mold in the tiles and a stain around the edges of the tub. I scrub the tiny bar of motel soap all over my body, suds up my hair. I want to cry, it feels so good. It's not perfect, but it feels good. When I'm finished, I pull on a T-shirt and then I stand in front of the mirror over the sink. I press my fingers against the tender skin of my face, hissing from my reflection, my black eye and swollen nose.

I turn the bathroom light off and stumble to the bed, crawl under the blankets. The comforter is heavy and the sheet beneath it scratchy. My eyes close and I feel the empty around me, something I can finally fall into.

But a small part of me just won't let go.

I don't know how long I drift in that in-between place when I hear the soft *click* of a door opening. The threat registers slowly, and even when it does I can't seem to surface for it. Then, the soft, shuffling sounds of someone moving across the room. I feel the gentle dip of the mattress as he weighs it down.

His hand touches my ankle.

"Sadie. Sadie, girl . . . I'm just coming to check that you said your prayers." The voice is soft and lulling, not quite a whisper or a lullaby. I keep my eyes closed, my breathing even. "Oh, you're asleep. Well, okay then." He sighs heavily. "I guess I'll go see if Mattie's said hers then."

I open my eyes.

# THE GIRLS

## EPISODE 5

**ANNOUNCER:**
*The Girls* is brought to you by Macmillan Publishers.

**WEST McCRAY:**
I arrive at Cold Creek in the very dark, very early hours of the morning. I don't anticipate meeting Claire until a more agreeable time of day—it's just not decent to visit a person before nine a.m., after all—but May Beth calls me as soon as I've set my bags down and tells me to, in these words, "Get here now." When I reach the trailer, I can hear the two of them arguing from outside.

*[MUDDLED SOUND OF TWO WOMEN'S VOICES]*

**WEST McCRAY [STUDIO]:**
It's almost impossible to wrap my head around Claire being back. I want to talk to her, see what she has to say. I've only heard one side of her story and it wasn't related to me by her biggest fan. But Claire—

*[SOUND OF DOOR OPENING, SLAMMING BACK INTO PLACE]*

**MAY BETH FOSTER:**
She doesn't want to talk to you and she hasn't changed a bit.

**WEST McCRAY:**
What does that mean?

**MAY BETH FOSTER:**
Selfish as ever.

**WEST McCRAY:**
I'd really like to speak with her, May Beth. This might be our chance at getting a lead on Darren.

**MAY BETH FOSTER:**
I'll go back in shortly. She's having a smoke right now.

**WEST McCRAY** *[STUDIO]*:
May Beth tells me she was getting ready to go to bed when she looked out her window and saw a light in Mattie's room. Her first thought was *Sadie*. It wasn't Sadie. It was Claire, curled up on Mattie's bed. She'd broken the locks to get in. When May Beth goes back in for attempt number two, I only hear the occasional furious rise in volume between them. It's a chilly night. The stars above Sparkling River Estates are spectacular. I don't see them much in New York and I wonder if residents of Cold Creek are so used to the view, they don't really see them either. I end up waiting nearly two hours before Claire finally comes out.

**CLAIRE SOUTHERN:**
So you're the reporter May Beth's been telling me about.

*[THE GIRLS THEME]*

**WEST McCRAY** *[STUDIO]*:
Claire Southern is not what I'm expecting.

She's clean, for starters, and that's one of the first things she tells me. At a glance, it could be true. She's different from the pictures I've seen. She's put on weight, quite a bit of it, actually. Her complexion is a healthy pink and her eyes are alert. Her hair is long, past her shoulders, shiny. She chain smokes—the one vice she can't give up. She refuses to go back inside May Beth's to sit at the table and talk. She wants to stand in the dark, where she'll consider my questions and, if I'm lucky, answer them. May Beth hovers at the screen door, shifting in and out of view, listening to us both, though I don't think she knows we know that.

**CLAIRE SOUTHERN:**
The only reason I'm talking to you is because I figured it out; May Beth doesn't want me to. And if the only person you've heard about me from is her—well, I can just imagine the bullshit she's been feeding you.

**WEST McCRAY:**
The last May Beth knew, you were using and then you were gone.

**CLAIRE SOUTHERN:**
When I heard Mattie . . . when I heard Mattie died last October, I tried to kill myself. I tried to OD. I just wanted to be with my little girl. It didn't work, though. I figured it was a sign. A friend helped me find a rehab—a spin dry. It wasn't the best place, but it worked. So far, it's stuck.

**WEST McCRAY:**
May Beth said she found you in Mattie's room.

**CLAIRE SOUTHERN:**
I got a right.

**WEST McCRAY:**
How did you find out Mattie died?

**CLAIRE SOUTHERN:**
Heard it on the news. A . . . a friend told me to turn on the TV.

**WEST McCRAY:**
Did you know Sadie was missing?

**CLAIRE SOUTHERN:**
Not until tonight.

**WEST McCRAY:**
Why are you back now, if you knew Mattie was dead and you knew Sadie was by herself?

**WEST McCRAY [STUDIO]:**
Claire surprises me, then. She starts to cry, and it seems to take every last ounce of her willpower to stay where she is. She looks like she wants to run. She doesn't. But it's a long time before she's able to speak.

**CLAIRE SOUTHERN:**
Why do you think I got clean? You said it yourself—Mattie was dead. I knew Sadie was here alone. I wanted to be with her.

**WEST McCRAY:**
Do you love your daughter?

**CLAIRE SOUTHERN:**
[PAUSE] Sadie deserves to hear the answer to that question more than you do and you got no right to ask me it.

**WEST McCRAY:**
Her car—

**CLAIRE SOUTHERN:**
She got herself a car?

**WEST McCRAY:**
Just before Sadie left Cold Creek, she did. That was in June. A month later, it was discovered abandoned in Farfield with all her belongings in it. Sadie hasn't been found.

Does Farfield mean anything to you?

**CLAIRE SOUTHERN:**
No.

**WEST McCRAY:**
We're trying to figure out its significance. May Beth reached out to me for help. I've been trying to find your daughter.

**CLAIRE SOUTHERN:**
Why?

**WEST McCRAY:**
Why what?

**CLAIRE SOUTHERN:**
Why are you looking for her?

[DOOR OPENING]

**MAY BETH FOSTER:**
Good Lord, Claire.

**CLAIRE SOUTHERN:**
I knew you wouldn't be able to keep yourself out of this. *[TO WEST]* What I mean is, why are *you* looking for her?

**WEST McCRAY *[STUDIO]*:**
Before I can answer, May Beth puts herself in front of Claire. She's waving the postcard Claire sent from L.A. in her hand.

**MAY BETH FOSTER:**
Why even send this, if you were never going to come back, huh? *Why?*

**WEST McCRAY *[STUDIO]*:**
Claire takes the postcard and squints at it in the dark. After a long moment, her face just seems to cave in. She begins to cry again.

**MAY BETH FOSTER:**
You know what Mattie was like after you left? She cried for you—

**CLAIRE SOUTHERN:**
No, no, no, you had your time to talk and this is mine—

**MAY BETH FOSTER:**
She *cried* for you. She cried for you every damn day and night. She wouldn't eat, she couldn't sleep—she had nightmares . . . when she got that postcard, it was like a light—it was like a light went on. She had something to live for. But still, she wanted *you.* They think Mattie got into a truck with a killer because she wanted to make her way to *you.*

**CLAIRE SOUTHERN** *[TO WEST]*:
Get. Her. Back. Inside. Now.

**WEST McCRAY** *[STUDIO]*:
It takes quite a lot of persuading to get May Beth to go back inside. Claire is agitated and refuses to talk until she burns through two cigarettes, tears silently streaming down her face.

**CLAIRE SOUTHERN:**
You know what everyone likes to forget about me?

I was a kid. I was a kid when I got into all that shit. I was a *kid* addict. I was a kid when I had Sadie. And my mother—my mother dying. I was a kid for that too. I was an orphan. I'm not making excuses but I don't understand why Sadie was too young for everything I put her through, but I . . . I was just somehow old enough for the shit that got thrown at me. Soon as she was born, May Beth ripped Sadie out of my arms and started turning her against me. It broke my *heart*. And I let it happen because I was just a kid and I was fucked up and I didn't know how else to be. My mom was dead. There was no one. Sadie hated me, and all I could do was let her. And then Mattie came and—Mattie, she loved me.

**WEST McCRAY:**
Claire, do you know a Darren M—?

**CLAIRE SOUTHERN:**
What?

**WEST McCRAY:**
I've retraced a lot of Sadie's steps from Cold Creek to Farfield—I'm not done yet, but I'm getting there—and so far,

it seems she was looking for a man she claims is her father. She's been telling people his name is Darren. He exists, but I haven't managed to track him down either.

**CLAIRE SOUTHERN:**
Then what good are you exactly?

**WEST McCRAY:**
If it's not Darren, who is Sadie's father?

**CLAIRE SOUTHERN:**
I don't know.

*[PAUSE]*

I think that's all I can take tonight.

**WEST McCRAY** *[STUDIO]*:
Claire excuses herself for a final time, holing herself up in May Beth's spare bedroom. I won't get any more information out of her for the time being. May Beth joins me outside a few moments later. She's been crying and she's doing her best to pretend she hasn't been.

**WEST McCRAY:**
What was Sadie like after Mattie disappeared?

**MAY BETH FOSTER:**
What? . . . How you'd expect. Frantic.

**WEST McCRAY:**
I mean after. After they found Mattie's body.

**MAY BETH FOSTER:**
She wouldn't come back to her trailer until she knew. And half the time she stayed at mine, I'd find her outside, right where we're standing now and I don't . . . I don't think she ever slept. She was out looking for Mattie when the police came around to tell us the news and I can't even describe watching her walk up . . . walk up to them. Two officers, just waiting. And when they told her, she just . . . I'm sorry.

**WEST McCRAY:**
It's okay.

**MAY BETH FOSTER:**
She just collapsed. It sounds so dramatic, but it wasn't like that. She wasn't screaming or wailing or anything, it was like her body couldn't stay standing under the weight of it. It was almost like watching a person getting pulled underwater, just being taken. And then she stayed at her place and she wouldn't leave and I was a coward about it. I let her alone for . . . days, because I didn't want to see it on her face. I didn't know if I could handle it.

When I finally braved it, she was on the couch and I fed her and I cleaned her face and I brushed her hair and I put her to bed. And when she woke up, she was just . . . there. But something inside her was gone. I couldn't reach her. Every day, since that one, I couldn't reach her.

**WEST McCRAY [STUDIO]:**
You can hear it, the devastation in her recollection. But now I want you to imagine it said to the universe, to the millions of silent stars above us.

**MAY BETH FOSTER:**
I hate Claire. I know it's not Christian of me, but I do.

**WEST McCRAY:**
I'm going to have to ask you to keep her around. There's more I need to talk to her about, when she's willing. And call me, if there's anything. Can you do that for me?

**MAY BETH FOSTER:**
I guess I can, but God help us both.

Where are you headed next?

**WEST McCRAY:**
Place called Langford.

**MAY BETH FOSTER:**
What do you think you'll find there?

# sadie

Weak light filters through the blinds. The room comes into slow focus.

Waking up in the backseat night after night never feels this strange, this lonely. At least I know what I have to do when I get up: Climb into the front seat. Drive. Find Keith. But this, the soft pillow under my head, the springy, but semi-comfortable mattress under my body, the assuring weight of blankets on top of it, reminds me of being back home and all the things I'm not doing—will ever do—again. Tiptoeing into Mattie's room, shaking her gently awake. Ripping the blankets off her none-too-gently ten minutes later if she hadn't managed to get her ass out of bed before then. She always made it to the table by the time her scrambled eggs had cooled into rubber and she always bitched about it, but after a while I realized she was just a freak who liked them that way . . .

Those were my mornings.

He took them from me.

My nose is throbbing in a way I need to do something

about. I force myself from under the covers, pull on a pair of jeans and that's when I notice the clock on the nightstand says it's five in the afternoon. Jesus.

I slip out of the room barefoot. The ground is cold, makes my toes numb in the way I want my face to be. The parking lot isn't as empty as it was last night. Now it's my car and one other at the farthest end of the lot, a little shinier, little newer. I pass a cleaning woman leaving one of the empty rooms. She's tall, is the first thing I notice about her. Tall and sturdy, with wavy, sandy hair. She stares at me a little too long as I pass, her forehead crinkling in something that could pass for concern. I duck my head, can only imagine what my face looks like, and feel a little guilty. I want to turn around and tell her *I'm fine.*

I'm fine.

I grab a bucketful of ice from the machine and head back to my room where I dump the ice in a hand towel. I hold that to my face until I can't feel it anymore. The ice melts and the cold water seeps through the minute gaps between my fingers. The room is uglier in the colorless late afternoon light. I throw the sopping towel in the shower, change my shirt, put my shoes on and open the window blinds before I get to work on the rest of me. There's nothing I can do for my nose—it just needs time to put itself together, I guess. But I brush my hair, which feels softer and frizzier for the wash, and run my hands over it. I enjoy that feeling while I have it. I pull my hair back into a ponytail. I shove all my things into my pack and sling it over my shoulder. I've got another night here, but after what happened in Montgomery, I'm thinking it's just always better to be ready to run.

When I step into the front office, the man I saw last night isn't there and I realize I never got his name. A boy has taken his place. He looks to be in his midtwenties. He has the kind of baby face that looks too young to be attached to the rest of his body, which is muscular and lean. Dimples in his cheeks. He has curly brown hair and a light tan, like he's already spent a good amount of this barely-begun summer outdoors. He wears a uniform as devoid of bluebirds as the rest of the place and is twirling a key ring around his finger— or trying to. It slips off and hits the floor with a *thunk*. He ducks to pick it up, and when he straightens, his face is bright red. He clips the keys back onto his belt. His eyes drift over my wrecked face, all the way down to my chest. I'm not wearing a bra. I stare at him, watch as his idle curiosity turns into something that knows it shouldn't be looking before he finally remembers to ask if there's anything he can do for me. He's got a raspy voice. Hearing it makes me feel breathless. I clear my throat and walk forward, lean against the counter. He's wearing a name tag. ELLIS. The TV's on behind him, but tonight it's playing the news.

"Is D-Darren around?"

He blinks at my stutter, recovers quickly—in his mind. You can't really recover from the moment you make someone else feel like a freak. You just have to hope the person you made feel that way extends a level of grace toward you that you probably don't deserve.

I force a smile at him that he doesn't deserve.

"What? He's back? I haven't seen him and Joe didn't mention it . . ." He looks past me, like he's expecting Keith. "Usually Darren says when he's gonna be in town."

"He t-told me h-he was here sometimes."

"How do you know Darren?"

"An old f-family friend." I pause. "He's only here s-some of the t-t-time? How d-does that work?"

"He's got a permanent room. Him and Joe have been friends for years. He stays in ten and keeps all his stuff there, so we don't ever rent it out."

"S-sounds like a p-pretty shit deal for Joe."

"Nah, Darren's a good guy. Saved Joe's life once," he says

proudly, like he had anything to do with it. "But I don't think he's around 'less you know something I don't."

"Well d-damn."

"How long you here for?"

"Another d-day."

"I guess he could always show up, maybe, but if you wanna leave a note or something, we can keep it for him until he gets back."

I chew on my lip for a moment. "You c-couldn't l-let me in his room, could you? What I w-want to leave is m-more . . . a s-surprise."

"You can leave it right here, and we'll get it to him."

Fuck.

"Do you know w-where he is? If it's near enough, I c-could just head on down th-there and g-give it t-to him in p-person."

Ellis stares at me a long moment. "What's your name again?"

"Uh." I sniff and wince, bringing a hand to my nose. "Ow."

"Mind if I ask what happened to you?"

"C-car accident."

"Looks like it hurts."

"It d-does."

I eye his belt loop, those keys on it. I wish I could just sneak them away from his body, make some small part of this easy.

"You need anything?" Ellis asks.

I raise my eyes to his face. "What k-kind of m-motel is this?"

"I mean." He shrugs, scratching his head self-consciously. "If someone looks like they need help, I'm gonna ask 'em if they need it, that's all."

I don't like how that makes me feel. I never know how to

meet people's kindness or consideration, unless wanting to tear my skin off is the right reaction. I clear my throat, and change the subject back to what it needs to be: "H-how well d-do you know Darren, anyway?"

"Got this job, thanks to him," he says. "We met online a while back. I was in a tough spot, he helped me out—got Joe to give me work. Joe let me stay here until I had enough saved for my own place. He's a great guy."

I step back, wondering if Keith has walked me to the edge of another nightmare like Silas Baker. *Met online.* What the fuck does that mean? And if it means—

If it means what I think it does, will I hesitate this time?

"O-online?"

"Yeah."

"How?"

"We share a common interest, that's all."

"And w-what's that?"

He frowns. "You never told me your name."

"You're r-right. I d-didn't."

The TV *pop*s again, turning to snow. I leave while his back is turned, my fingertips tingling, trying to quell my building panic. As soon as I clear the office, I move down the row of rooms until I'm standing right in front of ten. I test the door. It doesn't open. It takes everything for me not to kick it. I run my fingers through my hair and I don't know why this has to be so hard, why I haven't been through enough. It should be easy. It should have always been easy. None of this bullshit with beautiful houses hiding ugly, sick fuck things that I can't get out of my head. Every mile I've put between me and Montgomery is someone I didn't save and my sister's dead. She's dead. I don't know why that's not fucking *enough*.

I punch the door with my scraped-up knuckles, hard, and hurry away from it, passing my own room. I keep moving, until I reach the end of the motel. There's got to be a way in to Keith's room. I stare at the highway beyond this place, at the scattered houses, some closer than others. Langford is small but there's something about the feel of it that reminds me of Cold Creek. Smoke crawls up the skyline, a barrel fire in someone's backyard. I think I can make out the faint shapes of people sitting round it, country music and laughter floating through the air.

I move around the building, to the back of the motel. This side of it is one long line of windows and you can tell exactly where the property line stops. The narrow strip of mowed grass suddenly becomes long enough to reach my waist.

I tiptoe over to the first window. They're all just a little wider and taller than me. I grip the crumbling wooden sill and pull myself up, falling back at the sting of it splintering off into my hand. *Goddammit.* After I finish fishing the pieces of it out of my palm, I force myself up again, until I can get a good view in and it's what I thought . . . bathroom.

I could fit through this. It'll be tight, but I can fit. I push against the glass, can feel it give a little. Not enough to shatter. I jump down again and then start counting until I pass my own room and I'm standing at the back of Keith's. Maybe this is the easy part.

Breaking glass should be easy.

I comb the ground for something heavy enough to force against it. It takes a while. I have to wade into the long grass until I find a rock hefty enough. As soon as its rough weight is in my palm, I flash to the house, Montgomery, the lockbox . . .

I don't know if I can go through that again.

It's getting darker out. I go back to Keith's window, pulling myself up. I have to make this count and I have to make it quick. I don't know what Ellis can hear from inside the office, but the cleaner the break the better. I lever my arm back and force the rock against the glass.

Through the glass.

*"Oh fuck, oh fuck, oh fuck—"*

I hop back down. My arm looks like a fucking suicide attempt, just red, red, red, and torn raw. The pain is *exquisite.* I'm stupid, I'm stupid, stupid, stupid, *stupid . . .*

"Oh, fuck . . ."

I choke back a sob and listen through the pounding in my skull because having your fucking arm ripped open fucking *hurts,* but that's going to be the least of my problems if Ellis heard me. I wait. Nothing happens. I think it's safe. I don't even know what the glass breaking sounded like, if it was loud. All I know is my hand reached back and the next thing I was in this immediate, bloody aftermath.

"Okay," I whisper. "Okay, okay, okay . . ."

How cruel is it that the only person I can muster the steadiness of my own voice for is the one who will be least reassured by it.

I just need—I just need to get into that room.

I use the rock to clear the window frame of what's left of the glass, throw my bag through and then get to the excruciating task of maneuvering myself inside, trying not to scream at the pain in my arm, the torn, open skin assaulted by air, by any movement. Trying not to feel my own sticky blood everywhere I don't want it to be.

I end up in the shower. The room is dark and I can smell moldering towels. I step out of the shower and squint into the dim light and when I see a lump of them—towels—in the sink, I grab one and wrap it around my arm, my stomach revolting at the thought of it touching Keith before touching me. I move quietly across the floor and open the bathroom door, trying to ignore the furious throbbing in my arm and the way the towel is slowly turning red.

Keith's room looks like mine. That same bland wallpaper on the walls. Same table and chairs. He has a fridge, but I think it must be his own. This place is . . . has been lived in. The bed is unmade, blankets tossed aside so many mornings ago. There are clothes everywhere, thrown over the backs of chairs, on the floor beside the bed, hanging over the mirrored bureau. I don't know where to start. I get to work one-handed, opening and closing clothes drawers, digging my uninjured hand into the pockets of discarded pants, looking for something, anything, to tell me where he might be now.

*Come on, you motherfucker.*

I check the fridge—gagging when the curdled smell of rotting food assaults my nose—and then I pull the blankets off the bed and toss them on the floor, strip the pillows. It all takes too long being down one arm. I tear the fucking place apart as best I can and when I feel I've been through it all, I'm breathless and empty-handed. On the nightstand next to the bed, a matchbook catches my eyes. The logo on it. *Cooper's.*

I laugh.

Then I sit on the bed and try not to scream.

Enough.

Enough, Sadie.

I get up. I turn the table over, upend the chairs, try and fail to move the dresser away from the walls. I wriggle under the bed, choking on the dust, and there's nothing there. I scramble back until I'm eye level with the edge of the mattress. The mattress edge. I lift it up and a noise of triumph escapes me when I see the small envelope resting neatly in the middle of the bed frame. I reach my left hand out, the towel hanging limply over my bad one, blood no doubt dripping on the floor, and grab it. The mattress slams back with a *thunk.* I sit on the floor and stare at it, cradling my right arm to my chest. The envelope feels light as Silas's box and

a sick sense of déjà vu washes over me. I close my eyes, letting my fingers pulse against it, feeling the Bubble Wrap
inside.

*Make me strong,* I think to no one.

*Please make me strong enough for this.*

I turn the envelope upside down.

My heart is pounding so hard I'm scared my whole body
will quit before I know what I have. I close my eyes and force
myself to take a deep breath and when I open them, I'm staring at IDs and jagged strips of material. No photographs.
No photographs, thank God. I sift through the IDs, my
throat tightening as I make contact with this first real . . .
proof of Keith since I started this, proof beyond the way he
flickers in and out of other people's lives.

They're driver's licenses. They look real enough, excellent fakes. His picture in every one of them, and seeing it
makes my blood run hot, makes me want to swallow all the
broken glass in the bathroom just to free myself from it. He's
different now, time on him that makes him look somehow
less and more like the monster he was when he was in our
lives, when I was a girl. The lines at the edges of his eyes
are more pronounced, his skin sallow and tight to his skull.
Nearly all of the IDs have black markered *X*s over them,
places and personas he burned through and can't ever return
to again. He's known so many different names. *Greg, Connor,
Adam . . . Toby, Don . . . Keith.* I pick it up, hold it in my
trembling fingers.

This is the man I knew.

The *X* crosses over his eyes, obscures most of his face,
but I can picture him without it. I can see him across from
me at the breakfast table. Sitting on the couch in the living
room, his gaze fixed on the TV before moving to me. Outside, nestled in a lawn chair when we came home from school,
which was better than those days Mattie was sick and he'd

pick me up alone and pull us over to the side of the road just before we got up to the lot . . . I set it facedown on the grainy carpet and turn to the scraps of material on the floor. I pick one up. It's a pink piece of cloth, soft to the touch and ribbed along the edges like a . . . there's a tag on the underside, the prickly feeling of it against my thumb makes me realize exactly what I'm holding. Part of a shirt collar. I turn it over. There's a name written on it in thin black marker.

*Casey.*

I grasp at the next piece of material.

A delicate, flower print. Pink rosebuds.

I flip it over.

*Anna.*

The next one is plain blue.

*Joelle.*

Then a girl-plaid.

*Jessica.*

And, finally, soft peach.

*Sadie.*

I drop the tag and root through my backpack until I find what I'm looking for. The picture. The picture of him, Mattie, Mom and me and there it is, on me. That shirt on me.

That shirt on me.

I get to my feet slowly, my eyes never leaving my own small face, until I can't look anymore and then I let it drift from my grasp. I crouch down and start making a grab for the tags, the IDs, because I can't leave those girls here, alone, and the IDs are as good a list of places he's been and I can go to them. I can go to each one of them, ask if they've seen him, get them to tell me where he went and—a door opens behind me, slamming against the wall. *Shit.*

I whirl around, half-expecting *him,* Keith, finally, but it's not.

It's Ellis.

He stands in the doorway, his jaw to the floor.

The "What—" barely leaves his mouth before I have him shoved against the wall beside the door, have him pressed there, my body pushed against his. My bloody arm is tight across his chest, the towel slipped to the ground between us. His reflexes are no match for the surprise of me and it's all the time I need to get the switchblade out and I press it against his throat. The sound of us breathing fills the room. I put more pressure on the knife, so I can't tell where he ends and it begins. It's dizzying, how it feels to have a person like this and to know, just *know* that if he gives you a reason . . .

If he gives me a reason.

"A-are you l-like him?" I demand. He's sweating, trembling and so am I. I tighten my grip on the knife's handle and push into him with my hips. He yelps. *"Are y-you like him?"*

*"What?* Who?"

"K-K—" No, no. Not Keith. "D-Darren."

"I—"

"D-do you fuck little girls?"

*"What?* No! No—" He almost shakes his head but the force of the knife stops him. He swallows, his Adam's apple convulsing. "I don't know what you're talking about."

"Where'd y-you meet online? In s-some sick fuck p-place?" I push again and Ellis moans, near unintelligible with the fear I'm putting in him. "F-fucking *where?*"

"It was—was—" He takes a deep breath. *"Counterwatch.* It's a—it's a game, like a, a—an online game! We were on the same team. I don't . . ." His eyes frantically search the room and even in all its chaos, and with a knife against his throat, he spots the IDs and the smattering of tags on the floor. He says, "I don't know what you're talking about."

I can feel my body shaking, my hand shaking against his throat and I wonder if I could kill him that way, by accident.

Something about the way he said it, *I don't know what you're talking about,* is working through me in a way I don't like because I can hear a lie a mile away, and Ellis . . .

Ellis isn't lying.

"You're hurt," he says and I shake my head, because I don't want him to do what he's doing, talking to me like I'm some wild thing, like I can be calmed down with the gentleness he's dressed his voice in.

"N-no," I say.

"Are you gonna kill me?"

I press my lips together and feel the tears forming in my eyes.

*I'm dangerous,* I want to tell him. *I have a knife* . . .

The gravity of how fucked I am hits me.

My breath catches in my throat.

"I don't think you want to do this," he says.

"Don't," I beg him because what's going to happen to me when I move my hand. He's going to call the cops, he'll call the cops and all of this will have been for nothing. "D-don't—"

"Look," Ellis says. "Just put the—put the knife down. You're hurt. Let's look after that, okay? We'll just fix up your arm and you tell me . . . you tell me about Darren, okay?"

"N-no." I push the knife a little, like a promise to myself. *I could do this, if I have to. I can. I will.* "You're his f-friend. You'll c-call the c-cops and—" No, no, no. "It has t-to be me. I have t-to b-be the one—"

"Let me help you." He looks like he's going to cry. "Please."

# THE GIRLS

## S1E5

**WEST McCRAY:**

Langford is an in-between sort of place. In fact, you wouldn't think it was a town, driving through it. It's a smattering of houses and a few businesses here and there, no real order to it. Just a stop along the way. The address Cat Mather gave me—the one Sadie was headed to—turns out to be a motel called the Bluebird. The most diplomatic description I can give it is *rustic*, but really, it's holding on by a thread, the building doing a slow collapse in on itself. The siding is grimy, the roof badly in need of repair, if not outright replacement, and I spot a few cracked and broken windows here and there. It's got no avian aesthetic to earn it its name and in sixty days, its owner, Joe Perkins, will hand the keys over to Marcus Danforth, who will begin demolition. Joe will say a final good-bye to the place he's called home for more than fifty years. So I guess it's lucky I arrive when I do.

**JOE PERKINS:**
Well, it used to be called Perkinses' Inn before I took it over. My parents owned this place, my grandparents owned it before them, and my great-grandparents owned it before *them*. It's been in the family so damn long, but it just got to the point where it was more'n I could keep up with. It started getting away from me. Maybe it's more than I ever wanted to keep up with, if you want the truth. It was just handed to me, you know? I was a kid.

**WEST McCRAY:**
You never really knew what you wanted to do?

**JOE PERKINS:**
That's exactly it, man! I mean, I never got the chance to think about it. I don't want to sound ungrateful . . . I know it's fortunate I was never in want of a job for most of my life. It's just, straight out of high school, I had this and I wish maybe my parents—God rest their souls—had asked me if I even wanted it. I don't mind it, but it was never my plan.

**WEST McCRAY:**
Joe Perkins is fifty-five. He has a shock of white hair, a weather-beaten face and tattoos covering both his arms and legs. Each one of them means something, he tells me, but what they mean is between him and the ink.

**JOE PERKINS:**
I'll let you in on this one here, though . . .

**WEST McCRAY:**
It's a small bluebird on his left bicep.

**JOE PERKINS:**
First tattoo I ever got, and that's how the place got its new name. Everyone asks me, "Where's the bird?" And I say right here. *[LAUGHS]*

**WEST McCRAY:**
When I told Joe I wanted to talk about a girl who might have stayed at his motel about five months back, he told me he'd do his best, but the people who tend to spend the night are like a motion-blur through his life. They never stay long enough to make an impression. Still, when I show him a picture of Sadie, he remembers her instantly.

**JOE PERKINS:**
Oh, yeah, she was here. She talked a little funny. She was looking for a friend of mine. Both those things are how come I remember her.

**WEST McCRAY:**
The friend was Darren?

**JOE PERKINS:**
Yeah, Darren. She came here asking if he was around, but he wasn't, at the time. I don't know what she wanted him for. I don't think she ever said. I only saw her the once, though. I think she stayed one night . . . might've paid for two? I don't know. I trashed the records when we sold.

**WEST McCRAY:**
Tell me about Darren.

**JOE PERKINS:**
He saved my life.

**WEST McCRAY:**
Did he?

**JOE PERKINS:**
Yeah. I was driving along the highway here, headed back to this place. Got hit by some drunk asshole. The car rolled a few times, ended up in the ditch. Drunk kept going. Still don't know who did it but I hope that fucker rots. Well, Darren was right behind me and saw the whole thing. He pulled over . . . I was out cold and I'd sliced up my thigh. Anyway, the hospital told me later he kept me from bleeding out before the ambulance arrived. We been friends ever since. After that, I said any time you need a room, man, you got it.

**WEST McCRAY:**
Where is he now?

**JOE PERKINS:**
I don't know. He ended up taking me up on the offer about the room. Number ten. That's his. I didn't let anyone else stay in it. He was free to come and go as he pleased, and he did. He was rarely here more than a few weeks at a time.

**WEST McCRAY:**
That's awfully generous of you.

**JOE PERKINS:**
Well, my life's worth more than a room. Anyway, he'd head off for a while, but he always came back. He was a great guy, just never had his shit together. One of those, you know? This is the longest I've gone without hearing from him . . . I've been trying to get hold of him to let him know we sold. I can't put him up anymore.

**WEST McCRAY:**
You have a number?

**JOE PERKINS:**
Yeah, I can give it to you, but it's been disconnected.

**WEST McCRAY:**
He's right.

I call it and nothing gets through.

**JOE PERKINS:**
I've had a bad feeling about it, to be honest. Got worse when you called me, wanting to talk. A girl's looking for him, he's missing. You're looking for her, she's missing. *[PAUSE]* Who is this girl, anyway?

**WEST McCRAY:**
She says she's his daughter.

**JOE PERKINS:**
*[LAUGHS]* All the time I knew him, Darren never mentioned no daughter.

**WEST McCRAY:**
It's what she says.

**JOE PERKINS:**
I just don't . . . *[LAUGHS]* If he had a daughter, he shoulda been where she was because he wasn't the kinda guy . . . he wouldn't step out on his family. He *saved* my *life*.

Jesus, the more you tell me, the worse I feel about all this.

**WEST McCRAY:**
Could you show me Darren's room?

**JOE PERKINS:**
I don't know, man. I mean, I gotta pack it up . . . I been putting it off, but I don't want to go in there until I know for sure I got no choice. All he asked is we left it alone when he wasn't here and I respect that but . . . you really think he's in trouble?

**WEST McCRAY:**
I can't say for sure. All I know is that I'm looking for Sadie and she was looking for him and like you said—now they're both missing.

**JOE PERKINS:**
What's his room gonna tell you about that?

**WEST McCRAY:**
I won't know unless I see it.

**JOE PERKINS:**
*[SIGHS]*

# sadie

"This could use the hospital . . . stitches, like."

We're in the main office, out of view of the window, my arm stretched across a table atop a towel, ugly and open and still bleeding under the fluorescent lights overhead. I can't look at it for too long without wanting to be sick. It didn't seem so bad in Keith's room. Here, it looks bad. Ellis has an ancient-looking first-aid kit between us. He raises his eyes to me, awaiting some kind of confirmation, like *yes, a hospital.*

"N-no."

I couldn't kill him.

It nauseates me, that I couldn't, because he's all that's standing between me and Keith now. I have risked everything for this kindness, or whatever it is, and that makes me worry that I'm too starved, too broken, to do anything right. I know I am. I just thought I could be better than it for once. I close my eyes briefly.

There's a phone near us. Ellis hasn't made a move toward it.

In a neat little pile in front of me, the tags, the IDs.

"Didn't think so," he says.

He cried when I took the knife from his neck. That's the comfort I'm clinging to; in *his* eyes, I looked like I could've done it. He feels like he walked away with more than he had before the moment I lowered my hand. I was dangerous. I had a knife.

When we came back into the office, he rooted around under the desk and found a bottle of Jim Beam. He took a shot and offered me none. I want to ask him what he gets out of this. What he's going to make me do for him so I can finish what I've started.

"It'll h-heal f-fine."

"It'll heal ugly."

But most things do.

He unscrews a bottle of isopropyl alcohol and says, "This is gonna hurt," and then upends it over my arm, a little bit of revenge in the action. There's about a microsecond of nothing before all of my skin is on fire, I'm on fire. I press my lips together and scream through them, black dots in front of my eyes and I think I can hear Ellis saying, *easy, easy, easy,* and I gasp, didn't even realized I'd stopped breathing. My skin calms down a little at a time, not enough that I stop feeling it.

"Okay?" he asks.

He doesn't wait for an answer. He rummages through the kit and I get the feeling he's just trying to find things that make sense to him but he doesn't actually know what he's doing. After a long moment he settles on some butterfly bandages, and puts them where he thinks is right, pulling my skin as together as it'll get.

From there, he finds a bandage.

"Lift your arm," he says.

I raise my arm and he wraps the bandage around and around and around it. He does it with just a little more care than he did the disinfecting. And then it's done. It feels snug.

We stare at each other.

"I'm . . ." Ellis pauses. "I don't know what to do here."

"You said y-you'd h-help me."

"I just did. You pulled a fucking *knife* on me—"

"You s-said you were his f-friend!"

"I—" He stops, doesn't know how to finish. He presses his hand against his forehead. "Look, the only reason I'm not calling the cops right now is because . . ." He pauses. "Is because you think Keith's hurtin' . . . little kids. And you think I got something to do with that."

"I kn-*know* he is," I say. "You said y-you w-were his friend! S-said you m-met online! What else was I s-supposed t-to think?"

"It was a stupid MMO *game*! It wasn't any of the—any of the—" He waves his hands, floundering. "It wasn't any of the stuff you're talking about. That's not the guy I met. That's not the guy who got me this job. It's—you know how crazy you look? You broke into his room and trashed the fucking place! The only reason I didn't call the cops after you calmed some was because out of all the shit that coulda come out of your mouth, for it to be that fucked up . . . I don't know. I just don't fuckin' know." He scrubs a hand over his head and then reaches over and pushes his fingers through the IDs. "That's him, though. But that's not his name . . ."

I find the one with KEITH on it, slide it forward.

"Th-that's who he w-was f-for me."

He points to the tags. "What are the . . . what are those?"

"T-trophies. K-kids he's hurt."

Ellis turns pale, his hand drifting toward them and just stopping before his fingers can graze those tainted pieces of fabric, those lost girls. I watch him mouth each name, the curve of his lips for each one. I turn my face when he gets to mine.

"How do you know?"

"—" I close my eyes briefly and clench my hands together. "He d-did something t-to my s-sister."

"Then shouldn't you tell the police or something?"

"I w-will after I s-see him."

"No," Ellis says firmly. "You need to tell the cops now and let them—"

I slam my hand onto the table, the force traveling up my sore, hurting arm. It startles him enough to skitter back in his chair.

*"N-no."*

Silence. Ellis grabs the bottle of Jim Beam and gets to his feet, takes a swig. Then he wanders over to the window looking out over the parking lot and laughs.

"Darren, Keith—whoever the fuck he is—he got me this job. He really helped me out. He saved Joe's *life*. He's only ever been decent to me. I don't . . . I can't believe it."

"Then t-tell me I'm l-lying."

He doesn't say anything.

"D-do you know w-where h-he is?"

He tenses and it's the answer I need.

I am. So. Close.

I get up slowly, carefully. He eyes me warily.

"Ellis, I d-don't know you and I'm s-sorry about what h-happened in th—in that room, but I n-need you t-to tell m-me w-where."

"So you can ruin a guy's life?"

"Or p-put a sick f-fuck where he b-belongs."

"But if you're lying to me—"

"W-what's it gonna c-cost *you?* You gonna b-bet on some l-little g-girl's life? You g-gonna risk them?" I wish I'd followed through. I wish I'd cut his heart open. I pick up each tag. "C-Casey. Anna. J-Joelle. Jessica . . . S-Sadie."

"Then let me call the *cops!*"

"I n-need to *see* it myself. I *h-have* to."

"I just . . ."

"P-please."

It makes my stomach ache, how, at a time like this, I can't make that word come out of my mouth perfectly enough to convince him. I can't describe how bad it feels, this inability to communicate the way I want, when I need to. My eyes burn, and tears slip down my cheeks and I can't even imagine how pathetic I look. Girl with a busted face, torn-up arm, begging for the opportunity to save other girls. Why do I have to beg for that?

"If y-you knew what he d-did to my sister you wouldn't b-be doing this t-to me. You h-have to let me g-go. Tell me where he is. P-pretend I w-was never here."

His shoulders sag and he exhales slowly. He squints his eyes shut and squeezes the bridge of his nose and I realize, after a moment, that he's crying too.

I hold my breath.

I watch him age.

# THE GIRLS

## S1E5

**JOE PERKINS:**
Jesus Christ.

**WEST McCRAY:**
Wow.

**WEST McCRAY *[STUDIO]*:**
Darren Marshall's room looks like it . . . exploded, for lack of a better term. The air is thick, stuffy, attesting to the fact that he hasn't been here for a long time. But whenever he was here last, he apparently tore the place apart. There are clothes all over the bed, the floor, every available surface. The bed has been stripped of its sheets and the furniture has been upended and pulled away from the walls. Every drawer in the place is open, except for the fridge. Joe wanders over to it first. When he opens it, the stench of spoiled food fills the room.

**JOE PERKINS:**
Oh, goddammit . . .

*[SOUND OF A DOOR SLAMMING SHUT]*

**WEST McCRAY:**
What happened here, Joe?

**JOE PERKINS:**
It looks like a fuckin' crime scene . . . Jesus . . . *[SOUND OF A DOOR OPENING, CRUNCHING GLASS]* Oh, Christ, don't step in here! The bathroom window's fuckin' broken.

**WEST McCRAY:**
You didn't notice that until now?

**JOE PERKINS:**
You seen this place? How'm I supposed to notice one more broken window? Jesus.

**WEST McCRAY:**
So this isn't how Darren usually left the place?

**JOE PERKINS:**
I hope not . . . but I honestly don't know. He didn't want cleaning in here, and I trusted that he'd look after it and I didn't have a reason to doubt that, you know? But this . . . looks wrong. It looks like there was a fight or something . . . is that blood?

**WEST McCRAY:**
There are a few suspect stains on the floor, but it's hard to tell what exactly they might be. I move carefully around the room, taking photographs of it with my phone. The first thing that catches my attention is the matchbook. It's sitting neatly on the nightstand. I pick it up because it's familiar to me, but at that moment, I'm not sure why. It says *Cooper's* on the front. Before I can think too hard about it, there's something else:

A photograph on the floor, half-hidden under the bed.

I know the place it was taken. And I know the people in it. There are four of them, and the first one I recognize is Claire. She's younger, sicker. She's standing next to a man who is holding a small child against him. Mattie. To the right of the photo, at its very edges, is Sadie.

She's about eleven years old.

**WEST McCRAY** *[TO JOE]*:
Hey, Joe, is this Darren?

**JOE PERKINS:**
What's that? . . . Well, I'll be damned. That's him. And that's—

That's not the girl you're looking for, is it?

**WEST McCRAY:**
Yeah, it is.

**JOE PERKINS:**
What the hell is going on here?

**WEST McCRAY:**
Excuse me a minute, Joe . . . I'll be right back.

**WEST McCRAY:**
I step outside and send the photograph to May Beth over text. She calls me immediately.

**MAY BETH FOSTER** *[PHONE]*:
Oh my Lord, that's the picture. Where did you find it?

**WEST McCRAY** *[PHONE]*:
What?

**MAY BETH FOSTER** *[PHONE]*:
That's the photo that was missing from my album . . . when I was showing you those pictures of the girls, remember, I got to the page with nothing on it? A photo was missing. *That* was the photo that was on it. The girls, and their mother and—

**WEST McCRAY** *[PHONE]*:
Darren.

**MAY BETH FOSTER** *[PHONE]*:
What?

**WEST McCRAY** *[PHONE]*:
That's Darren.

**MAY BETH FOSTER** *[PHONE]*:
No, it's not. It's Keith.

# sadie

When I was seven, and Mattie was one, she whispered my name.

I was her first word.

When Mattie was seven days old, and I was six, I stood over her crib and listened to her breathing, watching the rise and fall of her tiny chest. I pressed my palm against it and I felt myself through her. She was breathing, alive.

And I was too.

Langford is miles behind me, a place called Farfield in my sights. *Keith is there,* Ellis told me. *Last I heard from him, he was there.* I don't know if he's called the police or warned Keith since I left, but any head start I had for myself is gone. I lost it when I realized I'd left my photo in Keith's room. My stomach turned and then it turned again and next thing I knew, I was jerking the car onto the shoulder and then I was out of the car and on my knees, on the ground, throwing up bile into the dirt.

I crouch back on my heels and wipe my mouth on my sleeve. I dig into my bag and find the IDs, the tags, and sit there with them, spread them out on the side of the road. It feels wrong to have them together. I separate his faces from their names.

I don't want to take them with me.

They're too heavy to carry.

When I was eleven, and Mattie was five, I didn't sleep for a year. Keith and Mom would come home so late from the bar—him sober, her wasted—neither of them trying to be quiet, but her especially. I'd listen to her shuffling steps to the bedroom, to the clatter of Keith tidying up the kitchen, and when all that sound was gone, I knew what would happen next and I knew what would happen if I refused. If it wasn't me, he'd go to Mattie unless I said, *W-wait* . . .

Wait.

Until one night, I couldn't.

And I'd had the knife that night, had it tucked under my pillow, my fingers clutched around it and instead of doing what I should have, I sent him to her. The next morning, Keith was gone, and the dirty shame of my weakness was all over me and I think Mattie sensed it somehow, that there was some part of me that had given her up, that I couldn't protect her.

I held on tighter to prove myself wrong.

I felt her breathing, alive.

And I was too.

When Mattie was ten, and I was sixteen, Mom left and took Mattie's heart with her. Mattie spent every night crying herself awake and was it really so bad, Mattie, just the two of us together?

And then that postcard—

Mattie returned with her heart in her hands, there, breathing, alive . . .

And I was too.

When I was nineteen and Mattie was thirteen, Keith came back.

*Guess who I saw,* she'd announced, still angry, always

angry for the lengths I wouldn't go for Mom, and never seeing the ones I went to for her. *I told him about Mom. He said he'd take me to L.A., to find her.* And I asked her who she thought raised her, because in that moment, it couldn't have been me.

When Mattie was thirteen, and I was nineteen, she crept away into the night, to the truck parked under the streetlight on a corner in Cold Creek, and climbed into the passenger's side. I don't know what happened next. If, when the apple orchard appeared on the horizon to mark the growing space between us, she finally felt the distance and changed her mind. If Keith wouldn't let her change her mind, and dragged her, kicking and screaming, out of the truck and between the trees, where he had her, breathing and alive, until she wasn't.

And I wasn't.

I am going to kill a man.

"I *am*," I whisper into the ground, over and over again. *I am, I am, I am.*

I have to.

I'm going to kill the man who killed my sister.

And I'm not leaving the side of the road until I can make myself believe it.

I sit on the ground, feel the gravel press into my jeans. It's windy, air pushing my hair from my face. I listen to the way it moves the world around me; the trees off the road, leaves rustling their soft song into the night. I stare up at the sky, its stars. Small miracles.

Looking at the stars is looking into the past. I read that once. I can't remember where and I don't know much about it, but it's strange to think of the stars above as from a time that is so far removed from Mattie and me, from Mattie being dead.

From the thing I am about to do.

# THE GIRLS

## EPISODE 6

*[THE GIRLS THEME]*

**ANNOUNCER:**
*The Girls* is brought to you by Macmillan Publishers.

**WEST McCRAY:**
Keith is Darren. I share the photograph with Ruby and she tells me it's the exact same one Sadie showed her when she came to Ray's Diner, asking after the man she said was her dad.

**RUBY LOCKWOOD *[PHONE]*:**
That's it. That was the one.

**WEST McCRAY *[PHONE]*:**
And you still doubted her?

**RUBY LOCKWOOD *[PHONE]*:**
Was I wrong?

**WEST McCRAY** *[ON PHONE WITH MAY BETH]*:
There's no possibility whatsoever that Keith is Sadie's father?

**MAY BETH FOSTER** *[PHONE]*:
I can ask Claire when she gets back in, but I doubt it.

**DANNY GILCHRIST** *[PHONE]*:
Tell me what you got.

**WEST McCRAY** *[PHONE]*:
Sadie was looking for a man from her childhood—her mom used to date him. She knew him as Keith, but everyone else I've talked to has called him Darren, which is why I never made the connection. Sadie was telling people he's her father, but that's not likely.

**DANNY GILCHRIST** *[PHONE]*:
Okay, so who is he?

**WEST McCRAY** *[PHONE]*:
Can't find anything on either name. I got my team on it. Get this, though—in Langford, that motel, the Bluebird. Keith's room was trashed . . . just hold on, I'm gonna send you the photos . . .

*[KEYBOARD SOUNDS, MOUSE CLICKS]*

**DANNY GILCHRIST** *[PHONE]*:
*[WHISTLES]* Wow.

**WEST McCRAY** *[PHONE]*:
Yeah. The photograph Sadie's been carrying around was in that room. It was from May Beth's album of the girls—she took it with her. So I'm going to guess she was in that room too. I

don't know if it was like that before she got there or after she left or while she was there. According to Joe, Keith wasn't there when she was, so I don't believe they met.

**DANNY GILCHRIST** *[PHONE]*:
She broke into his room.

**WEST McCRAY** *[PHONE]*:
That's what I'm thinking but . . . wait a second . . .

**DANNY GILCHRIST** *[PHONE]*:
What?

**WEST McCRAY** *[PHONE]*:
I forgot—I got so distracted by the photo. There was a matchbook in the room. *Cooper's.* That's a bar outside Montgomery.

**DANNY GILCHRIST** *[PHONE]*:
Montgomery . . . the town Sadie passed through on her way to Langford.

**WEST McCRAY** *[PHONE]*:
*[PAUSE]* Wait.

**DANNY GILCHRIST** *[PHONE]*:
What?

**WEST McCRAY** *[PHONE]*:
It's owned by Silas Baker.

**WEST McCRAY:**
Silas Baker, the man charged with sex crimes against the children he coached on his T-ball team. At first, it feels coinci-

dental, but when I dig deeper into his case, I find a news clipping where Baker's family was pressed for comment. I discovered Marlee Singer is his younger sister.

She refuses to answer my calls.

**WEST McCRAY** *[PHONE]*:
I should've done Montgomery first. Goddammit.

**DANNY GILCHRIST** *[PHONE]*:
So you go back.

**WEST McCRAY** *[PHONE]*:
This isn't—I have a bad feeling about this, Danny.

**DANNY GILCHRIST** *[PHONE]*:
You have to follow those too.

**WEST McCRAY:**
Silas Baker's crimes were uncovered when a local boy, eighteen-year-old Javi Cruz, called 911 and reported a dead body in an abandoned house fifteen miles outside of town. When the Montgomery Sheriff's Department arrived on the scene, they didn't find a body. Instead, they found a collection of pornographic photographs of children. One of the officers recognized the kids in them and after that, all hell broke loose.

I head back to Montgomery to talk to Javi. He's an interesting guy. He's six foot three, lean, with light brown skin. He's lived in Montgomery his whole life. This is his last year of high school and college is on the horizon. This was supposed to be the year he lived it up, but things have taken a hard turn for him, at least socially, in the wake of his role in Silas Baker's arrest. Javi happened to be best friends with Silas Baker's teenage twins, Noah and Kendall, and was even on one of Silas's T-ball teams when he was a child himself. He says he was never abused.

**JAVI CRUZ:**
Everyone hates me now.

**WEST McCRAY:**
That's rough.

**JAVI CRUZ:**
Well, not *everyone*. And, I mean, I don't have it bad, compared to those kids, but I lost a lot of friends. There's still a lot of Baker loyalists. You see the comments sections on stories about him?

**WEST McCRAY:**
They're divided, to say the least.

**JAVI CRUZ:**
This city is never going to be the same.

**WEST McCRAY:**
And you didn't know about Silas? You never experienced any untoward or sexually aggressive behavior from him when you . . .

**JAVI CRUZ:**
*No!* God, *no*. It was T-ball. We just . . . played *T-ball*. I didn't know he was a freak. I didn't know about the house until—I told you, it was the girl.

**WEST McCRAY [STUDIO]:**
Sadie.

Javi met Sadie during her brief time in Montgomery.

JAVI CRUZ:
She told me her name was Lera.

WEST McCRAY:
Tell me how you two met.

JAVI CRUZ:
I was hanging at Cooper's bar with Noah and Kendall, and another one of our friends—but she doesn't want me to mention her name and she's still talkin' to me, so I'd just as soon not name her, if that's okay with you.

WEST McCRAY:
Sure.

JAVI CRUZ:
We were drinking. We never had a problem being served at Cooper's because Mr. Baker owns the place and I know that's not right but you can't tell me you never drank before you were legal. That's how we killed time in Montgomery in the summer. It was no different than any other night, and then—she came.

She was like . . . You're gonna think it's stupid.

WEST McCRAY:
Try me.

JAVI CRUZ:
It's hard to explain. The band was taking a break, and they put on some canned music, and Lera—*Sadie*—was . . . dancing, right in the middle of the bar by herself and I thought she was so beautiful, you know? I just wanted to know her. You ever met someone like that, and all you can think about is being near them? Just like . . . in their orbit?

**WEST McCRAY:**
Yeah. I married him.

**JAVI CRUZ:**
Right? That's what I'm saying. I mean, I should say—she wasn't a great dancer. *[LAUGHS]* She just didn't care and that's what made it beautiful to me. I'm not . . .

Noah calls—*called* me a benchwarmer.

**WEST McCRAY:**
What's that mean?

**JAVI CRUZ:**
It's the—it *was* the big joke in our crew. Like . . . I watch the action, but I don't get in on it. But I got up, and I asked her to dance.

I danced with her.

**WEST McCRAY:**
What happened?

**JAVI CRUZ:**
I brought her back to our booth.

The friend—the one who doesn't wanna be named—she thought Sadie was part of a family who had just moved into town and Sadie just went along with it. She and Kendall kind of . . . I don't know.

Kendall didn't like her.

**WEST McCRAY:**
Why?

**JAVI CRUZ:**
Because being that crazy chick that dances alone, the one everyone's lookin' at? That's Kendall's thing. She thought Sadie was creepy, because Sadie stalked Kendall's Instagram. Like she looked Kendall up, and came to Cooper's because she knew we'd be there.

**WEST McCRAY [STUDIO]:**
More and more, it seems I had reason to doubt Marlee Singer's insistence that she never spoke to Sadie. I believe Sadie talked to Marlee, who knew Keith. She sought out Marlee's brother, Silas Baker, and his family in Montgomery. It stands to reason Silas knew Keith too.

**JAVI CRUZ:**
She told us her family'd moved to town because her sister died.

**WEST McCRAY:**
Did she elaborate on that?

**JAVI CRUZ:**
No, but I could tell it really hurt her. I wasn't surprised when you told me that part was true. Anyway . . . I gave her my number and she promised to call me in the morning—we were going to go over to the Bakers' together. Then she calls me and tells me to meet her here.

**WEST McCRAY:**
*Here* is Lili's Café. It's a small coffee shop on the corner of Montgomery's main street, with a sweet, homey feel to it. Javi tells me it's insane in the mornings, wall-to-wall with people lining up for Lili's famous cold brew and sugar-glazed doughnuts. It's quiet now.

**JAVI CRUZ:**
I bought her breakfast and we ate and right away, I could tell something was really wrong. It's hard to describe, but she was quiet and looked . . . sick. I asked her what it was. She didn't tell me, though.

She showed me.

**WEST McCRAY:**
Sadie took Javi to the house fifteen miles outside of Montgomery and showed him the photos. Javi is visibly shaking when he tells me this part.

**JAVI CRUZ:**
I remember I came out of that house screaming. Because I knew those—I knew those kids. And those pictures were . . . I . . . I dream about them and it makes me wanna tear my brain out and—I can't.

I'm sorry . . . I'm sorry—

**WEST McCRAY:**
It's okay. Take your time.

**JAVI CRUZ:**
[EXHALES] I asked her how she knew. How she knew that stuff was there and she told me she'd been parked outside the Bakers' house all night and she saw Silas leave his place really early in the morning, and she thought it was weird so she followed him all the way to that house . . . she said she hid 'til he left and went looking and that's what she found. I don't know if that's true, but she wanted me to call the cops.

I want to say I did the right thing right away, I wanna tell you that I did that but . . .

**WEST McCRAY:**
Javi was too overwhelmed, too distraught, to understand the scope of what was happening. Sadie demanded immediate action.

**WEST McCRAY [TO JAVI]:**
Was Sadie willing to call the cops?

**JAVI CRUZ:**
That's the thing! She wouldn't do it herself. She said she was scared.

**WEST McCRAY:**
You didn't think it was odd that she was parked outside the Bakers' house all night? You didn't ask her to explain that? It sounds like she might have had an inkling something was going on from the outset.

**JAVI CRUZ:**
Once I saw those pictures, I wasn't thinking about anything but that. This fucking broke me. I'm in therapy about it. And that's why I couldn't call the cops at first . . . Kendall and Noah were my best friends, and Mr. Baker—I'd known Mr. Baker since I was a *kid* and it didn't—none of it made sense. We drove back into town, and she just kept telling me I had to do this because if I didn't . . .

**WEST McCRAY:**
If you didn't, what?

**JAVI CRUZ:**
I don't know. We got back into town. She pulled up to the Rose Mart—a convenience store down the road. It's got a pay phone . . .

She said if I couldn't do it outright, to call the cops and tell 'em I wanted to report a dead body, hang up without ID'ing myself and let the police find it all.

**WEST McCRAY:**
You refused, initially.

**JAVI CRUZ:**
I was fucked up. Scared out of my mind.

**WEST McCRAY:**
When you told Sadie that, how did she react?

**JAVI CRUZ:**
She left me there.

**WEST McCRAY:**
But you ended up making the call right after.

**911 DISPATCHER *[PHONE]*:**
911, what is your emergency?

**JAVI CRUZ *[PHONE]*:**
Uh, I want to report a dead body.

**WEST McCRAY:**
Javi did as Sadie suggested: he left directions to the house and hung up before he could identify himself.

After the pornography was found, the Montgomery Sheriff's Department pulled security footage from outside the Rose Mart and identified their mystery caller. I got to look at it. Sadie isn't with Javi as he braces himself to make the call. It was after she drove off. He stands in front of the phone, pacing back and forth for ten minutes, before finally bringing the receiver to his ear. He makes the call and he goes home, where he shuts himself in his room and won't talk to anyone until the police knock on his door.

Sadie ended up at Silas Baker's.

**JAVI CRUZ:**
Kendall and Noah blew up my phone about it. I never answered their texts, but . . .

**WEST McCRAY** *[STUDIO]*:
The Bakers are not granting any media requests.

**JAVI CRUZ:**
They said Sadie showed up at their place because I told her to meet me there, which was a lie. Noah tried to get ahold of me, but I wasn't answering my texts.

I guess it was fine, for a little while, and then Mr. Baker came home. They told me Sadie wasn't who she said she was and that I was a dumbass for falling for her. They said she stole Mr. Baker's phone and attacked him—

**WEST McCRAY:**
Attacked him?

**JAVI CRUZ:**
Yeah, with a knife. In their driveway.

They said she got in her car and cleared out before anyone could do anything about it and that Mr. Baker didn't want to press charges because it was obvious she was "disturbed."

All the time that was happening, the police were at that house.

**WEST McCRAY:**
So Kendall and Noah suggested it got physically violent between Mr. Baker and Sadie. Did they say that he hurt her?

**JAVI CRUZ:**
They didn't say anything about that. Doesn't mean he didn't,
though, just that they knew not to put it in writing, if he did.

**WEST McCRAY:**
And Sadie wasn't hurt when you met her the previous night
at Cooper's or that morning at Lili's?

**JAVI CRUZ:**
Like hurt . . . how?

**WEST McCRAY:**
According to a young lady who met up with Sadie when she
was in the process of leaving Montgomery, Sadie was injured.
She had a bruised face, suggesting a broken nose, and a
scraped chin.

If it didn't happen at the Bakers' house, it would have happened shortly thereafter.

**JAVI CRUZ:**
Jesus.

**WEST McCRAY:**
Did Sadie ever mention a man named Darren or Keith to you?

**JAVI CRUZ:**
No . . . no, not that I can remember.

You think she's okay?

**WEST McCRAY:**
That's what I'm trying to find out.

**JAVI CRUZ:**
But do *you* think she's okay?

**AUTOMATED FEMALE VOICE** *[PHONE]*:
You have reached the voicemail of—

**MARLEE SINGER** *[PHONE]*:
Marlee Singer.

**AUTOMATED FEMALE VOICE** *[PHONE]*:
Please leave a message at the tone.

**WEST McCRAY** *[PHONE]*:
Marlee, West McCray here.

Look, I know you don't want me to keep calling you, but here's the thing—I have mounting evidence that suggests you saw Sadie, that you directed her to your brother, Silas's, house. You knew Darren. I think it's likely Silas did too. I would really appreciate if we could talk about that. I'm just trying to bring a girl back home to a family who misses her.

Please call me.

**WEST McCRAY** *[PHONE]*:
Hey, May Beth. Is Claire around?

**MAY BETH FOSTER** *[PHONE]*:
No. She's still . . . she hasn't been back.

**WEST McCRAY** *[PHONE]*:
Since I last called? Are you kidding me?

**MAY BETH FOSTER** *[PHONE]*:
No. I don't know if—I mean, she's got some things here I'd like to think she wouldn't have left without, but . . .

**WEST McCRAY** *[PHONE]*:
I'm headed back to Cold Creek. Call me if she turns up in the meantime.

**MAY BETH FOSTER** *[PHONE]*:
Why, what have you found?

**WEST McCRAY** *[PHONE]*:
I don't know.

# sadie

Farfield, Colorado.

I feel every single mile like a cut across my skin. This drive has been the hardest. The ache of it, the ugliness. The pain of holding the same position for hours, the way the joints in my fingers have started to seize from gripping the wheel so tight that when I finally stop the car, I know I'll still feel it there in my hands.

When the town sign comes into view at last, there's no relief in it.

Farfield makes up the averages of all the places I've been; not so riddled by poverty it hurts to look at, or as painful as Montgomery was in all of its shine. Here, some parts are ravaged, others only a little down on their luck, then it turns into this economic gradient going up: nice, nicer, nicest. The place Keith is living is on the Down on Its Luck side of town, a kiss in the direction of something nicer, except it's facing the wrong way. It's a plain two-story with flaking white paint on its worn siding.

I park across the street.

My heart pounds, my blood flows through my veins,

everything working how it's supposed to. I watch the house for a long time, like I did outside of Silas's, steeling myself for that moment I'll have to see him before I do anything else.

All I have to do is survive that moment to get through the rest.

I'm hot, sweating. I lean my head against the seat and close my eyes briefly, or maybe longer than that because the next time I open them, there's a little girl on the front stoop. She's surrounded by papers, scribbles all over them, but at some point she abandoned drawing for the well-worn book in her hands. She looks so much like something out of a Norman Rockwell painting that I don't believe she's really real. She's small. Ten, maybe. She's wearing pink denim shorts, a striped shirt and her brown hair is tied in pigtails so lopsided, I can only guess she's done them herself. The book is a paperback and she's clutching it like it's a lifeline. She's getting close to the end. She has Band-Aids on each of her knees.

The unexpectedness of her is more than I can bear. I don't know why I wasn't expecting her. I don't want to feel it, but I can't keep myself from feeling it.

I pull the sleeves of my red hoodie down. It's too warm to wear, but it's all I had to cover the bandage. My arm has been hurting since Langford, little dots of red creeping through the gauze, but I don't want to think about it. I check my face in the mirror. It's turned colors I can only liken to bruised fruit. Purples and browns and hints of yellow. I hate looking at it because it reminds me of Silas Baker, out there, still.

But maybe after Keith, I could go back.

Get it right this time.

I step out of the car, my body protesting every part of this simple act.

The girl looks up as I approach. The closer I get to her,

the more I see that she's frail, a little feral. Her milk-white skin is dotted with freckles. Her face is sharp with a long nose, small, brown eyes. I stare at her and she stares back. She closes the book—a copy of *The Baby-Sitters Club.* I offer her a small smile, and she eyes me warily in return. I don't blame her. I look scary, ghoulish.

"H-hi th-there."

"You talk funny," she says immediately, and she sounds smaller than I was expecting. Her voice is thinner, even, than Mattie's.

"I st—I stutter."

"What happened to your face?"

"I'm c-clumsy as hell."

I bend down until I'm roughly her height and point to the *BSC* book in her hand. On its torn-edged cover, Stacey runs toward the other members of the club with her arms outstretched. I remember that one and it's strange to remember it. I forget that at times, I was a kid, that I did kid things. That I read about the girls I dreamed of being. That I did things like play in the dirt and make mud cakes. Drew pictures myself. Caught fireflies in the summertime.

"St-Stacey was my favorite, but I always w-w-wanted to dress like C-Claudia."

"I hate Stacey."

Tough crowd. "Who's your f-favorite?"

"Mallory," she says after a long minute. "And Jessi. I'm almost as old as them. I like reading about girls being . . . my age."

She lowers her gaze and I can feel how old she thinks she is because I felt it then myself, years on me no one else could see, craving those moments where adults treated me like I was as young as I was. I wonder if Keith has her tag, all ready to take that part of her with him when he goes. I want so badly to have arrived in time but if he's already here, that means I'm too late.

The girl brightens suddenly, says, "Someone sold their entire *BSC* collection to the bookstore downtown. I'm tryin' to get them all before someone else does, but I don't have the money."

I pick up one of the drawings. They're better than they have any right to be at her age, I think. Moody landscapes and sad little girls who all look just a little bit too much like her. It's painful when pain like that is so obvious. I bet her mother hangs these on the fridge, proud, looking at them without ever really seeing. All the pictures are signed by NELL.

I see you, Nell.

"N-Nell," I say. "That's y-you."

"I'm not supposed to talk to strangers," she says.

"I'm n-not a st—not a stranger. I know your mom's b-boyfriend."

"You know Christopher?"

How she sounds, when she asks me this, makes me want to burn the world down. The sudden, fearful light in her eyes tells me all I need to know. I watch her hands tremor, watch her tighten her grip on the book to stop it, to hide it.

She's ten years old and she's already fighting her own cries for help.

I wish I could tell her that soon she won't have to worry about it. That *I know what's happening, it's going to be okay.* She's never heard those words before, I'm sure of it, like I never heard them, and I know she has to be starved for them, just like I was.

"H-he around?"

I move toward the house and she says, "No!" I turn to her. "He's sleepin'. This is quiet time. I'm not supposed to wake him up for anything or he'll be mad."

"Th-that's why you're out h-here?"

"I can get through a whole book nearly, by the time he wakes up."

This, she says with pride.

"That's a-a-amazing." She beams. "W-where's your m-mom, Nell?"

"She works at Falcon's."

"W-what's that?"

"A bar."

Of course. I straighten. My knees crack.

"When's she h-home?"

"After I'm in bed."

It's almost too perfect. I could let myself into his house and find him, stretched on a couch or a bed, prone and sleeping. I could stand over him, his switchblade in my hands, poised over his beating heart, and plunge it down, ending him. I imagine his eyes flying open just so I'm the last thing he sees before he dies. Painting an entire room red, leaving. And when they ask Nell if she saw anything, she'll say, *No, I was outside, I'm not supposed to be inside during quiet time* . . .

The thought, the heady thrill of it, guides me to the door and then my hand is on its handle, making the turn, when she panics. Nell runs to me, putting her small hands around my wrist. Hands as small as Mattie's were at that age. *She's not Mattie,* I think to myself, but my heart wants to take me to that place where she could be. *She's not Mattie, she's not Mattie, she's not Mattie, she is not Mattie* . . . but her hands are small . . . and warm . . .

"You can't go inside," she says urgently.

And alive.

"C-come with me," I tell her. She stares at me, dumbstruck. But what if she did? What if I just take *her,* what if I could take her away from what's beyond this door?

"N-Nell, c-come with me." She lets go of my hand and moves away from me. I reach for her, and she steps back again and I reach for her again, because I can't stop myself, because we know what's inside. I can feel my stutter's hold strengthen as the desperation inside me grows. "I-I think you should come w-with me. It's n-n—it's not—"

*Safe.*

So come with me.

Please.

"My mom will be home soon," she says, shaking her head, forgetting that she just told me her mom is at work, that she doesn't come home until late. "My mom—" I move in a way she must not like because she opens her mouth wide and screams, *"Mom!"*

It rips me out of the fantasy, forces me back into my body. My sore, bruised and tired body. My tired heart. I take a fumbling step away and she's scared out of her mind.

"I'm s—I'm sorry." I dig into my pocket, my wallet, and hold out a twenty to her. "W-wait. Here. T-take th-this."

She closes her mouth and eyes me suspiciously, while I glance up and down the street. If anyone heard the little girl screaming, they're not coming. I swallow and wave the bill in her face. *Take the money, Nell.* She has to understand money. I did, at her age.

"You c-could get a lot of *BSC* b-books w-with this."

She steps forward, hesitantly, doesn't want to get too close to this monster girl with the mottled face. She rips the twenty out of my hands and then she runs down the street. She doesn't look back. I blink away the threat of tears and make a promise at her retreating figure.

I'll finish this.

I face the house.

I let myself inside.

It's quiet but for the low hum of electricity and a clock ticking. I stand in a small hallway, which leads to a door at the back of the house. To the left, a kitchen, and to the right, the stairs leading to the second floor. I close the door behind me quietly and then I lean against it, forcing myself to take deep, even breaths in and out. There's a glass of milk and a half-eaten sandwich on the kitchen table. Dishes drying on a rack. There's a room beyond the kitchen and that's where I move to next, surprised at the silence of my own body, how made it was for this moment. It's a living room, and this is where the clock is, the television, the couch I imagined Keith on, one leg hanging off it, mouth wide open as he sleeps.

But he's not there.

So upstairs.

Everything is easy until the moment my right foot meets the first step. The stairs are old, and they let me know it, groaning loudly under the weight of my body. Each time it sounds, I feel like I did when I was driving and the car would take the curve of a hill, that strange anxious rising and falling sensation in the pit of my stomach.

When I reach the landing, I exhale. I don't realize how hard I'm shaking until the moment before I grip the banister, and I catch sight of my trembling fingers.

There are three doors, the closest one open, revealing a bathroom, leaving two left. I push the first door open and find myself in Nell's room.

I thought I might.

I hoped I wouldn't.

Her room is neat, in the way I kept my room neat, like everything was put into place by small, uncertain hands. There's faded pink wallpaper on the wall with yellowing seams that I think has been here longer than she has. A small bed with a mint green comforter, a little too deflated, second-hand. I cross the threshold and move to the tiny desk across from her bed. This is where she makes her masterpieces. A sketchbook and colored pencils with dollar-store stickers on them. I move to her closet, next to the bed, and open the door where I'm met with the scent of baby-soft detergent and all of Nell's impossibly small clothes.

I was this small once.

A lifetime ago.

I sift through them almost unconsciously. This wasn't something I set out to do, but now that I'm doing it, I can't stop because I know. I know I'll find exactly what I don't want to find, and it's there, in the back. A shirt with the tag cut out of it. I take it off the hanger and press it against my face and a fierce, near unbearable wave of grief follows. *I'm going to save you, Nell. I'm going to save you,* but everything after that, I think, is beyond saving. I can stop Keith but I can't undo everything that's already been done. How do you forgive the people who are supposed to protect you? Sometimes I don't know what I miss more: everything I've lost or everything I never had.

"Always wondered if you'd show up on my doorstep one day."

I take a faltering step forward and then steady myself, his quiet, edgeless voice turning me small, like that, turning me into a small girl, sick with the knowledge that she's done this wrong. I've done this wrong because when I turn Keith is standing right in front of me.

I wish his darkness lived outside of him, because you have to know it's there to see it. Like all real monsters, he hides in plain sight. He is tall, has always been tall. He's wearing jeans, scruffed and ratty at the bottoms, threads hanging against his bare feet. His legs stretch up to his torso, his arms taut and muscular in a way I don't remember them being when I was young. His face is as sharp as it ever was, shadowed and in need of a shave. The lines beside his eyes are so much deeper now than they were when I was eleven, and they were harsh even then. Eight years. It's been eight years since I saw him in the flesh, but I feel that time between us disappear. *I'm not small, I'm not small, I'm not small . . .* The floor creaks under him. He positions himself against the door frame, leaning against it and blocking my way out. I keep Nell's shirt pressed to my face. The skin of my hands is stretched so tight over my knuckles from my grip. I close my eyes. I listen to the sound of him breathing, remember the sound of him breathing late at night, I remember . . . *I'm not small* . . .

The floor creaks, shifting under his weight . . .

I open my eyes and raise my head.

He's gone.

I would think he was never here, if I couldn't hear him rushing through the house, running from me, and I feel frayed at my own edges, trying to understand what just happened, what I let happen. I drop Nell's shirt and leave her room, hurrying down the stairs, not quietly, because if he's here and he knows I am here, there's no point in being quiet anymore. I reach the bottom of the stairs. The back door is open, leading to the backyard, the woods beyond it.

I move to it. I step through the door, take that first step outside and the world explodes into a beautiful black night sky with more stars than I've ever seen in my life. I watch them flash and sparkle before my eyes, brilliant bright and white and then red, before they begin to slowly disappear, until all that's left is black. My skull feels like it's coming apart, throbbing from the impact of some unknown force. *He hit me,* I realize vaguely . . .

And then: a pinprick of light, a single star reappears on the horizon to keep time with my heartbeat, pulsing faintly, alive. I want to reach for it, but I can't move my arms. I fall through it instead, feel my body hit the ground. I'm on the ground, my head firing thought after thought that can't seem to complete themselves and they all begin with *Mattie* . . .

And they never seem to end.

# THE GIRLS

## S1E6

**WEST McCRAY:**
When I finally get back to Cold Creek, Claire still hasn't returned.

It's been a few days.

**MAY BETH FOSTER:**
I called all the bars within twenty-five miles. Nobody's seen her, I don't know how much that's worth. She's got money here . . . maybe she's on a bender in some dive I don't know about and got somebody else to pick up the tab.

**WEST McCRAY:**
It's easy to believe Claire would jeopardize her sobriety by returning to Cold Creek, but when she came back, she was motivated by her grief, not self-destruction. That grief should remind us Claire Southern is more than the sum of her failures. She's not a perfect person—but she *is* a person. A mother.

I find her in the orchard where they recovered Mattie's body.

*[FOOTSTEPS, CARS IN DISTANCE]*

**WEST McCRAY:**
Claire?

*[LONG PAUSE]*

**CLAIRE SOUTHERN:**
You recording this?

**WEST McCRAY:**
If that's okay with you.

**CLAIRE SOUTHERN:**
I was driving around . . . just driving the same roads, over and over. I wasn't sure what I was doing. Wound up here a few hours ago and now it's taking me forever to leave.

I just can't seem to make myself do it.

**WEST McCRAY:**
I'm sorry for your loss.

**CLAIRE SOUTHERN:**
That's the first time anyone ever said that to me.

**WEST McCRAY:**
I'm sorry about that too.

**CLAIRE SOUTHERN:**
It's different when you think someone's always going to be around. You think you got all the time in the world to make it right.

**WEST McCRAY:**
You thought you could make it right with Sadie?

**CLAIRE SOUTHERN:**
I doubt I could have. It's just a comfort, having the option.

You got kids?

**WEST McCRAY:**
Yeah.

**CLAIRE SOUTHERN:**
How many?

**WEST McCRAY:**
Just one.

A daughter.

**CLAIRE SOUTHERN:**
How old?

**WEST McCRAY:**
She's five.

**CLAIRE SOUTHERN:**
That's a good age.

**WEST McCRAY:**
Is it?

**CLAIRE SOUTHERN:**
Yeah. They're really starting to be people at that age but they're still clingy, like a baby. Sadie was—Sadie went through something like that.

**WEST McCRAY:**
That right?

**CLAIRE SOUTHERN:**
She never remembered it. It's probably amazing I do. But she went through this phase where she wanted me to tuck her in at night real bad, begged me to do it, so I'd go in her room and I'd run my hands through her hair 'til she fell asleep and this one time . . . she looks up at me and she says, *You made me.* And I—I said, *Yeah. Yeah, baby, I did.*

**WEST McCRAY:**
You love your daughter.

**CLAIRE SOUTHERN:**
My daughter hates me.

And let me tell you something else about Sadie. She was clever. When she was seven, she was signing her own permission slips and, as she got older, Mattie's too. May Beth would buy the gifts for Christmas, for birthdays, and Sadie would sign my name to the cards and Mattie, she never knew the difference.

You know something else? I was—I was in Harding's Grove since I left. For the last three years. Harding's Grove is about three hours away from Cold Creek.

**WEST McCRAY** *[STUDIO]*:
Of all the things I've learned since I started peeling back the layers of Sadie's story, this seemed the most certain: Claire, tearing off into the night, heading for the City of Angels, abandoning Mattie and Sadie and sending one palm tree postcard back with a plaintive *Be my good girl* scrawled across its back for Mattie, and nothing, as usual, for her eldest daughter.

And Mattie, clinging to those words until they pushed her into the passenger's side of a truck driven by the stranger who would go on to kill her.

If I'm being honest, the enormity of what Claire revealed to me in that orchard still hasn't hit me yet:

She was never in L.A.

Sadie sent the postcard.

**WEST McCRAY:**
My God.

**WEST McCRAY [STUDIO]:**
Sadie's circumstances often forced her to compensate. When Claire left, Sadie saw Mattie sink into a deep, unreachable depression and threw out one desperate lifeline—a postcard in her mother's handwriting—and it worked. But it also became the crack between them, something their relationship would never get the chance to recover from. Because of that postcard—and though it's by no means Sadie's fault—Mattie ran away and was murdered . . . and Sadie has moved through every moment since her little sister's death knowing that.

Does any part of her believe she's responsible?

The weight of that guilt.

I can't imagine it.

**CLAIRE SOUTHERN:**
I loved my mother. She never gave up on me. Loved me, no matter how bad I fucked up. And maybe that wasn't

the best thing for me, but God, when I think of her, I just think of that love. And when she died, it was gone. May Beth . . . she didn't have anything for me. So I thought Sadie—I thought Sadie would. And we all know how that turned out.

It hurt, her hating me. I couldn't stand it. I had to push her away, otherwise I'd want for her. And I've made my peace with that. And Mattie—Mattie was so much easier. And neither of 'em—neither of 'em deserved this.

**WEST McCRAY:**
We could still find Sadie.

**CLAIRE SOUTHERN:**
I might be far, far away when you do.

**WEST McCRAY:**
Claire . . .

**CLAIRE SOUTHERN:**
What happened to Mattie is killing me and that's all I'm willing to take.

**WEST McCRAY:**
I don't think that's how it works.

**CLAIRE SOUTHERN:**
Well, that's how I work. *[PAUSE]* You should be with your daughter. What the hell are you doing out here looking for mine?

**WEST McCRAY:**
Nobody else was.

**CLAIRE SOUTHERN:**
That's not why.

**WEST McCRAY:**
Well . . . having a daughter of my own has made me—

**CLAIRE SOUTHERN:**
Don't even finish that sentence.

**WEST McCRAY:**
Claire—

**CLAIRE SOUTHERN:**
You're doing this because your daughter opened your eyes, is that it? Having a little girl makes you realize, what, there's a whole big, bad, dirty world out there? So now you're going to try to save mine from it and pat yourself on the back for leaving it a little cleaner than it was?

**WEST McCRAY:**
No.

*[PAUSE]*

**CLAIRE SOUTHERN:**
I'm not an idiot, you know. I see the way you look at May Beth sometimes, when she's talking, like we're such poor little fools. You think you can take our pain, turn it into something for yourself. A show. A show . . .

I've been used by men my whole life, and if you want the truth, I don't think you're going to be any different.

**WEST McCRAY:**
Claire, if *you* want the truth, I didn't even want this story. And the more I have it, the less I want it because I don't think it's headed anywhere good. But I'm in this now, so I have to see it through.

**CLAIRE SOUTHERN:**
Well, that makes me feel so much better.

**WEST McCRAY:**
I don't know if I'm getting close with Sadie, but I've learned a few things. I need you to tell me about Keith.

**CLAIRE SOUTHERN:**
Keith?

**WEST McCRAY:**
The guy Sadie's looking for, the one she's been calling Darren? We've figured out that Darren is actually Keith. What can you tell me about Keith?

**WEST McCRAY [STUDIO]:**
She asks if we can go back to the trailer, where May Beth is waiting. May Beth isn't happy, but she takes one look at Claire and puts the kettle on.

**CLAIRE SOUTHERN:**
I need a drink.

**MAY BETH FOSTER:**
You can get right the hell out, you're going to be doing that.

**CLAIRE SOUTHERN:**
Jesus, May Beth, just because I want one, doesn't mean I'm gonna have one.

**WEST McCRAY:**
Whenever you're ready.

**MAY BETH FOSTER:**
Ready for what?

**WEST McCRAY:**
To talk about Keith.

**CLAIRE SOUTHERN:**
Keith was a mistake.

**MAY BETH FOSTER:**
He did his best to help you and you threw it away, like you do everything.

**CLAIRE SOUTHERN:**
Can she leave?

**WEST McCRAY:**
May Beth, if you can't let Claire tell it the way she remembers it, I'm going to have to ask you to please give us some time alone.

**MAY BETH FOSTER:**
This is *my* house. Are you kidding me?

**WEST McCRAY:**
This isn't about either of you. It's about Sadie.

**MAY BETH FOSTER:**
Fine. Have the place, I don't give a damn.

*[DOOR OPENING AND CLOSING]*

**CLAIRE SOUTHERN:**
Let's get this over with.

**WEST McCRAY:**
Walk me through how Keith came into your life.

**CLAIRE SOUTHERN:**
I met him at the bar. Joel's. I don't remember it too well, but he followed me home like a . . . a sober puppy. He didn't drink. He never drank, all the time I knew him.

**WEST McCRAY:**
So why was he even there?

**CLAIRE SOUTHERN:**
Exactly. He was looking for someone like me.

**WEST McCRAY:**
Tell me what you mean by that.

**CLAIRE SOUTHERN:**
Lost, sick . . . I was sick with my addiction. He helped keep me sick. Always giving me money, making sure I got wasted . . .

He never asked me for anything. He just gave and gave and I was happy to take, so long as he was willing. He was trying to keep me out of it because . . .

**WEST McCRAY:**
Because why?

**CLAIRE SOUTHERN:**
Sadie hated him, you know.

**WEST McCRAY:**
May Beth mentioned that. She said Sadie felt threatened by Keith.

**CLAIRE SOUTHERN:**
She never liked anybody I brought home. You've got to understand, even if they were good men, she didn't like them. They weren't all bad.

**WEST McCRAY:**
Was Keith bad?

**CLAIRE SOUTHERN:**
I ended up kicking him out.

**WEST McCRAY:**
Why?

**CLAIRE SOUTHERN:**
Something about the way he was with the girls. He was always . . . too interested, you know? Most guys, you tell 'em you have kids, and they don't want nothing to do with you, so you gotta *promise* them they're always gonna come first. Keith never wanted that.

I didn't like the way he was looking at Mattie.

**WEST McCRAY:**
What does that mean?

**CLAIRE SOUTHERN:**
It means just what I said.

**WEST McCRAY:**
Claire?

**CLAIRE SOUTHERN:**
I found—I found him in her room one night. The last night.

**WEST McCRAY:**
Doing what?

**CLAIRE SOUTHERN:**
Nothing, no, I don't know . . .

It was wrong. Soon as I saw it, I knew it was wrong. He had no reason to be in there. None. And sometimes, when I think about it, I think his pants were undone but I was . . . I was wasted, I don't know. I had him out of the house that night, and the next morning Mattie was up and asking where Keith was . . . and every time after his name came up, she was fine, so I don't think—I think I must have got there in time.

**WEST McCRAY [STUDIO]:**
Claire is a hard woman to pin down by voice alone. She relates these things in a flat, distant way, as if to keep herself separate from them. You have to look at the way she shrinks in on herself with each word that passes her lips. The way she fidgets with her cigarettes, but can't quite make herself light up. Her hands shake. This upsets her deeply.

**WEST McCRAY:**
Claire, I have to ask you something else.

**CLAIRE SOUTHERN:**
Don't.

**WEST McCRAY:**
Did Sadie ever tell you—

**CLAIRE SOUTHERN:**
Don't.

I don't know.

**WEST McCRAY:**
Did Keith abuse Sadie?

**CLAIRE SOUTHERN:**
*[CRYING]* I don't know.

**WEST McCRAY *[STUDIO]*:**
It's clear Sadie had unfinished business with Keith. Was it that? Or did he succeed in hurting Mattie? Claire may have saved her daughter for one night, but Keith lived with them for a year.

**MAY BETH FOSTER:**
I just can't believe . . . I can't believe what you're saying about him.

**CLAIRE SOUTHERN:**
It's the truth.

**MAY BETH FOSTER:**
Sadie must've told me every time she saw me how much she hated him. I didn't listen. I thought she was being a *kid* but . . . she was never a kid.

**CLAIRE SOUTHERN:**
Don't start with me, May Beth.

**MAY BETH FOSTER:**
I'm not, Claire. Thank God . . . thank God you stopped him.

**WEST McCRAY:**
It sounds like Sadie was looking for Keith because she had something to settle.

**MAY BETH FOSTER:**
I don't know why she'd go after him now, after all this time.

**WEST McCRAY:**
There's something else. Keith was in a relationship with a woman whose brother was recently arrested for sexually abusing children. He was arrested because of Sadie. I'll walk you through that later, but without Sadie, it's safe to assume he'd still be preying on children. I don't know the extent of that man's ties to Keith, but from what Claire's telling me, it seems they have this predilection in common.

**CLAIRE SOUTHERN:**
Well, what's the sister got to say about it?

**WEST McCRAY:**
She refuses to talk to me.

**CLAIRE SOUTHERN:**
That's confirmation enough, isn't it. *[PAUSES]* Did Sadie really get him arrested?

*[PHONE RINGING]*

**WEST McCRAY:**
Sorry. I have to take this. West McCray here.

**JOE PERKINS *[PHONE]*:**
Hey, it's Joe Perkins from the Bluebird. I'm awfully sorry to be calling you so late, but you told me to get in touch if there was anything else . . .

**WEST McCRAY [PHONE]:**
It's fine, Joe. What have you got for me?

**JOE PERKINS [PHONE]:**
I was talking to one of the boys used to work at the motel . . .
I let him go, soon as I made the sale. Ellis Jacobs. Anyway, I
mentioned how you'd come along, asking questions, and he
says you need to get down here, soon as you can, and listen
to what he's got to say. It's about your girl.

# THE GIRLS

## EPISODE 7

*[THE GIRLS THEME]*

**ANNOUNCER:**
*The Girls* is brought to you by Macmillan Publishers.

**WEST McCRAY:**
Ellis Jacobs is a twenty-five-year-old white male, but his boyish face suggests he's five years younger than that. He's had a rough life and he'll be the first to tell you about it. He was kicked out of his house when he was seventeen. He insists it wasn't because he was a bad kid. His mother's boyfriend at the time just wasn't a fan.

**ELLIS JACOBS:**
They might be married now, for all I know. He was an abusive prick and he beat the shit out of me and that's the way it goes sometimes, I guess.

**WEST McCRAY:**
He was homeless until he was nearly twenty-four.

**ELLIS JACOBS:**
I didn't have it as bad as some people. I couch-surfed a lot. I had a lot of good friends. But I was having problems getting my feet under me.

**WEST McCRAY:**
And then he met Keith.

But Ellis knew him as Darren.

**ELLIS JACOBS:**
What happened was, I got into this game online, when I was at a pal's house. An MMO. Massive Multiplayer Online game. You can talk to people while you're playing, and that's how I met Darren. There was nothing sinister about it, we just struck up a friendship and he told me he knew what it was like, drifting from place to place. He wanted to help.

**WEST McCRAY:**
Just like that? You barely knew each other and he was offering you help?

**ELLIS JACOBS:**
I'm condensing it down for you. A lot. We had over a thousand hours in that game. It's a lot of time to get to know someone, or at least feel like you have.

**WEST McCRAY:**
What did he tell you about himself?

**ELLIS JACOBS:**
Well, it's just like I said—he said he was a drifter, that he was estranged from his family most of his life too. His dad used to beat him . . .

Now I wonder if any of it was true, but I don't know. He got me my job at the Bluebird when I needed it the most. He never gave me any reason to think he was . . . bad. I mean, he was good to me.

He saved Joe's life, for God's sake.

Joe talked about Darren like he was a brother, like he was one of those guys that'll do anything for you if you ask, but can never quite figure out how to get his own life together, you know?

**WEST McCRAY:**
Tell me about meeting Sadie.

**ELLIS JACOBS:**
I was working that whole night. I hadn't heard a word about her when I changed off with Joe. She came into the office late, and her face was all busted up. She didn't look good. First person she asked for was Darren.

**WEST McCRAY:**
But he wasn't there that weekend.

**ELLIS JACOBS:**
Nope, but he hadn't been around a long time before that either. Longest stretch we'd gone without seeing him. We still haven't seen him.

**WEST McCRAY:**
Did Darren ever keep his whereabouts hidden from you?

**ELLIS JACOBS:**
Not from Joe, not from me. But we understood . . . you know, it was understood not to bug him about wherever he ended

up, or share it with anyone who asked. That's what Joe told me, anyway.

**WEST McCRAY:**
What happened with Sadie?

**ELLIS JACOBS:**
She said she was a family friend. She asked a lot of questions about him. The thing that stood out to me at the time was she was real persistent. I offered to leave a message for him, she refused. She asked if she could leave something for him in his room, I said no. She asked if I knew where he was and I wouldn't tell her that either. After that, she gave up. Least, I thought she did.

**WEST McCRAY *[STUDIO]*:**
That broken window in the bathroom?

Sadie.

**WEST McCRAY *[TO ELLIS]*:**
And you didn't hear the window break?

**ELLIS JACOBS:**
If I'm shut up in here, and the TV's on . . . I didn't hear it.

**WEST McCRAY:**
What made you decide to check the room?

**ELLIS JACOBS:**
She put it in my head. She was acting so fucking weird about it . . . I couldn't shake it. So an hour or so later, I guess it was, I got up to look. My gut just told me to. From the front of the motel, it didn't look like anything was going on, but I went

right up to the window and I looked in. The curtains were drawn, but I could make out what I thought was some kind of . . . something moving around.

I opened the door, and there she was.

**WEST McCRAY:**
Tell me everything you remember.

**ELLIS JACOBS:**
It was . . . a lot to take in. The place was trashed. She'd done it. She was bleedin' bad from her arm—

**WEST McCRAY:**
Bleeding?

**ELLIS JACOBS:**
She broke the bathroom window, and she didn't get through it clean. It tore up her arm.

**WEST McCRAY:**
You never told Joe about that window. You didn't tell Joe about any of this until he told you about talking to me.

**ELLIS JACOBS:**
Yeah, that's right.

See, Darren's room is off-limits and I figured I'd lose my job if Joe got wind. I got like, no rules working there except that *one* and it's the easiest rule in the world *not* to break so . . . I just left it. I didn't know how long it was gonna be before Joe had the sale and I needed that money 'til it wasn't there anymore. Soon as the Bluebird got bought, he let me go and I just . . . they're gonna tear the place down. It seemed pointless to me to bring it up.

**WEST McCRAY:**
Okay, so let's keep going from the point where she broke the window and cut her arm and you found her.

**ELLIS JACOBS:**
She cut it up enough it needed stitches. She didn't get any, but it looked deep enough to warrant 'em and that's when I realized how bad she must've wanted in his room. So I get in there, and I see her and she sees me and she pulls out a switchblade and she puts it to my throat and she asks me— she asks me . . . Jesus, this is hard to say out loud.

**WEST McCRAY:**
What did she ask you, Ellis?

**ELLIS JACOBS:**
She asked me if I was like him.

**WEST McCRAY:**
Like Darren?

**ELLIS JACOBS:**
Yeah.

**WEST McCRAY:**
What did she mean by that?

**ELLIS JACOBS:**
She wanted to know if I . . . if I . . . how she put it was . . . God, it's ugly.

She asked me if I fuck little girls.

**WEST McCRAY:**
Those were her words?

**ELLIS JACOBS:**
Her exact words. She had a knife against my throat and she asked me if I was . . . like Darren, and that's what she meant when she asked. And of all the things she could've said, I wasn't—that wasn't anything close to what I was expecting.

**WEST McCRAY:**
What did you do?

**ELLIS JACOBS:**
I told her I didn't know . . . I didn't know about Darren. I told her how I met him online in a game and all that. She was . . . Okay, so when my parents kicked me out, I had to rely on other people seeing through me, you know what I mean?

**WEST McCRAY:**
Explain it to me.

**ELLIS JACOBS:**
Well, like when I was too proud or I was too angry . . . I was always putting on a front to keep people from giving me what I needed. I'd hurt them. Not—not physically, but I'd just put my pain on them because I didn't know how to ask for help. So I always try to remember that, about other people. I always try to see past them and give them help, if I think I can.

**WEST McCRAY:**
So you decided to help her?

**ELLIS JACOBS:**
A little. I mean—it was more that I was shitting myself and I had a knife at my throat and I really thought I was gonna die, man. She was crazed. She just had this . . . wild look in her eyes . . . and that was all I had to work with, so I worked with it.

**WEST McCRAY:**
You talked her down.

**ELLIS JACOBS:**
I guess so.

**WEST McCRAY:**
How did you do that, exactly?

**ELLIS JACOBS:**
I said she was hurt and I could help her and she could tell me about Darren, because I didn't know. I could kinda see that she . . . she was *tired,* man. She just looked like she was done. So I had that on my side. I think that was part of why she lowered the knife . . . but also, I guess—okay, so in the moment, I believed I was going to die. I truly believed that she was going to kill me. But after she left . . . I don't know. Hindsight's twenty/twenty. But *after,* I don't think she would've gone through with it. Still cried like a damn baby when she let me go, though.

**WEST McCRAY:**
Walk me through what happened next.

**ELLIS JACOBS:**
We went back to the main office and I fixed up her arm, and she told me about—she told me about Darren.

**WEST McCRAY:**
By all accounts, Darren had been a very good friend to you. I know you offered to hear her out as an act of self-preservation but was that all there was to it? Did you believe her?

**ELLIS JACOBS:**
I mean, when someone comes at you with a knife and they're not trying to shake you down for money or something like that,

and the first words out of their mouth are askin' if you mess with little kids . . . there's got to be something to that, right? And even though I . . . I swear I never knew the Darren she was talking about, she found this—she found this stuff in his room.

**WEST McCRAY:**
What kind of stuff?

**ELLIS JACOBS:**
She'd found a bunch of fake IDs and they were all—they were all Darren, the pictures on the IDs, but they all had different names. And none of them were Darren's name.

**WEST McCRAY:**
Do you remember any of them?

**ELLIS JACOBS:**
Just Keith, like you said. She said she knew him as Keith. And then the other things she had from his room were, uh . . . they were tags.

**WEST McCRAY:**
Tags?

**ELLIS JACOBS:**
Tags like . . . they were cut out of shirts . . . and they had names—girl names—he'd written girls' names on them. When I asked her what that meant . . . she said they were his trophies . . . his trophies from kids.

Sadie was one of the names.

**WEST McCRAY:**
Okay.

**ELLIS JACOBS:**
She didn't say she was Sadie, though, and I didn't even really think about it until you told me her name and then I remembered.

**WEST McCRAY:**
Okay, what happened after that?

**ELLIS JACOBS:**
Are you all right?

**WEST McCRAY:**
Yeah, just—what . . .

What happened after that?

**ELLIS JACOBS:**
She said Darren "did something" to her little sister, and he hurt kids, and that was the reason she was looking for him.

**WEST McCRAY:**
What did she mean by that?

**ELLIS JACOBS:**
She never said. I told her she should just call the police, get them to take care of it, if he was so bad . . . we fought about that.

**WEST McCRAY:**
She didn't want to?

**ELLIS JACOBS:**
She didn't want to. She made it out like she wanted to be sure he was there first, then she'd call the cops . . . but she had to

be there because after everything he'd put her through, she
needed to see it happen.

WEST McCRAY:
What did you do?

ELLIS JACOBS:
I bandaged up her arm . . . I mean, I bandaged it up as best as
I could, which wasn't very good, and then I sent her on her way.

WEST McCRAY:
You sent her to him.

You knew where he was.

ELLIS JACOBS:
Yeah.

WEST McCRAY:
Please tell me you called the police as soon as she left.

ELLIS JACOBS:
I didn't.

WEST McCRAY:
Why wouldn't you call them? Why talk to me and not the police?

ELLIS JACOBS:
Because I was—because I don't know! Because if I sent them
to Darren, and she was wrong, I betrayed a guy who was good
to me! I can't walk back from that! But if she was going there to
call 'em herself, and if he really was guilty, then it was all going
to work out anyway. I didn't—I don't know, man! It didn't feel

real, you know what I mean? I just wanted to forget about it. And then when Joe told me you were looking for a missing girl named Sadie, and I remembered that tag . . .

I don't know.

**WEST McCRAY:**
My God, Ellis.

**WEST McCRAY [STUDIO]:**
Farfield, Colorado, is a day's drive from Langford. When I'm done talking to Ellis, I prepare to drive there, but I'm stopped by the thought of Sadie, relentlessly moving from one place to the next, grief-stricken, guilty, exhausted and hurt. It's hard to think of someone so vulnerable and alone.

It's hard to think of her, so vulnerable and so alone.

**WEST McCRAY [PHONE]:**
I don't think I can do this.

**DANNY GILCHRIST [PHONE]:**
Yes, you can.

**WEST McCRAY [PHONE]:**
When Keith was in their lives, Mattie was about the same age as my—as my daughter. And Sadie was only eleven. He preyed on them and they're just—they're just kids, you know?

Who does that to a kid?

**DANNY GILCHRIST [PHONE]:**
You slept any?

**WEST McCRAY [PHONE]:**
Yeah.

**DANNY GILCHRIST [PHONE]:**
Liar.

**WEST McCRAY:**
When I arrive in Farfield, it's seven in the morning. Ellis told me the last place he knew Keith to be, the same address he gave Sadie, and when I pull up in front of that house, I don't wait for nine o'clock before I knock on its front door.

*[FOOTSTEPS, SOUNDS OF KNOCKING]*

*[SOUND OF DOOR OPENING]*

**FEMALE VOICE:**
Can I help you?

**WEST McCRAY:**
Hi, there. I'm West McCray. I'm a journalist with WNRK and I'm looking for a missing girl. I have reason to believe she was in this area, at your house, actually, and I would really appreciate if you could give me your time and let me ask you a few questions about that.

**FEMALE VOICE:**
I don't know anything about a missing girl.

**WEST McCRAY:**
It would've been a few months ago—

**FEMALE VOICE:**
Uh, look, I just got off work and I'm very tired and it's very early . . . but maybe you could—

**WEST McCRAY:**
Wait, I just need—just a—do you know this man?

**WEST McCRAY [STUDIO]:**
I show her the picture of Keith. Darren.

**FEMALE VOICE:**
Oh my God.

**WEST McCRAY:**
So you do know him? Is he here now? Was he?

**FEMALE VOICE:**
No. Yes—I mean . . . he was. But—

**WEST McCRAY:**
Where is he now?

**FEMALE VOICE:**
Well, he's—

He's dead.

**LITTLE GIRL:**
Mom?

# THE GIRLS

## EPISODE 8

*[THE GIRLS THEME]*

**ANNOUNCER:**
*The Girls* is brought to you by Macmillan Publishers.

**WEST McCRAY:**
It's been a year since I turned up on Amanda's doorstep and she told me Keith was dead. The next words out of my mouth were, "I think we should call the police." In the time since, I've been collecting the pieces of everything that's left, trying to put them together in a way I can understand. Amanda agrees to meet me to go over what happened that day. She's a white, thirty-year-old mother of one. She has asked me not to use her last name.

**AMANDA:**
I don't know where to start.

**WEST McCRAY:**
How did you meet him?

**AMANDA:**
He came to the place I worked at the time.

**WEST McCRAY** *[STUDIO]*:
Amanda no longer lives in Farfield. She lives in a new town, a different state. She's trying to put her relationship with Christopher—the name Keith was going by at the time—behind her. It hasn't been easy. She is haunted by everything that happened then. She's finding it hard to cope.

**WEST McCRAY:**
You worked at a bar.

**AMANDA:**
Yes. He showed up one night, and then another. He was nice, attentive. He didn't drink, he just ate there. He kept coming back. There was something about him—I felt like I could talk to him, and I felt whatever I said, he understood. I'm a single mom and it's difficult to find people—I found it difficult to find people willing to listen.

**WEST McCRAY:**
You have a daughter.

**AMANDA:**
*[PAUSE]* Yes.

**WEST McCRAY:**
How old was she at that time?

**AMANDA:**
She'd just turned ten.

**WEST McCRAY:**
How long did you know him, before he moved in?

**AMANDA:**
About a month and a half. He was there for every one of my shifts, and every one of my breaks. My days off. I was—I thought I was in love with him. I remember thinking that was ridiculous, to feel that way, but at the same time, why couldn't one good thing happen to me?

If I had known that bringing him home . . . if I had known what I was bringing home . . . my daughter never said a word to me. She never told me something was wrong. You'd think, as her *mother*, I would've known. You'd think that I—

**WEST McCRAY:**
He targeted single mothers of young girls, women who were alone and had to look after more than their fair share. He preyed on them as much as their children. You can't blame yourself.

**AMANDA:**
I know that, but knowing it and . . .

Knowing it and believing it, those are two different things. *[PAUSE]* He didn't have a job. Any other time, that'd be a red flag for me. But he was so nice and so good with my girl that I thought having someone around more often, someone who, at the time, she seemed to *like*—I thought that would be good for her.

**WEST McCRAY** *[STUDIO]***:**
Amanda's daughter is in therapy now. Twice a week.

**AMANDA:**
So I'd be working and he'd be home. With her.

**WEST McCRAY:**
Tell me how he died.

**AMANDA:**
One of the girls at the bar asked to switch shifts with me, so I went in a little earlier than I usually do, and came home a little earlier than I usually did. When I got home, my daughter was there and he wasn't. She told me she'd been at the bookstore and when she got back, he was gone. I was absolutely furious because I didn't want her home alone because I didn't think that was . . . *[LAUGHS]* I didn't think it was sa—

I'm sorry.

**WEST McCRAY:**
Take as long as you need.

**AMANDA:**
Anyway, he came in around nine o'clock that night. He looked awful. He was . . . dirty. Just filthy. He was pale, he was trembling, favoring his left side. I was horrified. Couldn't believe my eyes.

**WEST McCRAY:**
What did he say happened?

**AMANDA:**
He told me he got mugged. He said, how did he put it . . . "I got jumped, they took all my money, they took me for a ride." But he never said who *they* were and when I asked, he got real vague about it. He was in pain, though, and something *had* happened to him—that much was true.

**WEST McCRAY:**
You didn't go to the police.

**AMANDA:**
I wanted to. I begged him to. He refused. I told him we should at least go to the hospital and get him checked out, because he was clearly hurting, but he was adamant that he was fine, he was just a little sore, he just needed to sleep it off. And, as if he was trying to prove his point, he sat down and he had a late dinner with me. Then he took a shower. He went to bed. He was alive. The next morning, I checked on him, he said he was fine, he just wanted to sleep. So I let him sleep. I sent my daughter to a friend's house, to stay the day and night, so he wouldn't be disturbed. I went to work. When I came back home, around midnight, he was unresponsive, still in bed. I called 911.

**WEST McCRAY:**
He had tried, unsuccessfully, to treat a stab wound in his left side. It became infected. He died in the hospital of sepsis a few days later.

**AMANDA:**
When he died, I was devastated and completely out of my depth. I had no idea who to contact. I couldn't afford a funeral. He didn't really mention a family . . . so I went through his things. I found . . . in his wallet—he had money in it. That tripped me up because he told me "they" had taken it. His muggers. In his truck, I found an ID. It had a different name on it. It wasn't Christopher.

**WEST McCRAY:**
Jack Hersh.

**AMANDA:**
I didn't understand it, but I managed to get in touch with his parents, Marcia and Tyler. They'd been estranged since Chris—Jack was eighteen. They came down and identified

and claimed the body after the police released it and I was left with this . . . grief for a man I thought I knew and this utter shock of not really knowing him at all.

**WEST McCRAY [STUDIO]:**
Before Jack Hersh was Keith, Darren or Christopher, he lived in Allensberg, Kansas. After high school, he moved on, like many often do. No one there ever saw him again. But they remembered.

Residents of Allensberg described Jack as a loner, creepy. His parents were devout Christians who often kept to themselves. There were rumors, though, that things weren't great at home, that Jack's father drank too much and had a temper.

His parents refuse to talk to me.

There was an incident when Jack was twelve; he exposed himself to a group of girls at the elementary school.

Marlee Singer was ten years old when her brother, Silas Baker, became best friends with Jack. They were both seventeen. It happened suddenly, seemingly without explanation.

**MARLEE SINGER [PHONE]:**
I think it was that they probably recognized themselves in each other.

**WEST McCRAY:**
Marlee has finally agreed to talk to me.

**WEST McCRAY [PHONE]:**
You knew Jack long before you were romantically involved with him. You sent Sadie to your brother, to find this man, and

you knew or at least suspected both of them shared the same predilection, didn't you? So my only question for you now, Marlee, is *why?* Why did you send her to them and why did you lie to me?

MARLEE SINGER *[PHONE]:*
Because if you'd seen the look in her eyes, you would've known absolutely nothing was going to stop her. And I never . . . I've never been able to stand against my brother. And I didn't tell you, when you came, because I was afraid and I felt like I had something to lose.

*[TODDLER CRYING IN BACKGROUND]*

AMANDA:
When Jack died, my daughter—I had this thought she wasn't upset enough about it but I reasoned that kids work through those kinds of things differently. Now I know.

She was relieved.

WEST McCRAY:
What happened after I came to your house?

AMANDA:
We called the police.

WEST McCRAY:
While we waited, I showed you a picture of Sadie, in case you had been in contact with her without realizing it.

AMANDA:
My daughter was there, between us, and she said, "I saw her."

**WEST McCRAY [STUDIO]:**
Amanda's daughter told us that Sadie had appeared the same afternoon that Jack said he was mugged, as best as she could remember. What she related of their encounter was unsettling.

**AMANDA:**
My daughter said Sadie tried to . . . take her? She had my daughter's arm, and wanted her to come with her and when my daughter wouldn't, Sadie gave her money to buy books. My daughter was reading voraciously then, she was always down at the used bookstore. You said you think Sadie might have been trying to remove my daughter from the house. To save her.

**WEST McCRAY:**
That's what I choose to believe.

**AMANDA:**
When I asked my daughter why she didn't tell me about Sadie, she broke down. She said I had enough to worry about, that she didn't want to upset me. I found out later that was something Jack said to her a lot, to keep her quiet. That if she came to me, and told me anything was wrong, that I would be furious with her . . .

I'm glad he's dead.

**WEST McCRAY [STUDIO]:**
Amanda's daughter's account put Sadie in the area at the time Jack Hersh was killed. I called Danny that night.

**DANNY GILCHRIST [PHONE]:**
How are you doing?

**WEST McCRAY** *[PHONE]*:
I just told a mother there was a high possibility her daughter was being sexually abused by the man she let into her house. She . . . screamed, Danny. I can't even describe to you the sound.

**DANNY GILCHRIST** *[PHONE]*:
I'm sorry, man.

**WEST McCRAY** *[PHONE]*:
I've told the Farfield PD what I know. They want to review all my material—I've got copies, but . . .

**DANNY GILCHRIST** *[PHONE]*:
Give them what they want, and take the time you need.

**WEST McCRAY** *[PHONE]*:
I just—where is she, Danny? If they met, and he walked away from it—until it caught up with him, at least—where is *she*?

**WEST McCRAY** *[STUDIO]*:
After I was interviewed by the Farfield PD, I headed back to Cold Creek to explain to May Beth and Claire all that had happened—what I knew, and everything I didn't.

**MAY BETH FOSTER:**
Oh, Sadie. Oh, my girl.

**CLAIRE SOUTHERN:**
So where is she?

**WEST McCRAY:**
I don't know, Claire.

**CLAIRE SOUTHERN:**
That's not good enough.

**WEST McCRAY:**
I don't know what happened to her after she arrived at Jack's house. I don't know where she went. Jack was there when she arrived. I think it's safe to assume they met each other. I don't know what happened after that. They must have left the house at some point. Jack returned. Sadie didn't. Her car was found on a dirt road. He died. She's still missing. The police are looking into it. That's all I know.

**CLAIRE SOUTHERN:**
No. May Beth said you'd find her. May Beth said that's the whole point of this—that's why you're *here*. You're supposed to find her—

**WEST McCRAY:**
I've tried.

**CLAIRE SOUTHERN:**
What does that mean? You're just—you're just giving up? You think there's no one out there to look for, is that it?

**WEST McCRAY [*STUDIO*]:**
At that point, my mind was circling the state Jack was described as returning home in: dirty, pained, injured and then dead. I believed an altercation occurred between him and Sadie.

I wanted to believe Sadie survived it.

But I couldn't say for sure.

**WEST McCRAY** *[TO CLAIRE]*:
I've got to review everything I have and figure out where that leaves us. I'm headed back to New York.

**CLAIRE SOUTHERN:**
Of course you are.

**WEST McCRAY** *[STUDIO]*:
The trip back to the city was heavy.

I spent the weekend with my daughter and she could tell something was wrong. I didn't want to let her out of my sight, but at the same time, I almost couldn't bear to look at her. I felt as restless and reckless as I imagined Sadie was back then, like I had a need to run, to get back on the road, to drive until I fulfilled my purpose. I was supposed to find her, and bring her home to May Beth and her mother. I could barely cope with the failure stopping seemed to symbolize. It was too final. But I was in a position where the only thing I was able to do was go over what I had and wait for the next something—anything.

**DANNY GILCHRIST:**
Okay, assuming they did finally encounter each other, what do you think happened between them?

**WEST McCRAY:**
I think they met. Sadie was about to blow the lid off on Jack's life and it went badly from there. The way Amanda described Jack to me when he returned, it didn't sound like their encounter went down without a fight. I think his stab wound was an act of self-defense—for Sadie. Amanda didn't say there was anything out of place at the house, no suggestion of violence. I think wherever Jack came back from, that's where it happened.

**DANNY GILCHRIST:**
Maybe where they found the car?

**WEST McCRAY:**
Possibly. If Sadie didn't drive it there herself, Jack could have.

**DANNY GILCHRIST:**
Where do you think that leaves Sadie, if Jack did drive it?

**WEST McCRAY:**
Are you asking me if I think he killed Sadie, ditched her car on a dirt road and managed to get himself back home before dying?

**DANNY GILCHRIST:**
Yeah, I guess I am.

**WEST McCRAY:**
Ask me something else.

**DANNY GILCHRIST:**
You think he killed Mattie, don't you?

**WEST McCRAY** *[STUDIO]*:
If I've learned anything about Sadie Hunter, it was that she was almost a secondary player in her own life. She lived for Mattie, lived to love, care for and protect her little sister, with every breath.

It seems likely now that Jack abused Sadie, but I have a hard time accepting that this alone would inspire her to relentlessly pursue him the way that she did. And I don't know how she knew that Jack was responsible for Mattie's death, but, as she told Ellis at the Bluebird, *He did something to my sister.*

And if that is the case, why did Jack come back to Cold Creek? And was it always in his plan to return, years later, to find Mattie there, to steal her away from her family—forever?

These are the questions that keep me up at night.

*[PHONE RINGING]*

**WEST McCRAY** *[PHONE]*:
West McCray.

**MAY BETH FOSTER** *[PHONE]*:
It's May Beth.

**WEST McCRAY** *[PHONE]*:
It's good to hear your voice. What's going on?

**MAY BETH FOSTER** *[PHONE]*:
They matched the DNA from Mattie's crime scene to Jack.

**DETECTIVE SHEILA GUTIERREZ:**
The Farfield PD, in conjunction with the Allensberg PD and the help of the FBI, were able to match the DNA evidence from Mattie's crime scene with a sample we had on file from Jack, from a previous felony, a burglary. It was in the state database. Norah Stackett also confirmed the truck she saw Mattie get into was his. We're still looking for Ms. Hunter. Our investigation is ongoing, so if anyone has any information regarding either Jack Hersh or Sadie Hunter, we ask them to please call us at 555-3592.

**WEST McCRAY** *[PHONE]*:
I'm coming down there.

**MAY BETH FOSTER** *[PHONE]*:
No . . . no. It's okay. Please don't.

**WEST McCRAY** *[PHONE]*:
I'd really like to talk to you—

**MAY BETH FOSTER** *[PHONE]*:
I'm sure we'll talk again. But right now, right now, we just need some time.

**WEST McCRAY** *[STUDIO]*:
So I give them time.

A lot of time. I spend the winter and spring working on the show, and when I'm not doing that, I continue my work for *Always Out There*. Sadie's story starts coming together, building toward—well, that's the problem. I still don't know to what end. I ask May Beth if she and Claire would be willing to talk to me to figure that out. By then, it's June.

She agrees.

It's a bit poetic, arriving in Cold Creek a year after Sadie first left. This must have been what it looked like when she stepped out of her trailer and said good-bye to what remained of her life without Mattie. The flower beds are in full bloom and surprisingly, Claire still lives with May Beth. She helps manage Sparkling River Estates in exchange for the room and she's clean, still.

**MAY BETH FOSTER:**
I don't know. It's not always been easy—sometimes I just wanna . . . sometimes, I just can't stand her and I know sometimes, she can't stand me. But it feels like the right thing to do. If she wants to stay, I guess I want to let her.

**WEST McCRAY:**
How are you doing?

**MAY BETH FOSTER:**
Depends on the hour. *[PAUSE]* I'm angry. I'm angry at a lot of people, for a lot of reasons—most of all myself and what I failed to see—and sometimes that's the only thing that gets me out of bed.

**WEST McCRAY:**
I'm sorry.

**MAY BETH FOSTER:**
And you're winding everything up? I guess that's it, huh?

**WEST McCRAY:**
Not entirely. But I think if not much new is happening, the next step is getting Sadie's story told. I'd like to privilege the world with knowing her, the way you did for me.

**WEST McCRAY** *[STUDIO]***:**
May Beth tries, and ultimately fails, to hold back tears.

**MAY BETH FOSTER:**
Claire's inside. She'll talk to you.

**WEST McCRAY** *[STUDIO]***:**
May Beth insists on having me for dinner and heads to Stackett's for groceries, leaving Claire and me alone to talk.

The inside of May Beth's place looks exactly like it did when I was first here, all those many, many months ago. It's like stepping back through time, to our first meeting, poring over the photo album of Sadie and Mattie before reaching the page with the missing picture.

Claire stands at the kitchen sink with her arms crossed, looking more and less sure of herself since we last talked. We're
silent for a while, as though we're both holding out hope
Sadie will miraculously show up, will appear, walking up the
drive, disrupting the narrative one final time.

**WEST McCRAY:**
Where do you think she is?

**CLAIRE SOUTHERN:**
L.A.

That's a joke.

**WEST McCRAY:**
I'm surprised you've stuck around.

**CLAIRE SOUTHERN:**
Me too.

But you know what I keep thinking about?

**WEST McCRAY:**
What's that?

**CLAIRE SOUTHERN:**
She dyed her hair blond.

Sadie had naturally brown hair. She looked just like my mother,
and I had a hard time with that. It was too much for me.

Sometimes I think I'd like nothing better than to get out of
this place, and that I'm the last person in the world that'd deserve to see her if she came back. But then I think, *She dyed
her hair blond,* and that's Mattie's color, but it's mine too. And

if any part of her doing that had even a little bit to do with
me, I feel like I should stay here, just in case.

Just in case she wants to come home to me.

Just in case she's able to.

**WEST McCRAY:**
I hope . . .

**WEST McCRAY** [STUDIO]:
I hope.

**CLAIRE SOUTHERN:**
Have you thought about what you're gonna call the show?

**WEST McCRAY:**
I was thinking maybe *Sadie & Mattie*. Did you have a different
idea?

**CLAIRE SOUTHERN:**
I think you should call it *The Girls*. I think you should call it that
for every girl I figure Sadie must have saved.

You call it *The Girls* and you make sure the people who hear
it, you make sure they know Sadie loved Mattie with everything she had. You let them know that she loved Mattie
*so much*, that's what she turned her love into. You let them
know.

**WEST McCRAY** [STUDIO]:
I often think about what Claire said to me in the apple orchard
in Cold Creek. How when she asked me why I was looking for
Sadie, I told her I had a daughter of my own because it felt

like the most noble thing I could offer her at the time. Claire got mad at me, rightfully, for using my daughter as a reason to see the pain and suffering in her world, and as an excuse for my fumbling attempt to fix it.

But I was lying at the time.

I told Danny I didn't want this story because I didn't think it *was* one, and that was a lie too. I don't know that the truth is much better. Girls go missing all the time. And ignorance is bliss. I didn't want this story because I was afraid. I was afraid of what I wouldn't find and I was afraid of what I would.

I still am.

I never got to meet Sadie Hunter, but I feel in some small though significant way, I've gotten to know her. Twenty years ago, she was born and placed in her mother's arms, and six years after that her sister Mattie was placed in hers, and her whole world came alive.

In Mattie, Sadie found a sense of purpose, a place to put her love. But love is complicated, it's messy. It can inspire selflessness, selfishness, our greatest accomplishments and our hardest mistakes. It brings us together and it can just as easily drive us apart.

It can drive us.

When Sadie lost Mattie, it drove her to leave her home in Cold Creek, to take on the loneliness and pain of all those miles, just to find her little sister's murderer and make the world right again, even, possibly, at the expense of herself.

We may never know what, exactly, happened between Sadie and Jack, but I know what I want to believe. And in this aftermath, it's Sadie's love for Mattie that remains, to fill in those gaps until—if, when—Sadie returns to tells us in her own words.

And Sadie, if you're out there, please let me know.

Because I can't take another dead girl.

# acknowledgments

Sara Goodman, an expert in the possibilities and potential of words, whose sharp, smart, and thoughtful edits always reveal the hearts of my books and make me a better writer. Amy Tipton, whose tireless enthusiasm, infinite patience, and perfect timing never fail to keep me on track and creatively inspired. They've championed my work for ten years and not only are they both truly excellent at what they do, they're genuinely good people. It's been a joy and privilege to know and work with them.

The entire Wednesday Books team, past and present. It's an honor to have them hustle so hard for *Sadie*. Jennifer Enderlin. John Sargent. Anne Marie Tallberg. Brant Janeway. Brittani Hilles, Karen Masnica, DJ DeSmyter and Meghan Harrington—a dream of a team. Kerri Resnick and Agata Wierzbicka, for *Sadie*'s stunning cover, and Anna Gorovoy, for *Sadie*'s sleek interiors. Lena Shekhter. Lauren Hougen and Naná V. Stoelzle, for their attention to detail. Talia Sherer, Anne Spieth and all of library marketing. Sales. Macmillan Audio. Creative Services. Jennie Conway.

Alicia Adkins-Clancy. Vicki Lame. Eileen Rothschild. Lisa Marie Pompillo. Their passion for and commitment to their work is unparalleled.

Ellen Pepus and Taryn Fagerness, for their stellar work behind the scenes.

Dustin Wells's keen insights were critical in strengthening this manuscript. I'm grateful to him for his time and his invaluable feedback.

Lori Thibert, Emily Hainsworth, Tiffany Schmidt and Nova Ren Suma's faith, feedback and—most of all—their friendship got me through this book and a whole lot more. I'm so glad to have them in my life.

I'm thankful for the feedback, support, friendship, time and kindness of these good hearts: Leila Austen, Alexis Bass, Lindsey Culli, Somaiya Daud, Laurie Devore, Debra Driza, Maurene Goo, Kris Halbrook, Kate Hart, Kody Keplinger, Michelle Krys, Steph Kuehn, Amy Lukavics, Samantha Mabry, Phoebe North, Veronica Roth, Stephanie Sinkhorn, Kara Thomas and Kaitlin Ward. Brandy Colbert. Sarah Enni. Kirsten Hubbard. Damon Ford [ash]. [Veroni]Kelly Jensen.~*Whitney Crispell, Kim Hutt Mayhew, Baz Ramos and Samantha Seals. Carolyn Martin. Susanne and Meghan Hopkins. Meredith Galemore. Brian Williams. Will and Annika Klein. I couldn't have seen *Sadie* to its end without them.

Somaiya Daud and Veronica Roth, for their wisdom and wicked senses of humor.

Thank you to my readers, booksellers, librarians, educators, book bloggers, vloggers and 'grammers who have found a place for my books in their hearts and on their shelves. They're a huge part of why I'm able to do what I love—and why I love what I do.

My best friend, Lori Thibert, again, always. One of the best, most talented people I know. I can't imagine any of

6

this without her longtime friendship. I have learned so much from her and I aspire to navigate my life with the same grace, kindness, humor, generosity and cleverness as she does her own.

And last but never, ever least, my family—immediate and extended, from Canada to the U.S.—who loves, encourages and believes in me unconditionally. My mom, Susan Summers, whose strength, ingenuity and sense of wonder are just three of many amazing traits she possesses that make her my hero. My grandmothers, Marion LaVallee and Lucy Summers, two unstoppably loving and strong ladies. My big sister, Megan Gunter, the toughest of cookies, who I'll never stop looking up to; my brother-in-law, Jarrad Gunter, the sharpest of tacks; and my niece, Cosima, who, every day, exemplifies the best of her parents. I love and miss David Summers, Ken LaVallee, Bob Summers and Bruce Gunter, but what I learned from them makes up no small part of the writer I am today.

Thank you.